Jackie's Climb

A TWIST UPON A REGENCY TALE
BOOK 10

BY JUDE KNIGHT

ARE YOU SIGNED UP FOR DRAGONBLADE'S BLOG?

You'll get the latest news and information on exclusive giveaways, exclusive excerpts, coming releases, sales, free books, cover reveals and more.

Check out our complete list of authors, too!

No spam, no junk. That's a promise!

Sign Up Here

www.dragonbladepublishing.com

Dearest Reader;

Thank you for your support of a small press. At Dragonblade Publishing, we strive to bring you the highest quality Historical Romance from some of the best authors in the business. Without your support, there is no 'us', so we sincerely hope you adore these stories and find some new favorite authors along the way.

Happy Reading!

CEO, Dragonblade Publishing

Chapter One

Tissingham, a small village in the Midlands, 1820

J ACKIE WAS LATE, and he was going to be in trouble. She was, rather. At her morning job, everyone thought she was a boy, but in the afternoons, Jackie went back to being a girl. A girl who sat inside on a glorious day like today and sewed, dammit. To be sure, since it was fine, Madame might permit her to sit in the little garden at the back of the cottage, with sheets spread out on the ground and over the garden seat to protect the precious gowns she and Madame were making.

Or shirts. Jackie was currently sewing two dozen white shirts for the viscount. Horrid man, and horrid shirts. Shirts were so boring.

That was not why she was late. One of the squire's horses had come up lame. Jackie had applied a poultice first thing this morning and needed to change it for another before she came home. But someone—Dan Whitley, she was prepared to bet— had hidden the epsom salts, and no one could tell her where they were. She eventually found the jar tucked into the feed trough in one of the empty stalls. By the time she'd made the poultice and applied it she should have been home already.

Dan Whitley was a problem. Ever since he'd been threatened with dismissal for tripping Jackie up, he'd been out to make Jackie's life harder. Of course, he'd thought Jackie was a boy and didn't know why Tom Harris, the stable master, made a fuss about a little bit of rough housing.

For the moment, the bigger problem was Madame La Blanc, the dressmaker, who had expected Jackie home thirty minutes ago. And Jackie still had to change from trousers into skirts without anyone seeing her!

Some days, even Jackie was confused about who she was. In the little cottage just outside of the village where she lived with her mother, she had two identities. During the afternoon, she was Miss Haricot, the dressmaker's apprentice. But when the customers had all gone home and Madame La Blanc had shut all the curtains and locked the doors, she was Mademoiselle Jacqueline de Haricot du Charmont, and Madame was Madame *la Comtesse de Haricot du Charmont* and her Maman.

Maman spent the evenings in the thankless task of transforming Jackie into a lady fit to be presented at court. In Maman's daydreams, someone would one day appear at the door of their cottage with the fortune that Maman and Papa had left behind in France twenty-six years ago, one step ahead of Madame Guillotine.

"And then we shall leave this village and brush its dust from our shoes. We shall go to Paris, and you shall be presented at court, Jacqueline, *ma cherie*, where I fancy the name of *de Haricot du Charmont* will still command some respect. You shall make a grand marriage, Jacqueline."

Jackie had no desire to live in France. She had been born in England and had spent her entire life here. And she did not want to be a seamstress or a lady of the court. As for a grand marriage, she would not know what to do with such a thing. She much preferred her morning job, as a stable boy in the stables of Squire Pershing, but if she could have anything she wanted, she would have a home of her own from which no grasping landlord could eject her, a husband who cherished her, and children to love.

At Squire Pershing's place, she was Jackie Bean. Nobody except Squire Pershing and Mr. Harris knew that Jackie was a girl.

They both went along with the ruse because she was useful.

"Young Jackie has the best hands with a horse of anybody, man or woman, I've ever seen," Mr. Harris said to Squire Pershing eight years ago when Jackie was fourteen, after she'd managed to deliver a foal that both men had given up on. And Squire Pershing replied, "You can keep him then, as long as no one finds out that he is a she."

The Pershing stables would do, since she loved working with animals. For the dream of home, husband, and family was just about as likely as her mother's triumphant return to the French court. The village men avoided her as too educated, and the upper-class men had only one use for a seamstress, and it did not involve marriage. Well, too. They were not, after all, going to sew their own shirts.

Jackie also had a fourth identity. A year ago, she had begun to go out at night, disguised as a young man. Not every night. Once a month. More recently, once a week.

Jack Le Gume played the games of chance that Jackie's father had taught her. The games of chance with which her father had supported them and ruined them. But the rheumatics had seized Maman's fingers so she could no longer sew for hours at a stretch, and what Jackie could earn at the stables did not make up for Maman's diminished income.

Jackie was careful. Unlike her charming, irresponsible, impossible father, she never gambled with money she did not have. When the luck went against her, she left when she was empty-handed. When the luck smiled on her, she left when she was still winning. She won more often than she lost, and she had managed for the past few quarters to pay the rent, even to save a bit to pay for a doctor.

Rent day was coming round again, and the rent jar held nearly enough money. If the viscountess once again withheld the money she owed Maman, Jackie would put in the pound that Jack La Gume used for stake money. One way or another, they would meet the rent, thank goodness. The viscountess would not hesitate to turn them out of their cottage, and her son the viscount—Jackie shuddered. What Viscount Riese wanted from Jackie he would never have. She would kill herself first.

No. If it came to that, she would kill the viscount.

Even as she had the thought, she came within sight of the cottage and stopped. She recognized the curricle standing outside, the high-bred pair in the traces shifting impatiently as they waited under the groom's firm hand. Viscount Riese was just entering the cottage. Surely, he had not called for his shirts? They would be delivered to him at the end of the week, as Maman had promised.

Whatever his errand, Jackie did not want to see him. She went back around the corner out of sight, climbed over a stile into the field where they kept their cow and ran alongside the hedgerow, keeping low enough not to be seen over the top.

At the far end of the field, another stile allowed access to the Haricot's back garden. Jackie made her way to the back door and let herself into the workroom, being careful to make no noise. She could hear voices from the front room. Maman and Viscount Riese.

"Double the rent?" Maman was saying. "But that is not what was agreed, Monsieur."

"You were told at the last quarter." That was Lord Riese, sounding bored. "Five pounds. On Lady Day. Or you will be evicted."

"*Impossible!*" Maman exclaimed, giving the word its French pronunciation. Maman always reverted to French when she was upset. "*Non.* That is not what was agreed."

"You are not, I hope, calling me a liar, Madame La Blanc." Riese's tone had changed to low and dangerous.

"*Comment allons-nous payer?*" Maman's low mutter was to herself, but Riese answered.

"How are you to pay? Do you know what, Madame? I have an idea. You have something I want, and I am prepared to pay to get it." Now he sounded amused.

"Monsieur, I think it is time for you to leave," Maman said. She had guessed what the viscount had in mind, as had Jackie.

He said it anyway. "Dismiss your seamstress, Madame. I will make sure she can find no other work in the district. Except the work I have in mind for her." He chuckled. "On her back."

"Out, *Monsieur*," Maman told him, her voice taut with anger and distress.

"Better yet," said the viscount, "Convince her to be my mistress, and I will allow you to live rent free for as long as the arrangement continues. I will even give you a sum of money for yourself. I cannot say fairer than that." He sounded very pleased with himself.

"Monsieur!" Maman's voice was sharp. Jackie wanted to peek, but she did not want the viscount to see her.

The viscount's voice was harsh in response. "I will leave, but remember what I have said. If you cannot pay me, one way or another, you will be out on your ear. You, and your seamstress." The last word was cut off as Maman shut the door with a bang.

Jackie opened the workroom door just as Maman sank onto their parlor chair—the white one with the ornate carving and luxurious padding that was just for customers. When she caught sight of Jackie, she held out her hand.

"Jaqueline! *Ma cherie.* Did you hear that? That *cochon!*" She moaned. "Double the rent!"

"I am sorry I was late home, Maman. There was a horse…"

"Ca ne fair rein. The *cochon* searched for you. It was good you were not here, *ma cherie.* Double the rent!"

"Can he do that?" Jackie asked. "Surely we can appeal to the law?"

Maman turned to French entirely, which Jackie recognized as a measure of her distress, for though her English still echoed with the intonations of her birth language, and she peppered her speech with French expressions, she generally insisted she and Jackie spoke English unless they were alone in the evening. It was a habit she and Papa had adopted during the long war with

France, to stop some villager from denouncing them as spies because they said things that others could not understand.

"Who is to stop that *cochon*?" she asked, in French. "He and his *mere*—they own this village. Will the magistrate believe me instead of the viscount? He is an English nobleman. What am I? A Frenchwoman and a seamstress. Never mind that my family and your father's are far more noble than his. Besides, the magistrate is friends with the viscountess."

The magistrate, if village gossip told true, was the viscountess's lover. But Maman would never mention such a thing to any unmarried girl, let alone her daughter.

"What of Mr. Allegro, Maman?" Jackie asked. Mr. Allegro was the viscount's cousin, secretary, and assistant to the steward. But if he had any influence with either the viscount or his mother, Jackie had never heard of it, and apparently neither had Maman, because she dismissed the secretary with a shake of her head.

"How much do we have, Maman?" Jackie asked.

"Not enough, Jacqueline. Not nearly enough. Even at the old rate, the quarter's rent depends on Lady Riese paying her bill, and each time I present it, she complains, or orders something else, or makes another delay." She shrugged, her shoulders slumping in despair. "Double it, in just five days? It cannot be done."

Well then. They would need to make up the difference. Jackie knew how and where if she could just nerve herself to do it. The Crown and Pumpkin had a high stakes gambling room once a week that attracted the gentlemen of the district. Jack Le Gume had been avoiding it, because they were dangerous men, and if they recognized her as a woman, she was unlikely to escape an even worse situation than the one Viscount Riese intended.

"We must sell the cow," Maman decided.

"Bessie, Maman? Sell Bessie?" They had bought the cow as a heifer when they first moved here, when Jackie was fourteen, shortly after they'd lost Papa. Bessie was not just their cow; she was Jackie's friend.

"She is giving less and less milk, Jackie. She needs to be put to a bull, and no one will allow us to rent theirs." Because of the viscount, Jackie was sure. Ever since she refused his first offer, he had been finding ways to make it hard for Maman and Jackie to make ends meet. Though at least he had not been able to prevent the ladies of the district from employing Maman, who was the best modiste for at least a day's journey.

"Nor can we afford to have her eating the grass and giving us nothing in return," Maman pointed out. "She needs a new home where there is a bull with the herd, and we need the money. Then, when the rent is paid, we can perhaps buy a goat or two."

Jackie argued, but Maman would not be moved. "Enough. Tomorrow, there is a market in Civerton. Jackie Bean shall take Bessie to market, for a boy shall be safer than a girl. Get the best price you can for her, *cherie*."

Chapter Two

"THAT SHALL BE all for today, Allegro," Lady Riese said.

Apollo Allegro inclined his head politely and began to gather the neat stacks of paper into a file basket. Completed correspondence awaiting the viscount's signature. Bills the viscountess had authorized him to pay. A pile of bills and correspondence that he'd been ordered to investigate further.

In theory, he was secretary to Lord Riese, the lady's son, but the viscount had no interest in his lands and business affairs, and no head for them either. Oscar's mother and Pol ran everything between them, Pol doing all the preparatory work and the management, Lady Riese making decisions.

Decisions that Oscar, Lord Riese, seldom overturned, except when his own interests were affected.

"About the dressmaker's rent—" Pol began. Oscar had given him the order last night. Madame La Blanc's rent—already double what it should be and due in less than a week—was to be doubled again. The dressmaker had already been told.

Lady Riese interrupted him. "My son has made up his mind," she said.

Of course, Oscar had. The rutting villain wanted Madame's seamstress. He probably had no idea that the girl was also Madame's daughter. Pol made it his job to know everything there was to know about the people of the estate and the nearby village, the better to protect them from Lady Riese and her son.

Pol had no intention of sharing any of their secrets with his employers. Who were also his relatives, but a man didn't choose his family. He tried another tack with the viscountess. "It will unsettle the other tenants, my lady."

Lady Riese fixed him with her icy glare. "They will not question the viscount's decision. Nor shall you. Remember your place, Allegro."

Pol picked up his basket, bowed, and left the lady's sitting room. He knew his place in the Riese household. Far beneath the viscountess and her children. Not quite a servant and certainly not part of the family. Required to be grateful for every bite of food and every thread of clothing.

He had been made aware of where he fitted in the Riese household from the first. He had arrived from Italy as a child of not quite ten to discover that the uncle to whom he had been sent after his mother's death had also died.

Finding himself in the care of strangers after his mother's death, missing his mother and the only home he had ever known, another death—and that of a stranger—was of little moment. In the face of his grief, the loss of his surname was no more than a blip. He still remembered the moment, though, when he ceased to be Apollo Riese and became Apollo Allegro.

"Your name is not Riese," the viscountess had told him, her voice cold and harsh. "Your father never married your mother. You have some claim on us, for your father was my husband's brother. You may stay as long as you obey orders and make yourself useful."

Or, at least, those were her sentiments. He had been only nine years of age, and perhaps his memory of the exact words was faulty. What was certain was that he had been called Apollo Allegro from that time, and he had been sent to the housekeeper to be put to work.

From that moment, Pol cleaned pots in the kitchen, polished

silver, and emptied chamber pots. He initially slept in a little nook off the kitchen, although later he was given a room upstairs, near the family. He obeyed orders and made himself useful.

It could have been worse. The estate's steward, the house-keeper, and the butler remembered his father, and though they expected him to complete the tasks they gave him, they also made certain he had time to play, plenty to eat, and as much affection as they could provide without the viscountess noticing.

He grew up in the servants' hall, progressing through roles and taking on more and more responsibility. Lessons also had to be fitted into his busy day, for his grandmother, Clara Lady Riese, as she was known, had insisted he have the education of a gentleman. Or, rather, all his other activities had to be fitted around the lessons that he shared with his cousin Oscar, who—despite being the same age as Pol—was already the Viscount Riese.

Oscar was a bully, a sneak, and not very smart. The first two were a problem. The last was an opportunity, and Pol soon found himself trading help with homework for immunity from mean tricks and nasty tattling. "Help" being another word for doing the homework for Oscar.

"I won't need to know all of this stuff," Oscar insisted. "You shall be my secretary, Polly, and will deal with all my correspondence and other rubbish of that nature."

Sure enough, by the time of Pol's first open rebellion when he was twenty, he was Oscar's secretary and also his part-time house steward and assistant to the land steward. He was also the unofficial protector of his grandmother, who suffered chronic ill health and was living in the dower house attended by a companion, a devoted maid, and other servants.

Then the viscountess—Pol was not encouraged to call her "aunt"—decided Pol would justify the costs of his piano and harp lessons by becoming music teacher to Oscar's little sister, who had been a baby when Pol first arrived at Riese Towers.

Pol said it was too much work on top of everything else he

did, and if she wanted to give him another task, it was time he was paid for at least some of them.

"I have been providing you with bed and board since you were a small boy," the viscountess had pointed out.

"I worked for my keep from the day I arrived," he had retorted, and had listed all the positions that would have cost her wages if not for him. His heart had been pounding in his chest so hard he could not understand how she had failed to hear it, but years of standing up to Oscar and others had taught him the victory often went to the one who best feigned calm and determination.

"Out," she had screeched. "Out you go, you ungrateful brat."

"If you wish, my lady. But consider that I am only asking to be paid as Lord Riese's secretary and Lady Amanda's music teacher. If I leave, you will need to pay someone else. You will also need to hire a house steward and an assistant to the land steward."

He had calculated she'd need to replace him with at least two people, plus the part time music teacher, and that she would not do it.

He had not actually intended to leave back then, six years ago. A decade of finding ways to work around the viscountess and her son had given him a set of skills essential to those who worked in their household and on their land. Besides, his grandmother needed him—not only was she ill, but she had also recently lost both her companion and her maid, and the replacements were strangers to her.

He flattered himself that even Amanda, spoilt though she was, would be worse if he was not there.

Lady Riese sulked for weeks and then gave in.

Ever since that time, Pol had been saving every penny he did not have to spend on essentials. He had enough to support himself and Gran while he looked for a position. Soon, he would take Gran and her attendants and move away. Or perhaps just Gran. Pol did not trust the nurse, whom Lady Riese had hired since Gran had become so ill and confused.

Amanda would leave for her first Season in a few weeks. Lady Riese and her son would accompany Amanda to London and Pol would be left to run the estate. Once the weather was fine enough to be safe for Gran, he would seize his opportunity—he and Gran could be far away before the Rieses knew he was gone.

Meanwhile, he needed to deal with these papers and meet with the land steward. After that, he had a music lesson to deliver.

⇛⇚

BESSIE DID NOT attract much interest at the market. She was nearly ten years old and would not be in milk until she had been successfully bred and had given birth to the resulting calf, which meant no milk for at least nine months.

The first person to make an offer said he would pay two pounds, for he could get that much value out of her hide and her bones. "Not much value in the meat," he opined. "It might be fit for the dogs."

Jackie was horrified. "She has many useful years yet," she insisted. She could not sell her old friend to be made into handbags, dog food and glue.

She received three more offers in the next two hours, and all of them were insultingly low. "A good cow might fetch as much as twenty pounds," she told one man, indignantly, after he'd suggested that he could take Bessie away if she'd accept ten shillings.

"Aye, lad," the man agreed. "A good cow. But that's not what you have to sell now, is it?"

By the middle of the afternoon, Jackie was tired, hungry, thirsty, and discouraged. She hated the thought that she might have to take Bessie home and admit she had failed. Finally, a fifth buyer approached. Humbly, and without much hope. Poorly dressed and bent with age, she did not look like a buyer, but as she examined Bessie with gentle touches and soft murmurings, Jackie found herself warming to the woman.

"You've allowed her to dry off," the woman commented.

"She calved two years ago, and gave good quantities of milk for twenty months," Jackie explained. "We thought we would breed her again after we sold the calf, a lovely little heifer." She shrugged. "It was not possible." Though Civerton was not on Riese land, many people from the estate and the village came here for market. It would not be wise to explain that she and her mother were being victimized.

The woman asked about the quantities of milk and how well she behaved at the milking stool. "She seems sweet natured," she commented.

"She is," Jackie assured her. "She has a *very* sweet nature. Do you want her for yourself, Mistress?"

"I do. To join my little herd. I cannot pay much, mind. I'll have to feed her for nearly a year before I get anything back. Ten shillings, lad. What do you say?"

"I've been offered two pounds," Jackie said, honestly.

The old woman examined Bessie with narrowed eyes. "I could not go to two pounds," she said. "You should take it, lad."

"It was a knacker," Jackie explained. "I couldn't sell dear Bessie to a knacker."

"No," the old woman agreed. "It would be a great shame. I shall tell you what, young man. I will give you one pound and a packet of my never-fail heavy crop beans. Come up like magic, they do and taste delicious. I don't give them to just anyone, mind. But I do like a boy who wants a good home for his cow."

A pound. It wasn't enough. It wasn't nearly enough, but it was a better offer than any but the one from the knacker. "I'll take it," Jackie said.

It was on the walk home that Jackie had her idea. A pound wasn't enough to pay the rent, but it was the entrance fee to the Crown and Pumpkin's gambling night, which was on tonight. Yes, and Jack Le Gume had one pound of stake money hidden in a hollow oak just outside the village. Jackie had planned to give it to Maman with the price paid for Bessie, but even two pounds, with the two pounds they had already saved, would fall short of what was needed.

But what if she could double her stake? Or better? Riese was one of the habitues at the Crown and Pumpkin. How fitting it would be if his losses paid the extortionate rent he was demanding. *Yes.* Jack Le Gume would certainly be visiting the Crown and Pumpkin tonight.

First, she needed to face her mother and admit that all she'd received for the cow was a package of bean seeds. Maman was as upset as Jackie expected.

"Bean seeds? Jacqueline, how could you! You foolish, foolish girl. Even a few shillings would have been better than that!"

Almost, Jackie confessed to having the pound, but she clung to the picture she'd imagined—Maman's face tomorrow morning, when Jackie showered her with money and admitted she had withheld the pound the woman had paid in the interests of multiplying it.

It would all be worth it.

Maman snatched the little package of bean seeds from Jackie's hand, strode across the room, slammed the window open, and threw the seeds—package and all—out the window. "That for your bean seeds. Do you think we shall be here to see them grow? Or will have any ground to grow them in after that scoundrel Riese throws us out? Do you not understand what he has planned for you, you foolish child? Out. Get out now and find some work to do. Clean a few more horse stalls. Wash dishes at the inn. We need money, Jacqueline."

Poor Maman. She always got angry when she was upset. Perhaps Jackie should tell her about the pound, and how she planned to make more money. "It is not quite as bad as it seems, Maman…"

But Maman interrupted her. "You are just like your father. It was the same with him. Always, something would come along to save us. He was certain of it. Always. And always the same. He would gamble away our last coins and things would be worse. Get out of my sight, Jacqueline. I do not wish to see you."

Jackie left.

Chapter Three

POL MANAGED NOT to wince as he listened to Amanda Riese murder yet another perfectly delightful tune. Their usual music lesson had been postponed until after dinner, since the viscountess and her daughter had gone visiting this afternoon. Like the music lessons, making afternoon calls was part of the girl's preparation for her first Season.

If the viscountess hoped to find Amanda a husband after she was presented, then she had better not be permitted to play the pianoforte. Or perhaps somewhere out there was a potential suitor with cloth ears, or ears that were merely painted on?

When it came to music, Amanda's own ears were merely decorative, and Pol would have sympathized with her if she was prepared to admit to the defect. But no, Rieses were perfect in every way, and therefore, Amanda was musically talented and played the pianoforte with grace and style.

That, in any case, was what her mother and brother told the girl, though Pol noticed Oscar usually managed to find an excuse to leave the room, and often the house, before Amanda played.

Lady Riese saved her criticisms until Amanda was out of earshot, and applied them all to Pol. In vain did he explain that Amanda was just not musical. "What nonsense, Allegro," she insisted. "Amanda must be able to play creditably when she makes her debut, and you are here to see that she does. Try harder."

"Miss Riese," Pol said to her when she finished the piece and turned to him with a broad and satisfied smile, "you played all the notes in the correct order."

Her face fell and then her eyes sparked irritation. "You did not like it. But I did it all correctly. You said so yourself."

"If you wish to impress when you play in public," he said against growing evidence of her ire, "you will need to play all the notes, in the correct order, and with the correct duration for each note. Some notes linger." He had explained all of this to her before, but not recently. Perhaps today she would be willing to hear what he said. He leaned over her and demonstrated. "Some go quickly by. Watch me."

He sat next to her on the piano stool and played the piece, naming the notes as he did. Then he played it again, this time counting out loud so she could hear how some notes were left to linger on the air while others tripped quickly one after the other. If Amanda was unable to appreciate the music enough to hear what she was doing wrong, then she would have to learn by rote how to do it right.

Amanda grimaced when he was done. "But how am I to know what to do with which notes?" she whined.

Pol ignored the tone. Fortunately, he had not been charged with amending her personality. "Look at the music," he advised. "See this?" He explained, for perhaps the thousandth time, the shape and duration of a whole note, a half note, a quarter note and so on.

Perhaps it would work. She had, after all, learned the bar system well enough to actually play the notes. At least she seemed to be listening.

Lady Riese's harsh voice thundered, "Why are you sitting next to Amanda?" Pol leapt to his feet.

"We were reading the music, Lady Riese," he explained, keeping his stance and his voice humble.

She looked down on him, frowning. Pol was not a short man, but Lady Riese was an enormous woman—tall and broad. Her son was built on the same gargantuan lines and bore the same thick crop of black hair and steely-grey eyes. Amanda, fortunately for her, took after her deceased father, in a female version of the fair-haired, blue-eyed good looks Pol's own father had also had. Pol had to assume he took his dark hair and eyes from his Italian mother.

"The viscount has gone out, Allegro. Go after him and make sure he comes safely home," the viscountess ordered.

Not the job of an assistant steward, a secretary or a music teacher. But Pol would not argue. In Lady Riese's opinion, Pol was here, at Three Oaks Manor, to do anything Lady Riese wanted him to do. Teach Amanda. Supervise the household. Assist the land steward. Organize dinner parties. Run after Oscar and bring him home when he was too drunk to know the way.

"Yes, my lady," Pol replied. Any other response would be futile and unacceptable. "Miss Riese, try that piece again, keeping in mind what I said about duration." He bowed to both ladies. Lady Riese had not said where Oscar had gone, which meant Oscar hadn't told her or his valet. Or perhaps he had, and she wasn't prepared to name the place in front of her daughter. He must be whoring, drinking, or gambling, or all three.

All three, Pol decided. It was Thursday evening, so Oscar would be at the Crown and Pumpkin. "The fee for entry is one pound, my lady," he said.

He met her glare, careful to show nothing on his face but polite attention. He'd be damned if he'd spend his own money cleaning up after Awful Oscar.

"Do I not pay you, Allegro?" Lady Riese demanded.

"You do, my lady. As music teacher to your daughter, secretary to your son, and assistant to your steward." A calm and polite answer.

He waited, maintaining a calm silence while she glared at him.

"Very well. Take one pound," she grumbled.

He should have asked for money for a drink and something to eat. *No. That might have been pushing the old bat too far.*

Once he arrived at the Crown and Pumpkin, he paid his fee, checked that Oscar was at the tables in the room set aside for gambling, and ordered a glass of red wine of better quality than anything Oscar had in his cellars.

Oscar was, of course, absorbed in his game, his drink, and the two scantily clad women who were dancing attendance on him. He gave Pol one glance and then ignored him. He was winning. If only he applied himself to his estates with the same devotion he applied to his vices, Pol's job would be a lot easier! Not that Oscar's mother would cede control into her son's hands.

Pol moved around the room, watching the play, talking to those who appeared interested in conversation, and all the time he surreptitiously watched Oscar. His cousin was losing, now. Losing to a person Pol felt he should recognize.

The other player was a short, slender man whose face was obscured by the unfashionably long hair that fell around it. "Do you know the lad?" asked the man with whom he had been talking. "The one playing with Riese?"

"I don't think so," Pol said. "Yet there's something familiar about him." Something odd, too. Something that set every pore of Pol's skin alert and heightened his senses. If the player had been a woman, Pol could have given a name to his reaction, but he'd always been attracted to women, not to boys.

"I've not seen him here before," his companion commented, "but I've met him. Le Gume. That's what he calls himself, anyway. It seems an unlikely name, but there you go. Many names are unlikely, I've found."

"You've met him before?" Pol asked, wondering why the name, too, tickled at his mind, as if trying to attract his attention.

"That I have. Lost to him, too. He's good enough to be a professional, Allegro, and perhaps he is, but I've not seen him here before."

A professional card player. Pol resisted the urge to leap into action. Oscar would never agree to leave the tables at this time of night. And how much could he lose, after all? The Crown and Pumpkin had a top limit for IOUs, and the estate was prospering in Pol's care. Still, the situation bore watching.

Over the next two hours, the honors went back and forth. The pile of gambling tokens in front of Le Gume grew steadily larger, but each time Oscar came close to running out, the luck went his way, and he won a few hands.

It was clever play on the part of the young man. When he wanted to encourage Oscar to keep playing, he simply made the wrong choices. Not that the young man cheated. He was simply in control of the game, and Oscar wasn't. Oscar was completely outclassed.

The climax of the evening, then, was unexpected. Le Gume put everything he had in the middle of the table and won the lot. Le Gume should have taken his winnings and left. Hell, Oscar should have walked away, but the fool demanded a rematch and enough time to buy more tokens. With a graceful wave of his hand, Le Gume invited him to do so. The coat sleeve fell away, and Pol's attention was riveted to the delicate wrist suddenly on display. He shook his head. What was wrong with him?

Oscar had left the table. Pol followed, keeping behind him so he wouldn't be noticed. Oscar was not to be trusted. He put his head together with the innkeeper's nephew, who was the cashier for these gambling nights. Another mean-minded villain, and one of Oscar's sycophants. Pol couldn't hear what they said, but when the cashier produced a new pack of cards and Oscar unwrapped it and shuffled it, he knew what they were planning to do.

From the shadows, Pol watched Oscar slip several cards up his sleeve and then the cashier called another man over to watch the cash box while Oscar and the cashier returned to the table. Pol followed behind, knowing what was about to happen but unsure how to stop it.

If he spoke up and accused his cousin of cheating, Oscar and the cashier would deny everything. And no one would believe a poor relation over a viscount, especially a viscount who was the landlord of three quarters of the local residents.

The chances were one card would not make a difference. How could Oscar know what other cards would be dealt? That question was answered when the cashier replaced the house dealer at the table.

Pol could not let it pass. He stepped closer and opened his mouth, but before he could speak, he felt hard hands grasp his arms. "Not a word, Mr. Allegro." The person who spoke was behind him, but the prod in the back reinforced the command. Was it a gun?

The men holding his arms hustled him into another room and let him go. He turned to see the innkeeper shutting the door behind him.

"You wouldn't want to interfere, Mr. Allegro."

"Lord Riese is about to cheat, and your dealer is helping him," Pol declared.

"Well, you see, Mr. Allegro, Lord Riese owns the inn," said the innkeeper. "We have a deal, him and me. He don't put the rent up and he don't cheat the locals, and I don't object when he fleeces some stranger. Not that I'd get far if I did object, nor you neither, if you don't mind me saying so, sir. Catch him red-handed, and Lord Riese'll swear he's innocent."

Pol grimaced. The man was not wrong.

The innkeeper pressed his point. "Yes, and a dozen witnesses will swear to it right alongside him. He owns this town, sir, and most of the people in it. You'll finish up with no job and no home neither, and I'll lose my business, so you're not going back into that room until you swear to me that you'll keep your mouth shut."

Dammit. The man was right, but Pol hated it. Hated how Oscar used people and abused his position and hated that nobody was able to call him to account.

The innkeeper must have thought he needed further persuasion. "I've heard of this Le Gume," he said. "He hasn't been here before, but he has been all over the countryside. Winning wherever he goes, too. He's a hardened gamester, for all he looks like a boy behind that beard."

Something about the last few words struck a chord, but Pol could not decide what his mind was trying to tell him. "I'll not call Riese on his cheating," he said. Not this time. Not yet anyway. Not before he had Gran safely away.

The innkeeper nodded to the two men who still held Pol, and they released him. Pol nodded in acknowledgement. They could take it as thanks if they wished.

When he returned to the gaming room, the players were about to show their cards. At a glance, Pol could tell that Le Gume had bet everything he had on this last hand. *You should have walked*, Pol thought. Le Gume showed his cards. Oscar couldn't keep the gloat from his face as he placed his cards one by one before him and immediately began raking the tokens toward him.

Le Gume gaped, and then his eyes flashed, and he demanded, "What is up your sleeve, sir?"

The silence that filled the room, as all the bystanders stared at the gamester, lasted only a moment before Oscar roared. "How dare you! Do you know who I am?" He cast down the tokens he was holding and pushed to his feet. He continued his rant as, his fists clenched, he rounded the table.

Pol brushed past Le Gume, whispering, "Run. I'll try to slow him down."

The gamester hesitated, but sent a sweeping glance around the room and must have realized he had no allies here. He scrambled backwards, turned, and shot out the door.

He? Up close, Le Gume smelt of violets, and the scent made all the other pieces fall into place. The slight figure, the slender wrists, the unlikely beard. And yes, the way his hips moved as he—rather, *she*—ran. Le Gume was a woman.

More determined than ever that Oscar would not get his hands on the gamester, Pol turned and stumbled after her, pretending to be drunk. "I'll catch him," he shouted to Oscar. Then he lurched into the side of the door, tripped over his own feet, and crashed into Oscar.

Back on his feet again, he helped his cousin to rise and brushed him down, apologizing all the time. Oscar's impatient scorn was worth it. Le Gume, whoever she was, had got away.

Chapter Four

JACKIE DID NOT go home. She reached the old shack in the woods where she kept the clothes that she wore in her other identities, but she did not enter. Instead, she paced up and down the clearing outside the shack, fuming.

She had been so close! If only she had refused to play that final game. Although, if he was prepared to cheat, Lord Riese would probably have found some other way to get the money off her when she tried to walk away. He was a liar, a bully, and a thief.

Her mother's words echoed in her ears. "Your father would gamble away the last of his coins and things would be worse." Jackie shuddered.

But it was not her fault, even if Maman would never admit it. *Someone should rob Rotten Riese, so he could see how he likes it.*

The thought resounded in her brain, stopping her in her tracks. *I should rob him.* She walked on more slowly. It would not really be theft. She would simply be stealing back the money he had won by cheating. It was her money, by rights.

It would take planning, and to plan, she needed information. She would have to find out where the viscount might keep his money. His study? His bedroom? Where were those rooms in the castle? When was Riese most likely to be away from home? What time of night would be best for moving around without being detected?

Would some of those who had lost places in the castle be willing to help her? She would have to be careful—she could not risk letting them know what she planned lest someone betray her. But surely, if she talked to enough people, she could piece together the information she needed?

She had best get some sleep. She could not start asking questions until the morning. Tonight, the rickety bed in the shack would have to do, for she was not going home until she could pour money into her mother's lap. She was not like her father. She wasn't.

IT DID NOT take Jackie long to gather the information she needed. She made a start the following morning when she went to work at Squire Pershing's stables. One of the other grooms had worked for the viscount before he came to the squire's and was still walking out with one of the viscount's maids.

"How do the stables here compare to those at the castle?" she asked him, as they mucked out the stalls.

"You don't want to work up at the castle, young Jackie," the man said. And he began a series of hair-raising stories about how the viscount and his mother treated the servants. Jackie barely had to ask any questions, and she soon had a good idea of when the viscount made demands on the stable, and where he tended to go when he took out his curricle or a carriage. The same for the viscountess and also Miss Riese, her daughter.

"Mr. Allegro mostly takes his horse," the groom commented. "And he likes to groom the beast himself. He's a nice man, is Mr. Allegro."

Jackie had been trying not to think about Mr. Allegro. Until last night, she had only ever seen him at a distance. He was even handsomer up close. Far handsomer than Lord Riese, who was running to fat and who generally wore a scowl or a leer.

Mr. Allegro was tall and muscular, with dark brown eyes and hair that probably would probably have touched his shoulders, if not for the curl. She liked his eyes. They were kind, she thought. He looked as if he smiled a lot, though she couldn't imagine the Rieses gave him much to smile about.

It counted, too, that Mr. Allegro had helped her to get away. She hoped he didn't get into trouble with Lord Riese for it. But then again, he was some kind of cousin of the viscount. Presumably that would help insulate him from the worst Riese could do.

He had not been gambling last night. He had not been drinking either. Just watching. Jackie felt a shiver run through her. She had a feeling he saw a lot more than he revealed. Just as well that he did not sleep in the main house—according to her groom informant, he had a bed in the steward's cottage.

After the morning's work was over, she headed for her next informant, changing back into Jacqueline at the shack first, and then stopping at the bakery to spend the few coins she had left on buns and a loaf of bread.

Grace Campion had worked as a maid at the castle and would know the layout. The only question was whether she would share it with Jackie. She had been dismissed from her position when her pregnancy was too advanced to be hidden. She refused to name the father, but everyone assumed she had been forced by the viscount. She wasn't the first, by a long shot.

Turned off without a character or any wages, she lived with her mother and her little daughter in a small cottage just outside the village. The little family depended heavily on the goodwill of the villagers, including Maman, who gave Grace piecework. When Jackie arrived at the cottage, she met Maman at the gate into the Campion's small front garden.

"Jacqueline. You stayed out all night." Maman glowered at her, and her tone was accusing.

Jackie felt a surge of resentment. She had been doing her best, but it was never good enough for Maman. "You said you did not wish to see me," she pointed out.

"You will come home with me now," Maman told her. "I have given the shirts you did not finish to Grace, but I have some sheets that need hemming."

No. Not this time. She would not fall into heel at her mother's skirts, like a chastised dog. "I have things I must do, Maman." Adding, in the forlorn hope that her mother would understand. "I am trying to put matters right."

"Do as you please then. You always do." Maman brushed past her and headed off down the lane toward the village. "Just like her father," she muttered.

Grace was watching them from the doorstep. Jackie forced a smile. "Miss Campion, may I have a word?"

The former maid frowned with narrowed eyes. The heavens alone knew what she had made of the little scene with Maman. "Come inside, then," she said. "I need to finish peeling the vegetables."

Jackie followed her into the little cottage—the main room downstairs and a steep staircase up to the sleeping area above.

"Ma has taken Ruby for a visit with Mrs. White, and I am making stew," Grace explained.

She led the way past the small sitting area, where the basket of shirts that Jackie had been sewing was perched on one of the chairs. Grace waved Jackie to a stool at the kitchen table at the rear of the room. Cooking was done in the fireplace, which also provided the heat for the whole cottage.

The room was sparsely furnished but painfully clean and decorated with a few pretty touches—a bunch of spring flowers in a cracked vase, a colorful rag rug, a couple of samplers pinned to the walls that read "Bear ye one another's burdens" and "God bless this home".

Jackie picked up a paring knife and began scraping the outer skin off a carrot. Grace said her thanks and fetched a chopping knife to begin cutting those vegetables that were waiting ready.

"If you need the work back, Miss Haricot, I understand. You will need Madame's agreement, though."

"I haven't come about the shirts, Miss Campion," Jackie assured her. "Though I wouldn't blame you if you sewed ill wishes into every seam. I certainly feel like doing so. The viscount is a loathsome man."

Grace looked up from her chopping, the frown back in her eyes. "Is that monster after you now, Miss Haricot?"

What could it hurt to be honest? It might make Grace more likely to help her. "He wants to be," she admitted. "He made an offer, and when I refused him, he went to Madame. He is threatening to evict her if she does not make me submit to him."

"No! Is that what you and she have argued about? Is she trying to force you?"

"Never," Grace assured her. "We do not agree about how to stop him, though."

The former maid grimaced. "I certainly cannot help you, Miss Haricot. I wish I could. Just don't go anywhere you might meet him, especially alone. Though I daresay that if he hauled you off the street in front of half the town, no one would stop him." Her tone turned bitter. "Many of them would find a way to blame you, and not him."

"You can help me," Jackie said. The inspiration had just come to her, and she followed it, testing it with her mind even as it flowed off her tongue. "He is a villain, and there must be evidence of things he has done that even he wants to keep hidden. I am going to search the castle, but I have never been into the private parts of the house." It was even true, and she did not know why she had not thought of it before. "What can you tell me about his study and his private chambers?"

Silence from the other side of the table. Grace had stopped chopping and was staring at her, her jaw dropped. "Do you mean that?" she said, after a moment.

She really did. Stealing from the viscount would be satisfying. But it wouldn't hurt him half as much as losing the favor of those who ignored his wrongdoing. "If you don't feel you can help me, I am still doing it," she replied. "And I will understand. Even if I am caught, I will never tell anyone you have helped me. But you must do what you believe is best for you and Ruby."

Grace diced a potato before she spoke, wielding the knife with skill and speed. She swept what she'd chopped into the bowl where small cubes of carrot, turnip, and parsnip waited. Then she paused and looked Jackie directly in the eyes. "I will help," she declared. "What do you need to know?"

❋

"OSCAR, BEFORE YOU go out, I would like a word," Pol said after dinner. The ladies had withdrawn, and it was just the two of them and a couple of footmen in the room.

"I'll have a port then," Oscar said, waving a hand at one of the footmen.

Pol stood. "I'll get it," he said to the men. "Leave us, please. I will let you know when you can clear."

"Uh oh." Oscar grinned, mockingly. "I detect a Polly scold."

The topic Pol wanted to broach had nothing amusing about it. "If you wish to see it that way. I am looking out for your interests, cousin. And they won't be served by alienating the villagers and your tenants."

He handed Oscar his port, and the heathen tipped back his head and swallowed the lot. Pol doubted if he'd tasted it.

"If you are going to scold me, I'm leaving," Oscar threatened.

Right. Straight to the point then. "You've been trying to talk John Westerley's daughter into meeting you in private. She had the sense to talk to her father. He asked me to let you know that any man who touches her, whoever he might be, will lose his ballocks." Margaret Westerley was fifteen. If Oscar seduced her or worse, Pol might just hold his cousin down for the knife.

Oscar snorted. "Westerley is my tenant. He won't touch me."

"Westerley runs the biggest and most successful farm in the district. If he is hanged or transported for gelding you, you will lose not only your breeding equipment but also a third of your income. That is, if he gets caught. I tell you now, Oscar. If you turn up minus important body parts, I shall deny we had this conversation, and all your tenants and most of your villagers will make certain that Westerley has an alibi."

"She's ripe for it," Oscar protested. "You can't blame me if the tarts lead me on."

Rubbish. Margaret Westerley was modest, well-behaved and innocent. She was also clearly frightened of Oscar. Perhaps he thought her horror and disgust to be an act, but Pol did not know how he translated that into "leading him on."

Except that she was remarkably pretty, but there was no point in arguing that a girl's appearance was not an invitation to molest her. "You're an adult," Pol told him. "If you want to stay whole, think with your brain and not your pecker. Leave the tenants' daughters alone."

In a whiny singsong, Oscar repeated the last sentence and added to it. "Leave the tenants' daughters alone. Leave the villagers' daughters alone. Leave the maids alone." His sneer broadened. "You might be a eunuch, Polly, but I'm not."

"Keep on poaching other people's women and you will be," Pol promised, ignoring the insult. "That goes for the dressmaker's girl, too, by the way."

Nothing in Oscar's eyes or his expression hinted that he knew anything about what Pol had heard in the village—that the dressmaker was searching for her seamstress, who had not come home last night. So, it probably wasn't anything to do with Oscar. Pol hoped she was somewhere safe, but he greatly feared she might have fallen afoul of some of the other predators who thrived in this district. Oscar's example and the negligence of the magistrate saw to that.

"The dressmaker's girl is my business, not yours." Oscar was on his feet and pouring himself another port. "As for the tenants,

I'm the highest ranked peer in the district. They won't touch me. Little mice. Everyone is afraid, and they should be. You should be."

He tipped his glass up again, swallowing several times as the port ran down his throat. "I can destroy them," he added. "I can destroy you, Polly. So, stop trying to tell me what to do."

He stormed out of the room.

That went about as well as I expected. Honestly, Pol should let Westerley loose with his gelding knife. Pol couldn't think of anything else that would stop the viscount from his indiscriminate rutting.

He went out into the hall. "You can clear," he told the waiting footmen. "I will take my port through to the study." He'd been out about the estate all day and had come up to the main house to find a heap of paperwork waiting for his attention. His landlord, the steward, was away visiting a sister, and his cook-housekeeper had gone with him, since apparently the two women had been friends since they were children.

And while the company here at the Towers left a great deal to be desired, they had an excellent cook. He'd eaten a splendid dinner. If he stayed here tonight, he could expect a delicious breakfast.

Tired though he was, he'd not sleep until he'd managed to get at least some of the correspondence dealt with. After that, he'd probably catch a few winks on the sofa in the study—it would not be the first time.

Chapter Five

I N POL'S DREAM, he was chasing the gambler from the night before—Le Gume. Jack Le Gume, to be precise. Pol had asked a few questions and discovered that the man was well known in the area. And liked, too. He was remembered as a graceful winner and a cheerful loser. He won more than he lost, apparently. But not huge amounts, and those who had met the man swore to Pol that he was honest.

She was honest. Pol was certain of his impression from the night before, but now, in the dream, he tackled her to stop her from running away, and as she fell, the beard tore from half her face. Pol looked down into a face he knew. Jackie Bean, the stable boy from Squire Pershing's.

Was he wrong, then? And yet his body insisted that the lithe shape underneath him was female and desirable.

At that point, Pol woke up. He was in the study, lying on the sofa under a rug, half aroused. Suddenly, he realized what his dream had been trying to tell him. He should have guessed sooner, for she had done little to disguise her name. *Jack Le Gume.* Legume. A bean was a sort of legume. Jackie Bean. Yes, and Jacqueline Haricot, too. *Haricot* was French for bean, and the French born Miss Haricot, the dressmaker's apprentice and daughter, was very definitely a woman.

A lovely woman. Slender, but beautifully curved, with light brown hair that she usually wore tightly confined. But he had seen it loose, once, falling in soft waves to her shoulders. He had been riding past the field where she and her mother kept their cow, and she had not seen him, but the horse had stopped at a signal he did not know he had sent, and he had sat for a minute, staring at her with a dry mouth and an odd ache in his chest.

No wonder he had not guessed. The seamstress might be small, but she was all woman. However, now that he'd noticed it was obvious. She was also the stable boy, and the gambler.

A soft click came from the door, which he had locked before he went to sleep. A similar sound had reached through the mists of sleep to wake him, he realized. Someone was tapping metal upon metal outside the study door.

No. Inside the door lock, for the light from the embers in the fireplace was enough to see the door open, and he had locked it himself, before he had settled on the sofa.

He watched as a slender figure slipped through the opening and closed the door. Not Oscar, then. His cousin was the only person with a right to pick the lock, though it was not likely he'd try. In the unlikely event he even wanted to enter the study and found the door locked, his style would be to hammer on it and demand to be let in.

This person was twelve inches too short and more than a hundred pounds lighter. For the same reasons, it couldn't be the viscountess. Amanda, perhaps? But Pol already knew who it was. Perhaps it was the faint scent of violets, so vague he might have been imagining it. Perhaps it was the tightening of his body, already primed by the dream. *She is safe*, said a part of his mind, rejoicing far more than made sense, given they had not had even a single conversation.

Why was Jackie Haricot or Bean, or whatever her surname might be, breaking into Oscar's study?

She had made her way to the desk and was crouching down by the drawers on one side. He shifted the rug from his legs and swung his legs to the floor to sit up, watching her the whole time. Her focus was on the drawers, and she didn't notice him. The scratching sound suggested she was once again picking a lock.

He did not speak until he was ready, his weight balanced forward so he could make a spring for the door if she attempted to escape.

"Are you looking for anything specific?" he asked. "If it is the money Oscar cheated you out of, I'm afraid it isn't here. Probably Oscar took it with him. He has ridden over to Civerton, I daresay for gaming and… um… other things."

The girl froze when she heard his voice. As he kept speaking, she slowly moved, her head coming up, so she was looking at him over the desk. "Is it you, Mr. Allegro?" she asked, only a small tremble in her voice indicating what was probably a turmoil of emotions.

"Yes. And you are Jacqueline Haricot. Or Jackie Bean. Or Jack Le Gume. Or perhaps—since you are the dressmaker's daughter, are you not—Mademoiselle La Blanc? Are there any other identities I should know about?"

She had risen to stand, little more than a shadow in the dimly lit room. One shoulder lifted in a shrug. "You should not know about any of those identities, Mr. Allegro."

He smiled at the wry humor in the remark. No denial, he noted.

"Jackie Haricot will do," she said, and added, "If you know who I am, you know that Lord Riese doubled my mothe… my employer's rent. Did you know he was demanding me as payment? Madame La Blanc would not hand me over, of course, and so he doubled the rent. *Cochon.*"

Pig. Pol could not disagree with her assessment. The woman's rent was already high at ten pounds a year, though the cottage was large by the standards of the village. But the point was, twenty was extortionate.

"You are taking a risk, being so honest with me," he pointed out, as he poked a spill into the embers until he had a flame and then used it to light the candles in the holders on the mantelpiece. He could explain that he had tried to argue Oscar out of both the planned seduction and the rent change, but Miss Haricot had no reason to believe him.

"I have heard you are the best of the family, Mr. Allegro," the girl said.

The lady. From her bearing, her accent, and her choice of vocabulary, she had been educated as a lady. Pol's desire to learn more about the forces that shaped her was almost equal to his most improper urge to embrace and kiss her. To keep his urges in check, he lit the candles on the desk.

Even the more innocent desire was not to be satisfied at this moment, for the door handle rattled as someone opened the door, and Miss Haricot dropped into hiding behind the desk.

❊❊❊❊

JACKIE CONCEALED HERSELF just in time, for Lady Riese's voice boomed through the room.

"Allegro! What are you still doing here at this time of night?" She sounded accusing, as if she had caught him at some malfeasance.

In some ways—in many ways, in fact—Lady Riese was more dangerous than her son, for she was clever, and so concealed her true nature behind a facade of austere courtesy. Her voice told the true tale, however, as did her eyes. Both were harsh, especially when dealing with those she thought beneath her.

Mr. Allegro's reply in his warm baritone was courteous but firm. "I worked late, my lady, as quarter day is approaching. I will be here early for a meeting the steward organized before he was called away, so I decided to sleep on the sofa to make certain I am here in time."

"Quarter day, is it?" the viscountess grumbled. "Where is my son, Allegro? Why are you not watching over him?"

"He went into Civerton to meet some of his friends, my lady. I expect him to be gone all night."

Lady Riese snarled. "He needs looking after, Allegro. You know this."

She had directed that tone at Jackie when Jackie had come with Maman to take the lady's measurements or to do a fitting. It had the brutal weight of a large hammer and had left Jackie feeling bruised and shriveled.

Mr. Allegro sounded as if he was entirely unaffected. "I have instructed his groom to bring him straight home once he leaves the brothel, my lady," he answered. "I daresay he will be near insensible and will make no objection."

After a moment's silence, Lady Riese hissed, "You are insolent, Allegro. Remember, nobody is irreplaceable."

"Very true, my lady," the man replied.

"Hmmph," said Lady Riese.

"Is there something I might help you with, my lady?" Mr. Allegro asked.

"The accounts for the cottages in the village. Lord Riese has made some changes for the new quarter. I wish to review them."

"Of course, my lady. I shall fetch the book." He moved to the desk, stepping into Jackie's view. From her position on the floor, she could see him select a file book from the top of a neat stack of documents.

"Lord Riese has increased some of the rents and decreased others," he told Lady Riese, moving out of sight again. "Repaying gambling debts or favors in the latter case. At least one of the rents has been doubled because he wishes to force the tenant into allowing him sexual access to her employee."

A slap sounded, followed by Lady Riese's harsh voice. "It is not your place to ascribe motives to your master, nor to criticize his decisions. What happens to the Riese tenants is not your concern," she said.

Mr. Allegro's calm and courteous tones did not change. "I merely advise, my lady. The Riese estates depend on the wellbeing of the Riese tenants. As might Lord Riese's safety as he rides around the neighborhood."

"Are you threatening your master?" Lady Riese demanded.

"Not I, my lady. I merely advise. Desperate people do desperate things. Lord Riese would do well not to drive people to desperation."

Lady Riese's laughter was a grim sound, with nothing of humor about it. "Those mice? Those frightened cowering fools? They will mutter into their beer, but none of them will do anything. Besides, my Oscar could fight off a dozen of them and not disturb the set of his coat. And then Lord Barton would send them all to the assizes, to hang or to be transported." He probably would, too, for the magistrate was Lady Riese's lover. "No," she insisted. "Oscar is in no danger. Give me the rent book."

He must have complied without speaking, for her voice next came from farther away. "Do you have an eye for the dressmaker's girl, Allegro? That social-climbing little tart with her airs and graces? She thinks to tease Oscar until he provides a way for her to climb up out the muck that is her natural home. He will take her, of course, but she need not think above her station. Perhaps Oscar will allow you his leavings." This time, her chuckle did sound amused.

The bitch! Social-climbing tart, indeed! Even if Jackie were stupid enough to think Oscar could be trapped into marriage, she would not touch him with a very long and very pointy stick.

She heard footsteps and the click of the door latch falling.

"She has gone," Mr. Allegro said. "You can come out now, Miss Haricot."

Jackie discovered that her hands were locked into fists, so tightly that her nails had cut her palms. She relaxed them and used the desk to haul herself to her feet.

"Thank you for not telling Lady Riese I was here," she said.

Mr. Allegro shrugged. "I tell the Rieses as little as possible, although just now..." He rubbed his hand over his cheek. "You no doubt heard that Lady Riese has no sympathy for your plight, and no intention of standing between her son and the victims of his vices. I imagine you climbed up here with a plan. What is it, and how can I help?"

Could he be trusted? Would he really help? She looked into his steady brown eyes. Kind eyes, she thought again. But then she realized another fact about him.

He is not going to leave me to wander about the house on my own, and if he does not help me, I shall have to go home empty-handed. And I am running out of time.

"You were there last night when Lord Riese cheated me out of my winnings," she commented. He had helped her then, too, come to think of it, by stopping Lord Riese from seizing her. She shuddered at the thought of what might have happened had that ogre discovered she was a woman.

"Yes?" Mr. Allegro said.

"I need that money to pay the rent," she found herself saying. "I came to steal it back, and also to look for evidence of Rotten Riese's crimes so he can be stopped before he hurts more people."

Mr. Allegro's jaw dropped, and he stared at her. Jackie glanced toward the window. If he called for help, would she be able to get out that way? What possessed her to blurt out her plan like that? Why didn't he say anything?

As the silence endured, her discomfort grew. "Right," she said, taking a step to the side so that she could sidle around the desk and make for the door. "It was too much to ask. I'll just be off then."

Chapter Six

POL'S MIND WAS reeling. He was stunned by Miss Haricot's courage and honesty, and even more by her comment about stopping Oscar.

Why had he never thought of seeking evidence of the crimes his cousin had undoubtedly committed? It would have to be something that would see the man—Rotten Riese indeed—arrested. Oscar was right that his position as a peer gave him some protection, not to mention that Lord Barton, the magistrate, wasn't going to press charges, so it would have to be a crime that couldn't be brushed under the carpet.

Shame would not do it. Oscar felt no shame.

Pol, however, was ashamed to realize that he had thought only of leaving, and not of seeking justice for those Oscar and his mother had hurt.

Miss Haricot's words—and more, her movement toward the door—drew him from the whirl of his thoughts. "Wait," he said. "You're right. We need to stop him. Him and Lady Riese."

She turned to face him, her lovely eyes full of hope. Light eyes. Blue? Grey? Even green? He could not tell in the dim light, and he had never been this close to her before, but he could see the smile with which she blessed him as she realized what he had said. "You will help me?"

"Perhaps we can help one another," he said slowly as he ordered his own ideas, "Please. Have a seat and let us discuss what might be done. Would you care for a drink, Miss Haricot?"

But before she could respond, the door rattled again, and she dived back behind the desk. Pol pulled a couple of documents toward him and bent over them.

"You're still here," Lady Riese said, her voice heavy with disapproval.

"As you see," he replied.

She held out the rent book and pushed it toward him when he put his hand on it. "I have amended some of the figures. You will let Oscar know. If he wishes to know why, tell him to see me."

"Yes, my lady." Pol inclined his head in a shallow bow. It was not a time to ask questions. Let her leave, and quickly.

"Good. And Allegro? I will not be paying the dressmaker's bill until after Lady Day. Perhaps a week after. That should compensate Oscar for the alterations I have made to his cronies' rents." Her smile was both fierce and gloating.

"You would conspire with your son to ruin a girl?" Pol demanded.

His aunt made to slap him, as she had many times, but this time he caught her arm. "No, Madam," he told her. "You shall not strike me."

"Let me go!" she demanded.

"You shall not strike me," he warned again, as he let her go.

"You should be beaten for your impertinence." Lady Riese narrowed her eyes in a glare as she spoke, her tone making the words more of a promise than a wish. "How dare you touch me!"

"You shall not strike me, Lady Riese," he said for a third time. "Not ever again. If you do, I shall walk out of this house and never return."

Her eyes widened at that. "You shall not," she declared. "You will not leave the dowager."

"Try me."

Lady Riese stared at him as if she had never seen him before. For a moment, he could see indecision in her expression, then it hardened into the usual impervious mask. "You are a thankless brat. We should have turned you out when you first landed on our doorstep."

Pol had heard that many times before. He had long since stopped feeling guilty for his lack of gratitude. His labor over these many years had more than repaid the Rieses for taking him in.

"*Hmmph.*" His aunt tossed her head. "Such a fuss over a seamstress. She is no better than she ought to be, I'll be bound. She thought to put her price up by acting coy, but I put Oscar wise to that ploy. He'll have her in the end, and at his price, not hers. And you shall not interfere, Allegro, or I shall turn you out."

With another snort, she turned on her heel and left the room.

Pol shut the door and locked it so he and Miss Haricot would not be disturbed again. "I shall get you that drink and we shall sit down and talk," he said. "We need a plan if we are to get away with this."

She emerged from her hiding spot and sat in one of the chairs that faced the desk, and he brought her a glass of brandy and sat in the other.

"Oscar and his mother have proven over and over that they will be listened to while we lesser mortals are ignored," he said, "so we must not be discovered searching the house. I doubt there is anything here in the study. I am familiar with all the estate papers. But we must look. Also, in Oscar's chambers and Lady Riese's. Letters, perhaps? I'm sure you are right. There must be something."

"I don't have time," Miss Haricot pointed out. "Lady Day is nearly here. If I cannot pay the rent or force him to lower it, we shall be cast out."

"It is two separate problems. I shall find you enough money to pay the rent. Then we shall figure out how to search the house." It would probably be better for him to do it himself. If he was caught, he could probably talk his way out of trouble, but Miss Haricot could have no conceivable reason to be here.

As if she had followed his thoughts, she told him, "I need a reason to be in the house. Could you hire me as a maid?" She must have seen his refusal on his face, for before he had time to speak, she said, "You'll not keep me out of this, Mr. Allegro. If you won't let me work with you, I'll find a way to do it on my own."

"You do not trust me," he commented. And fair enough, too. She knew him only by reputation. Given his relationship with her persecutors, it was amazing she had been so honest about her intentions.

She wrinkled her nose. "It isn't that, precisely. I have trusted you. You could have me arrested for what I've told you. You could hand me over to Rotten Riese."

He had to smile. "I do like that nickname. It fits him like a glove." But this was not a laughing matter. Serious again, he leaned forward as if that would help him to convince the lady. "Miss Haricot, I am on your side, but I am worried about your safety. Especially as a maid, with Oscar in the house, and some of the footmen nearly as bad."

"Then, Mr. Allegro, we need to have a plan," she told him. Her smile was sweet, but he knew a determined jaw when he saw one. His heart turned over in his chest. *Her*, it told him. *She is the One*. Nonsense, of course. He hardly knew the lady.

His mouth took the next step without his brain's intervention. "If we are to be partners in this," he said, "you should call me 'Pol'. Apollo, really, but Pol for short."

She held out her hand. "Jackie. Jacqueline, as you know, but everyone except my mother calls me Jackie."

He took the proffered hand and fought to disguise the shock that zinged through him, reminding him of when he had stuck his fingers into a friction machine at the fair. Perhaps *thrill* was a better word than shock, and from the way her eyes widened, and her fingers tightened over his, she felt it too.

It was a worker's hand, firm and slender. He could feel the calluses from her various professions. No pampered maiden, this. *Her,* his heart said again. He forced himself to focus on his thoughts instead of his heart.

"First things first. Oscar will not be home tonight. Lady Riese is still awake, but once she goes to bed, her maid will do so, too. The rest of the servants are mostly in bed already—they start early in the morning. There'll be a footman in the front hall, but he has no reason to come upstairs. In half an hour, or perhaps a little more, we shall visit Oscar's chambers and fetch your rent money."

That should be safe. He hoped it would be enough to satisfy her.

Jackie heaved a deep sigh of relief, and her eyes glistened in the candlelight as tears started to her eyes. "I cannot tell you what this means to me," she said.

"While we are waiting, tell me more about yourself. How do you come to have so many identities? And which one is the real Jackie?"

"Truth for truth," she said. "Who is Pol Allegro? And why are you helping me?"

Fair enough, but not so easy to answer.

"I asked first," he pointed out, playing for time.

"Which is the real Jackie?" she repeated his question. "I hardly know." She shrugged. "I can more easily say who I am not. Not a stable boy or a gambling man."

Or a male at all. Even before he had realized she was a woman, his body had known she was not a man. "The dressmaker's daughter, then," he coaxed. "Your mother is a French *émigré*, is she not?"

"Maman is French," Jackie confirmed. She chuckled, "I do not suppose you will believe me, since most *émigrés* say the same thing, but she and my father really were aristocrats, and they really did escape France just ahead of the guillotine, or so Maman has always told me. I was born here in England. Your turn."

"I was born in Italy, in Tuscany. My father was the son of the then-Viscount Riese, and my mother was the daughter of a large Tuscan family." Lady Riese had always told him that his mother was an opera singer, said with her lip curled as if Mama was a disgrace beyond imagining, but what Pol remembered was a large, joyous family house, filled with uncles and aunts and cousins. And servants. He remembered nursemaids and governesses and tutors, as well as maids and footmen. And the stable boys, with whom he and his cousins had played raucous games of ball on Sunday afternoons, when even the servants had time off.

"Your turn," he told Jackie.

They filled the half hour with snippets from their past. Jackie talked about her little family's seesaw existence, in and out of funds, as her father's fortune at the tables waxed and waned, and how much harder but more stable their lives had been since he'd disappeared, ten years ago.

Pol told her about his uncle's decision to send him to England after his mother died, and about his cold reception and lonely boyhood in England. "I understand why I had to go after my mother died," he said, but it wasn't true. Part of him had always questioned it, especially when he recalled the close knit but large family he'd left. "Napoleon had gone to war with England again, and Uncle Giuseppe said that Tuscany was no place for an English boy. I was better off with my father's people, he said." Surely, his uncle could have pretended? Pol looked more Italian than English and back then he had spoken Italian better than he spoke English. After sixteen years, he only remembered a few words, but sometimes those were still the first words to come to his lips, and he had to stop and think of the English word instead. If the family in Italy had really wanted Pol, they would have kept him. "He promised he would write. But he never did."

The clock on the mantel gave its soft chime to mark the hour. *Midnight.* Time to leave the thorny memories and search the house.

Chapter Seven

THE HOUSE WAS the sprawling maze that Grace had described. Without Pol to show her the way, Jackie might easily have become lost, even with the map that Grace had helped her draw. Grace was more familiar with the servants' ways that riddled the walls, and that was the way Jackie had intended to go. But Pol conducted her up the main staircase and along several passages to a separate wing of the house.

Pol explained that the wing had its own door to the garden, which allowed Rotten Riese to come and go without alerting his mother. "His are the only occupied rooms in this part of the house," he told Jackie. "It used to be the bachelor wing when the family had house parties, but there hasn't been one of those since before I came here." He stopped in front of one of the doors. Jackie wondered what it was like to live in a house that had such long hallways and so many doors leading to so many rooms. It was so different than the cottages she and Maman had inhabited. "There. That's the one." He found the right key and unlocked the door.

He took back the candelabra he'd given her to hold. "I'll go first, if you permit me," he whispered. "Just to make sure Oscar's valet is not within."

Jackie did her best not to show any fear. If Pol realized how much her heart quailed, he would refuse to involve her further, and she was determined to be part of the search.

"No one here," Pol called, softly. "Come in, Jackie."

When she was a little girl, Jackie's mother had several times taken her along to the shop of a second-hand dealer who was also a pawnbroker. The shop had fascinated her, crowded as it was with color, shapes, textures—furniture, paintings, ornaments, fire implements, rugs, even drapes. There was no organization, just items piled on one another wherever there was a space. Nothing fitted with anything else.

Rotten Riese's living room reminded her of that shop, except with more expensive items and more glitter. Mirrors, crystals, and gilt abounded, reflecting the candlelight and dazzling the eye.

"Awful, isn't it?" Pol said.

"How on earth are we going to find anything?" Jackie wondered.

"Searching it would take hours," Pol acknowledged. "Maybe days. And there are two other rooms in the suite. But tonight, we are just taking the money you need for the rent, and Oscar always keeps his money in the swan." He pointed to the gilded bird, which graced—if that was the right word—a table by the window.

"Oh," said Jackie. "I thought that was a goose. Is it a money box?" She crossed the room and ran her finger down the ornament's long neck.

She was right. It did look more like a goose than a swan. "Oscar calls it a swan," he commented, and showed her how it worked. "If you pull the neck down, this aperture opens. You put anything you want to hide on the platform, and when you raise the neck, the object drops into the body of the swan."

Jackie experimented. "You can't get your hand in to retrieve what you've put in there," she discovered. "There's another mechanism?"

He nodded. "Twist the left wing clockwise," he said.

She did. Another aperture opened under the swan's tail feathers and a stream of coins dropped onto the table. "It lays gold!" Jackie exclaimed. She twisted the wing again and was rewarded with another stream of coins.

Pol pulled the pile toward him and began counting. "You can't empty it or he'll notice, but you can certainly take the rent and the money that the Rieses owe your mother. I need something to put this in." He looked around the room as if a pouch or purse was going to suddenly appear.

"I have one." Jackie opened her coat to unbuckle the pouch she wore on her belt. His eyes riveted on her chest, where her man's shirt molded to her breasts. She had not bound them tonight. She was wearing a coat that disguised her figure, and she figured that—if she was caught—her gender would not stay a secret for long.

As she stilled, her mind screaming at her to run before he seized her, he wrenched his gaze upwards. Even in the candlelight, she could see the color flooding his cheeks. "Thank you," he said. "Pass it to me and I shall put the money in it. Ten pounds. Will that be enough?"

For the rent. He is talking about the rent. She said, "Yes, perfect." and finished unbuckling the pouch to hand it to him. Five pounds for the rent, and a whole five pounds besides. Surely that would be enough to move them away from the Rieses?

"I shall walk you home," Pol proposed.

"That is not necessary," Jackie said. "I often go around at night dressed like this."

"You often go out at night? Does your mother not worry?" He must have seen her answer on her face, for he added, "Ah. I see. Your mother does not know."

"My mother threw me out of the house the evening before last," Jackie heard herself say. What was it about Pol Allegro that he drew such truths out of her?

Pol was obviously shocked. "Threw you out? But why?"

She had said this much. She might as well tell him the rest. "She sent me to sell our cow to raise the money for the rent. But she is not a young cow, and we could not afford the services of a bull these last two years, so she is not in milk. Maman thought I should have sold her to the knacker for two pounds instead of to a lady who gave me a pound but wanted her for her herd."

She was being unfair to Maman, telling a stranger such a story without explaining. "She is worried about what will happen to us, and particularly about Rotten Riese's intentions for me. That makes her irritable, and when she is irritable, she says things she doesn't mean. She will feel better once I give her the money. I will go home in the morning. It is too late now. She will be fast asleep."

Pol shook his head. "I doubt it. She has been searching for you. I've heard of it from several people today. From the sounds of it, she was out all day, and I cannot believe she will have gone tamely to bed."

His tone did not sound accusing but his words made her feel guilty, and in her own defense she snapped, "She knows I can look after myself. When will she stop treating me like a child?"

Pol disarmed her by commenting, "I envy you having some-one to worry about you. My grandmother is the only person who cares about me, and these days, she is as likely to take me for my father than remember me for myself. At least you have your mother, and she has you." He held up his hand in the way her mother did when she was pretending to be a gentleman about to escort Jackie onto the floor at a grand ball. "May I walk you home, Miss Jacqueline Haricot? Otherwise, *I* shall worry."

Was she touched or merely flattered by his claim? Whichever it was, she gave in. "Very well, Pol. You can walk with me while I go home." After all, she couldn't stop him from walking anywhere he wished. It wasn't as if he was courting her, or anything like that. She had no idea how such a ridiculous thought even entered her head.

She ignored his hand. She was not going to risk the disturbing sensation that had thrilled through her body last time they touched. "I take it we don't go the way I came in?"

He laughed. "Not quite." Cautioning her to silence with a finger against his lips, he led her out of Oscar's rooms, through the quiet house, down the servant stairs, and through servant passages to the breakfast room, which had a door that let onto the terrace.

Once they had crossed the lawn below the terrace and entered the first of the enclosed gardens, he spoke again. "The quickest way is through the maze and then the woods, I believe."

"Yes," Jackie agreed. "And we'll be out of sight most of the way, too."

"I asked before if you often go out at night, and you didn't answer. Is Jack Le Gume a regular thing with you?"

"I invented him a year ago, the first time Rotten Riese doubled the rent. My father taught me how to play most games the men around here are interested in. I used to go out once a month, and it was enough. But the shopkeepers in the village have had their rents increased, too, and so they have put their prices up, and Maman is having trouble with rheumatics in her hands, so is not able to complete the same volume of work. I have been able to manage with gambling once a week."

"Hmm," he said.

"I don't cheat," she assured him. "But I can usually win more than I lose. Especially if I can hold on in the game until everyone else has had too much to drink. I don't drink, you see, so if I can play for long enough, winning is almost inevitable."

"Except when other people cheat," he commented.

"I should have expected that of Rotten Riese. I should have left with my winnings as soon as I had enough to pay the rent. It is my first rule—walk away from the table before you've won enough to make the other players angry. It has made me welcome at games in taverns and inns in all the villages for miles around. I gave into the temptation to make your cousin suffer."

He cast her a sidelong glance, the corner of his mouth quirked in a smile. "I understand the temptation to thrash my cousin. It is ever with me."

She acknowledged his witticism with a chuckle. "However, you resist!"

They were through the woods, and sure enough, light shone from the windows of the cottage. Maman must be awake. Jackie stopped, uncertain how to tell Pol to come no farther. She had enough to confess to her mother without having to confess she had been out alone at night with a man.

Once again, he showed how attuned he was to her thoughts. "I shall wait here until you are inside. Do you work for the squire tomorrow?"

At her nod, he said, "What time do you finish? I shall meet you on the way home and we can talk about our next steps."

"I leave by noon and walk back along the lane that runs behind the village," Jackie said. "Good evening, Pol. Thank you." She rushed away before she did something outrageous like shake his hand—or hug him.

"My pleasure," he called after her, his voice so soft she only just caught the words.

Maman had latched the window by which Jackie normally escaped on her nocturnal adventures. She had to knock on the door, and to answer when her mother called out, "Who is it?"

"Maman, it is me. Jacqueline!"

"*Cherie!*" Her mother's voice had a sob in it, and Jackie could hear her removing the bar on the door and fumbling with the latch. She looked over her shoulder to see Pol standing on the edge of the wood, then the door opened, Pol faded backwards into the shadows of the trees, and Jackie's mother almost leaped from the house and seized Jackie for a ferocious hug.

"I was so worried, dear one." Maman was speaking French, a clear sign of how upset she was. "I could not find you. I worried that someone had taken you—that dreadful man, perhaps. Come in! Come in! Where have you been? How could you have worried me so?" She hauled on Jackie's arm, and Jackie let herself be pulled into the house.

"You sent me away, Maman," she protested. "I disappointed

you. I did not want to come back until I could pay the rent."

"I sent you out of my sight, not out of the house! But there, I should not have been so cross. You did your best, I know this. As for the rent, I spit on it! Do you think I love the rent more than my daughter? We shall go away, *cherie*. We will start again. It shall not be the first time. We shall find somewhere where the landlord is fair."

Jackie had been unbuckling her pouch. "I have the rent, Maman," she said, handing it to her mother.

Chapter Eight

POL REMEMBERED WHEN his grandmother had been a lively and compelling force in the manor. Back then, when he first arrived, she and the dower house where she lived had been his sanctuary from his cousin's bullying and his aunt's nagging.

It was thanks to her that he had been taken from the kitchen and given a room of his own—a small one, but on the family floor. She had insisted on him being allowed to take lessons with Oscar. He had even—back in those days—taken his meals with the family on the occasions that the older Lady Riese joined them, rather than in his room or with the servants.

She had begun to fade, though, losing focus, regularly stumbling, falling asleep throughout the day. Perhaps she had had some kind of fit or perhaps it was grief over the loss of her last surviving son.

By the time Pol escaped into an apprenticeship with the steward, she was barely in the land of the living, spending most of the day asleep and frequently mistaking visitors for other people she had known in her younger days.

Nonetheless, Pol visited her most days. Unless she was asleep, she was always welcoming, even if he had to reintroduce himself every time. Today, her sour nursemaid—more keeper than maid or nurse—reluctantly admitted the dowager was awake and would see him.

She was sitting by her window, looking out at the garden, but when he spoke, she turned to face him. "I know you, young man, do I not?"

He said what he said almost every day. "I am Apollo, Gran. The son of your son, Richmond."

"Richie's son. Oh, yes. Of course. He hasn't been to visit me. You look like him, a little. His eyes were blue, though."

Pol had heard that before. He had his Italian mother's dark brown hair and brown eyes. "How are you today, Gran?"

She waved a frail hand—her skin was crinkled and age spotted, the blue tracery of veins clear under the translucent skin. "Well enough, Apollo. Well enough." She frowned at him and then her face cleared. "Richie went to Italy," she declared. "He met a girl there." She grabbed his hands and gazed into his eyes, her own distressed. "Aaah. Poor Richie. He died. The poor girl had a baby. I told Frederick to write to her and invite her to bring her little boy home to England. He belonged with his family, the young man, even if he was half-Italian."

Frederick was the name of her husband, Pol's grandfather. Had grandfather written to Pol's mother? Then Mama had ignored the invitation. But perhaps that was the reason he had been sent to England after Mama had died. If so, the welcome he received had been far less than Gran remembered. He had come believing his parents were married. His mother had been addressed as Signora Riese, and he had been called Apollo Riese. Discovering he had no right to the name had been only the start of the shocks in store. She frowned. "Did he come? I think he came. Who did you say you were, dear?" She had forgotten him again already. Usually, once he had reintroduced himself, she remembered him for the rest of the visit.

"I am Apollo, Gran. Richmond's son. I did come."

"My lady has had enough, Mr. Allegro," said the maid. "She is becoming confused. It is time for you to leave."

Pol was prepared to argue, but she was right. Gran's brief

burst of energy had gone. Her hands slipped from his and her eyes drifted shut. "I will come back tomorrow," he said.

She was getting worse, and the tonics that crowded her dressing table didn't seem to be making any difference. It was time to take her away. In a little over a week the Rieses would be gone to London. After that, he needed to make his escape, and between when the Rieses left and when he did, he wanted to search the house.

Something that incriminated Oscar was what Jackie wanted. And Pol wanted that, too. He would leave, yes, and take Gran with him. But he would strike a blow for justice on the way.

POL RODE AROUND a curve in the back road that led to the squire's stable, found himself almost on a group of people—and set his horse bounding forward. Jackie, cornered between a shed and thick scrub, her back pressed to a tree, was facing off against two much larger youths. "Let's take his shirt orf," shouted one. "That'll tell we if'n he's a boy, or just pretendin'."

Like hell! Pol was on them before they realized he was coming, the horse pushing them away from Jackie as it forced its way between her and the bullies. "Leave the boy alone."

"It ain't a boy," one of her persecutors insisted. "I tell 'ee, she'm a girl. Takin' a boy's place, actin' likes she's as good as us'ns. She's cut 'er 'air! Tha's disgustin', that is."

Pol was more focused on the speaker's hair than what he said. He knew he had seen that straw-color before. That and those pale-blue eyes were the signifiers of a family he knew well. "You're a Whitely," he stated.

The Whitelys were one of the district's problem families. Casual laborers living on their wits—of which they could muster few—which mostly meant lending their muscle to anything that paid and supplementing uncertain wages by theft and poaching.

The father was a drunkard. The eldest son was away with the army. The remaining older sons were well on their way to following the father's footsteps.

"Wha' of it?" the boy sneered—for he was still a boy, though a tall and heavy one.

Time for an aristocratic eyebrow. Pol rubbed his hand thoughtfully up and down the stock of his whip as emphasis. "Contain your impudence, young Whitely. Shall I have a word with your father? The squire? Or beat you myself?"

The boy backed away, but his accomplice was stuck between Whitely and the shed. "And you are?" Pol demanded.

"It weren't me, Mister," insisted the other boy. "I didn't do nuffin'. I was just helping a mate."

"Your name?" Pol insisted.

Whitely, assuming Pol was distracted, took to his heels, and his friend scurried after him. Whitely was correct. Pol's eye had been caught by Jackie picking up the cap that had obviously been lost in the scuffle. Her coat rode up and her baggy trousers pulled tight over her shapely rear. Pol's mouth dried. If Whitely had seen the lady bending over, no wonder he had guessed she was a girl.

He averted his eyes and dismounted, by which time the boys were out of sight and Jackie had straightened, her cap on her head, her figure once again concealed by the shapeless clothes she wore.

"Thank you for chasing them off," Jackie said.

Blue. Her eyes were an intense and glorious blue, with a dark blue circumference to the iris. And she was still talking, so he should listen instead of staring at her like a lummox.

"Dan Whitely was threatened with the sack today, at the squire's, and he took it into his head that it was my fault," she explained. "He and his friend came after me, to teach me a lesson, Dan said. The friend is from the village and knows me from church. He wouldn't let Dan hit me till I proved I wasn't Jackie Haricot. They will tell everyone, Pol. I won't be able to go back to the squire's. He said I couldn't work there if people found out I was a girl."

So, Squire Pershing knew. Pol was relieved to hear it. "It wouldn't be safe," he said. Many men would feel entitled to take advantage of a girl who worked in a man's workplace while dressed as a boy.

"That's what the squire said." Jackie sounded disgruntled, but she perked up as she added, "Maman says it is time for us to leave this village, so I would not have been able to continue working there, anyway."

"You'll be sorry to lose the work?" Stable boys were the lowest in the stable pecking order and got all the dirtiest jobs. Pol had always been relieved that the Rieses had not seen fit to send him to the stables.

"Not the work so much as the money. Shoveling horse leavings pays twice as much as sewing miles of straight seams. Anyway, I like horses, and straight seams are boring. Besides, the pay comes every week, whereas people often don't pay their dressmaker's bills for months. Also, on days I work there, I can stay for the midday meal, which helps stretch the pennies at home."

By silent agreement, they had begun to walk toward the dressmaker's cottage, Pol leading his horse and Jackie keeping pace at his side.

"What work would you want to do if you had a choice?" Pol asked. Truly, though, a girl of her quality should not have to work at all. Not for wages. She should be looking forward to a home, a husband, a family, not thinking about how to help her mother to keep a roof over their heads and food on the table.

Jackie frowned in thought. "Not cleaning out stables," she declared firmly. She sighed. "Not sewing, either. One must buy the fabric and notions, then put in weeks of work with no guarantee that the customer will pay on time, if at all."

"Marriage, perhaps?" he asked.

She snorted. "Hardly likely. Who marries a seamstress? Men

assume that we are no better than we should be, just because we exist on pennies, and therefore many must sell themselves to survive."

They strode along in silence for a minute or so, while he struggled to suppress the urge to offer for her, then and there. She would laugh in his face, probably. And since when had he decided that marrying Jackie Haricot was a good idea?

Oblivious to the direction of his thoughts, Jackie continued, "Maman is convinced that somewhere there is a gentleman who will see past my current circumstances and elevate me to 'my proper sphere'. 'Which is what?' I ask her. I was born the daughter of a *Comte*, yes, but by the time I was born, he had lost everything except me and my mother and was living in England on his wits and his charm. Now I am a seamstress and a part-time stable boy."

She chuckled, but there was no amusement in the sound. "I am neither fish nor fowl, Pol. Too educated to be the wife of a man who would marry a poor seamstress; too poor and too sullied by work to marry a man of my parents' former class. In some ways, Maman is as much of a dreamer as my father was."

"I am planning to leave, too," he told her. "Once the Rieses have gone to London, and after you and I have searched the house, I am going to take my grandmother and go."

"Maman wants to go now," Jackie said. "Before Lady Day. But she is afraid Lord Riese will pursue us if we do that. Yet if we wait until he has gone to London, we will have paid five pounds for a cottage we don't plan to use."

"Perhaps she should refuse to pay the rent, and let him turn her out," Pol suggested.

Jackie shook her head. "She is afraid he will take me by force if she does that."

That was not going to happen. Pol would not allow it. "Will you introduce me to your mother, please, Jackie? I have an idea, but she will need to agree."

"Tell me," Jackie demanded.

The idea had sprung into his head because he was trying to think of a way to stay in touch with Jackie. It was still a good idea, though. "It's a way to make up that five pounds and also help me, at the same time. My grandmother is frail. She needs a woman to look after her, but I do not trust her maid. Do you think your mother would agree to us all traveling together until I can find a safe place to live and another maid for Gran? I would pay all traveling expenses and her wages."

"It seems a good idea to me. Don't be offended, though, if Maman is suspicious. When I told her how you had helped me, she warned me to be careful of you, in case you want..." She blushed.

"I shall need to convince her that I am a gentleman," Pol said. He hoped Jackie's mother could not read minds. He could guarantee his behavior, but where Jackie was concerned, he was not always in control of his thoughts.

They were at the cottage. Jackie showed Pol where to tie the horse and conducted him inside. "Maman, may I present Mr. Apollo Allegro? He has something he wishes to discuss with you."

The dressmaker put her sewing to one side and stood. Pol found it easy to believe she was nobility. It was in the way of the proud carriage of her head and her direct gaze. "Mr. Allegro," she said.

Pol bowed, as deeply as he would to any English countess. Deeper, perhaps, for this was Jackie's mother. "It is a privilege to meet you, Madame *la Comtesse*. Should I say *la Comtesse de Haricot*?"

"You should say 'La Blanc' in this village, lest we be over-heard, young man. In our next home, I shall be Madame Haricot, so that those who would ravage my daughter will know they are dealing with her mother! However, if not for the revolution, it would be Madame *la Comtesse de Haricot du Charmont*. But if not for the revolution, we would not be in this cottage. My daughter tells me that you have been of assistance to her. We thank you."

Pol would have known her for French by the cadence of her

sentences, and the way she pronounced some sounds, but her English was otherwise excellent.

"It was my privilege to be of service, Madame. You and your daughter have been badly treated by Lord Riese and his mother."

"Not as badly as he would like," said the lady. "That man will never touch my daughter. I shall kill him first."

"I'd prefer to make that unnecessary, my lady," Pol told her. "But I shall do it myself if need be. If that was the only way to keep Mademoiselle Haricot safe."

Madame Haricot regarded him with a jaundiced eye. "Fine words, *Monsieur*. Is that what you came here to say?"

Honesty might be his best strategy. "Your daughter warned me you would be suspicious, Madame. It is understandable. I do not ask you to trust me, but merely to give me time to show that I am worthy of your trust. I came here to ask you for your help with my grandmother, for I, too, want to escape the Rieses, and I cannot leave my grandmother behind."

"The old dowager Lady Riese," Madame Haricot said, thoughtfully. "The people of this place speak well of when she was viscountess here. Before her son and his wife took over. I make her dresses. She is not in her wits."

"She is confused, and very frail."

"Does the doctor visit her?" Madame Haricot asked. "The man here is an idiot. I would not trust him to care for a dog, if I had one."

Pol had to agree with her on that one. "He has prescribed all sorts of nostrums. I do not know what they are or what they are supposed to do."

"Hmmm." Madame Haricot looked like her daughter when she narrowed very similar blue eyes in thought. Or, Pol supposed, the other way around. "I do not like her maid."

"Nor do I," Pol agreed. "That is why I need someone else to help me care for her. Will you take the position? Just temporarily until I can make a new home for her and find someone else?"

"The maid shouts at her, and pinches her when she is slow, or if she speaks to me," Madame Haricot commented.

Bloody hell! How had Pol missed that? He had seen bruises on his grandmother's hands, but he had believed Crawford when she said that Gran banged into things and bruised easily. "I have to get her out of there," he repeated.

"Where do you intend to go?" Jackie asked. "And when?"

"I don't have a strong preference for where," Pol told her. "As to when, I want to search my aunt's and my cousin's rooms before I go. Madame Haricot, your daughter suggested that, if we can find evidence of crimes they have committed, we might be able to stop the Rieses for good. I'd like to try, but I don't want to stay too long after they leave for London. Perhaps a week?"

"Hmm," said Madame Haricot again. "Jackie, go and make a pot of tea. I wish to speak with Mr. Allegro in private. Mr. Allegro, come with me into my work room."

Pol followed, his conscience advising him that she had noticed his interest in her daughter, and sure enough, as soon as she had closed the door, she said, in a hushed voice, "What is your interest in my daughter?"

Only the truth would do. "I cannot have any interest yet," Pol said. "I have enough saved to keep us all for perhaps six months, and not in luxury, which is what your daughter deserves. I don't know whether I will be able to find work, or what even what kind of work I might look for. I think the steward here will give me a good reference, but finding a position without one will be hard. I have no right to any intentions when I cannot guarantee my wife and her mother a home and a measure of comfort for the foreseeable future."

That was all he could say on the matter. It was, perhaps, more than he should say, given that Jackie had no idea how he felt, but this was her mother. Madame Haricot had a right to be concerned for her daughter's safety.

"You intend marriage, then? On a few days' acquaintance?" The lady sounded scornful.

Again, Pol opted for honesty. "I am thinking of marriage, yes.

Your daughter is an innocent, if perforce somewhat wiser than most of those in the social rank to which she belongs by birth. It has to be marriage or nothing. But I have not spoken to her of marriage or anything else. You must see, my lady, that I have nothing to offer. Not at the moment. Hopes for the future, yes. But one cannot eat hopes."

She said nothing, but merely examined him, her expression thoughtful. Pol resisted the increasingly uncomfortable urge to shift under her gaze. It seemed a long time before she nodded and said, "Very well, Mr. Allegro. I accept your position. I will care for your grandmother on the journey and until you can make other arrangements.

"Thank you, Madame," he replied.

"We shall rejoin my daughter and discuss our plans," she decreed. "Be aware that I will be watching you, Mr. Allegro. And I will not permit you to hurt my daughter."

Pol had no intention of hurting Jackie, but he was increasingly aware that Jackie had the power to hurt him.

Chapter Nine

LADY DAY DAWNED cloudy and grim, but fortunately the rain held off as the tenants lined up to pay their rent. It was the Riese tradition that the rents were paid to the steward in public, at a table set up in the courtyard at the foot of the steps to the main entrance of the house.

Pol sat beside the steward, who was back from his sister's, and recorded the payments in the rent books for farms, village, and other properties as the steward received them and counted the money. Oscar watched from the parlor that overlooked the main entrance and appeared from time to time when a tenant he had a particular interest in—one of his cronies or one he was bullying—took their place at the front of the line.

He was there, a broad grin of expectation on his face, when it was the turn of Madame Haricot. "Well, Madame?" he said, gloating. "I do not suppose your circumstances have improved in the past few days? Where is your pretty seamstress?"

Madame Haricot ignored him and spoke to the steward. "Five pounds, *Monsieur*. Count them. I wish there to be no mistake."

Oscar, who was leaning against one of the pillars at the side of the steps, pushed himself upright and strode over to confirm the evidence of his ears. "Five pounds? How did the likes of you come up with five pounds?"

"It was not easy, *Monsieur*," the lady said. "The amount is extortionate. However, I am a skilled dressmaker, and I have friends. It is done. Paid and written in the book. Be aware, *Monsieur*, that I am never going to let you despoil my daughter."

"Paid? No. I forbid it!" Oscar shouted, ignoring what Madame Haricot had said.

"Madame is correct. It is paid and written in the book," Pol pointed out.

Oscar glared at Pol and then turned his scowl on Madame Haricot. "This is not over," he threatened, and stalked back up the stairs.

"Keep your daughter out of his sight," Pol advised. "It will only be for a few days. Until he goes to London."

"It is good advice, Madame," the steward agreed.

She nodded. "I know it."

"Here is your receipt for the rent," the steward said. "I have signed it, and Mr. Allegro has signed it."

The next in line was waiting. Madame Haricot left and the routine of rent day continued. Oscar came out of the house again and sloped off toward the stables. Ten minutes or so later, Pol glimpsed him riding down the carriage way. He was probably going to find some cronies to drink with.

By noon, the rents were all taken. Or, in the case of a few unfortunate people, marked as unpaid. Pol was helping to pack up the records when Madame Haricot came hurrying up the driveway.

"Mr. Allegro, is my Jacqueline with you?" Her face was drawn with worry and pale with distress.

"No, Madame." Pol's mind flooded with worrisome images. "I have not seen her since yesterday."

"She wanted to go to the squire's this morning. To explain she could not work in the stables anymore. I told her to go in girl's clothes. It would be safer, I thought, now those wicked boys know who she is. She has not come home, Mr. Allegro."

"May I go and look for her?" Pol asked the steward.

"Yes, lad. Go. I shall finish clearing up here," the steward assured him.

"I'll get my horse, Madame," Pol said. He strode toward the stables, and Madame Haricot kept pace. Fair enough. If his child was missing, he would want to join the search, too. "Do you ride?" he asked her. "Or do you want to come up behind me?"

"Pillion, *Monsieur*. I have not ridden in years, and then it was sidesaddle."

As fast as he could, he saddled Ajax and buckled a pillion pad to the saddle for Madame's comfort. Ajax was not his usual ride, but he had been used to carry pillion passengers before and could be trusted not to object.

Within minutes, he was swinging into the saddle. He rode the horse to the mounting block, and Madame took her seat, perched on the pad as if it were a chair, with her legs dangling side by side. She gripped the saddle with the hand nearest to it and said, "Ready, Mr. Allegro."

Ten minutes later, they stopped outside the squire's stable. Pol swung one leg over the horse's neck to make an awkward descent and then helped Madame Haricot down. "I shall speak to the stable master, Madame. Will you ask for your daughter inside?"

"The little miss left three quarters of an hour ago by the stable clock, Mr. Allegro," said the stable master. "She went her usual way, along the back road. I daresay, she's stopped along the way to talk to someone, or to sit a spell. No need to rush back to sewing. I wouldn't want to sit still all day sewing, and neither does she, I'll be bound."

"We came along that road from the Hall, but she might have been on the far section of the road, beyond where the bridle path from Westerville joins. Madame and I will check. I was in time to stop her being harassed by the Whitely boy yesterday, and one of his friends."

The stable master spat. "That one. He's been trouble from day one. Should have got rid of him months ago, but there. The squire wanted to help Mrs. Whitely and give the boy a chance." He shook his head. "Glad to see the back of him, but we'll be sorry to see Jackie go, and that's a fact. She might be small compared to some of the boys, but she's a hard worker. And she has a gift with horses."

Madame Haricot emerged from the house, shaking her head, her face creased with worry.

"The stable master says she left three quarters of an hour ago, Madame. Along the back road, he said."

"Hurry." Madame suited actions to words, picking up her skirts to run to the mounting block.

In less than a minute, they were on their way. "Pray God we find her before that devil does," said Madame.

SINCE JACKIE HAD to pass the shack on her way home, she stopped to collect the male clothes she had kept there, and the other items with which she had furnished the single room in the years since she first discovered the building.

She wrapped everything up in a blanket and made a parcel out of it, then found it was too bulky to carry and split it into two parcels, using her Jack Le Gume cloak for the other. She then decided to sweep out the shack. She was leaving it better than she found it, having done some basic repairs on the roof and the corners of windows, but something in her felt this final clean was a thank you to a place that had been both refuge and jumping off point for her adventures.

Carrying a parcel under each arm, she made her way back to the lane that led to her cottage. Maman had planned to go early to pay the rent at the manor, but even if she had been delayed, surely, she would be home by now. She and Jackie had a few minor sewing tasks to finish, but their main task today and for the next several days was to sort everything and decide what they would take with them, what they could usefully sell, and what to simply leave behind.

Composing lists in her mind, she was not paying much attention to her surroundings. Not until she heard someone shout, "There she is. Get her!"

That was sufficient warning for her to swing around, buffeting her would-be assailant with one of the parcels. Dan Whitely, curse him. The blow knocked him off-balance, and the second one she delivered with the other parcel sent him sprawling.

But then someone grabbed her from behind, wrapping his arms around her and locking her arms to her chest. "Take them parcels, young Dan," said a growl close to her ear. "There might be summat we can sell."

The man held Jackie up off the ground, so that her struggles had no purchase, and Dan dodged her attempted kicks and forced her to drop the parcels. Both assailants ignored her screams and her shouted imprecations in English and French as they dragged her into the bushes.

"Get us that there rope, Dan," the man behind her ordered. "And your kerchief. Her yellin's makin' my head hurt."

"Why my kerchief?" Dan whined.

His partner wasn't having any discussion on the matter. "Just do it."

Jackie didn't want either kerchief. Both assailants smelt as if they never washed, and heaven alone knew what other substances might have been wiped with or onto the disgusting object around Dan's neck. She renewed her struggles and managed a lucky kick on the man's knee that had him yelling and loosing his grip.

She almost slithered free, but he recovered quickly and fetched her a whack across one cheek that sent her tumbling to the ground. "Bitch," he snarled. "You'll pay for that."

He threw himself on top of her, holding her down by the weight of his body. He was another of the Whitelys—an older, dirtier, and meaner version of Dan. Fear almost swamped her, but she fought it back, determined to be ready to take any opportunity to escape whatever they had in store for her.

With Dan's help, the older Whitely forced her mouth open and shoved Dan's foul kerchief to ball up inside her mouth, then tied it in place with his own. If she vomited, she would choke, and not vomiting took all her focus when she should have been fighting to free herself.

All too soon, he had the rope bound around and around her, tying her arms to her sides so that all she could do was helplessly flap her arms.

The older brother sat back on her hips and grinned down at her. "Nice bubbies," he commented, grabbing one of her breasts in a meaty hand and squeezing hard. "That's for kickin' me, bitch."

She glared at him.

"We gotta take her to the viscount, Bill," said Dan.

"Not yet," said Bill. "How's he s'pposed to know if I have her first?"

Dan wasn't so sure. "He won't like it."

"Who's gonna tell him?" Bill sneered. "You?"

"Her, maybe?" Dan suggested.

Bill scoffed. "Her? Why would he listen to her? I'm 'is mate! She's nothing but a lyin' teasin' bitch. That's right, ain't it, bitch?" He squeezed her breast again.

Dan was not finished. "Pete won't like it, neither."

Whoever Pete was, the mention of him made Bill furious. "Pete ain't the boss of me," Bill snarled. "Comin' home, throwin' 'is weight around, tellin' me I have to get a job, tellin' Da to stop drinkin'. Who does 'e think he is?"

Grabbing one of Jackie's breasts in each hand he squeezed again, so hard that Jackie cried out. "You won't be tellin' no one nothin', bitch," he growled.

He got no further. Someone exploded out of the bushes and charged into him, setting him sprawling. She recognized Pol Allegro, even through the snarl that distorted his face as he punched Bill again and again, both fists flying with a speed and force against which the other man's attempt at a defense was swiftly overwhelmed.

Could he fight two of them? Dan was not yet an adult, but he was a big youth, and he had just picked up a large dead branch, which he was lifting as a club. Jackie tried to make a noise to warn Pol, but it was no more than a squeak.

Then a fourth player entered the scene. "Drop that branch, Dan Whitely," said her mother's voice.

Jackie managed to shift her head enough to watch her mother step out of the bushes, a pistol held steadily in her hand.

Dan almost obeyed the authoritative voice, but she could see him stiffen as another thought occurred to him. "You won't shoot. You're a woman."

"I am a woman," Maman agreed coldly. "I am the woman whose daughter you kidnapped and tied up. Drop that branch and untie my daughter, or I shall shoot you in the knee and untie her myself."

Something in her tone convinced him, for he did as he was told, kneeling beside her to fumble with the ropes. He was in between Jackie and the two men, and she could see little of the fight, but the sound of flesh thumping into flesh and the paroxysms of the legs she could see told her that it continued. Pol was still on top.

As the rope loosened, Jackie wriggled her arms out of it and clawed at the gag.

"Mr. Allegro, I think the man you are hitting is unconscious," Maman said.

Pol stopped to check, then stood, lowering his bloodied knuckles. Jackie's anxious eyes picked out a livid bruise high on one cheek. Apart from that, he bore no wound, and certainly nothing that could have supplied the red marks spattering across his light blue coat, high on one side, with a few splashes on his cravat. Jackie's assailant, whose face was a bloodied mess, was a more likely source.

His cheeks flushed with embarrassment. "Thank you, *Madame*. My apologies, ladies. You shouldn't have had to see that."

Jackie looked at Bill's battered face and her stomach gave up the fight. She scrambled to her feet and raced to lose her breakfast under a bush. Even that tasted better than Dan's kerchief. "So disgusting," she said, and turned on Dan. "Don't you ever get your clothes washed?"

"You're hurt," Pol commented, taking a couple of strides toward her, and putting up his hand as if he would touch her cheek. She suddenly realized how much it throbbed even as he checked his movement. "Did this pond scum hit you?" He poked Bill with his boot.

"Ye've killed him," Dan whimpered.

"He's still breathing," Pol told the boy. "He'll live to be hanged or transported." He scooped up the rope that Dan had dropped on the ground and used one end of it to tie Dan's wrists.

Dan's eyes opened so wide that the whites showed all the way around the pale irises. "It weren't our idea," he complained. "T'viscount told us to get her."

Pol cut the rope with a long tail, which he handed to Jackie while he began tying Bill with the rest. "I suppose it is not your fault, then," said Pol, kindly. "Just tell the magistrate that you were following orders, Whitely. I daresay he will take that into account."

Sneaky. Dan is fool enough to think he'd be allowed free with that excuse, so won't cause any trouble. Bill stayed unconscious—and he did not rouse as Pol hoisted him across Ajax's saddle, tied him in place, and fastened the tail of Dan's rope to the saddle.

"I'll take those pistols now," he said to Maman, and she handed over the one she'd held on Dan all this time plus another that she took from one of her pockets.

"We will have to turn this pair in to the magistrate," Pol said. "Ladies, do you feel able to come and bear witness to what happened?"

Maman nodded. Jackie agreed, but said, "I need something to

clean my mouth. It feels as if I have been eating garbage."

Pol had taken a pouch from his saddle and was loading one of the pistols from it. He handed it to Maman and felt around inside his coat, coming out with a flask. "Brandy," he said. "It might help."

It did. It burned her mouth and then scorched its way down her throat, but still, under the flavor of the alcohol, she could taste mud and corruption. She had another swig from the flask.

"Careful," said Maman. She shot a glance at Dan Whitely and lowered her voice. "We do not want to give the magistrate any reason to disbelieve you."

Pol put the flask away and loaded the other pistol. Jackie's eyes widened as she realized that Maman had held Dan at bay with an unloaded weapon.

"Maman?" she said. "Did you know it had no bullets?"

Maman shrugged and spread her hands. "What was I to do? Let that boy hit Mr. Allegro, and then have both brothers turn on us? *Non.*" She shrugged again. "It worked."

"It worked very well," said Pol. "Let's hope that handing them over to the magistrate also works."

Chapter Ten

BARON BARTON WAS of little use. First, he declared that any female who went around in men's clothing was asking for "it". Maman put on all the considerable hauteur of which she was capable and commented to the room at large, "I thought England a land of laws, but I see that this poor excuse for a gentleman has no interest in justice."

The magistrate sputtered.

Pol's contribution was diplomatic. "These two men assaulted Miss Haricot. That is illegal in England, and Lord Barton is the King's man. He will, of course, uphold the law."

"There are witnesses?" Lord Barton demanded.

"Miss Haricot, myself, and Madame de Haricot," Mr. Allegro said.

Lord Barton glared at Maman. "I thought you were Madame La Blanc."

Maman answered with her court curtsey. Not the full curtsey for monarchs, but the curtsey for another peer of her own rank. Lord Barton was only a baron, but Maman was clearly playing for effect. "Madame La Blanc is the name I use for my business as a modiste. I am Madame *La Comtesse de Haricot du Charmont*."

It did not have the expected effect. "An *émigré*," Lord Barton grumbled, and then turned to Pol and pointedly ignored Maman and Jackie.

"I shall lock up the Whitely brothers and refer them to the Assizes, but I don't believe their claims about Lord Riese. It's clear what they intended for the seamstress, whatever her name is. No need to involve the viscount."

"The viscount has made threats and demands regarding Miss de Haricot to her and to the lady her mother," Pol said. "He has also spoken to me of his intention to take her, by force if necessary."

"Heresay," the magistrate insisted. "And even if he did want the girl as his mistress, that's not against the law. I daresay we'd all be in jail if a man couldn't even look." He chortled at his own wit. "He was not present, and it is only heresay and supposition that he was involved. I can't accuse a man of a crime on the say so of a foreign dressmaker, her brat, and the viscount's bastard cousin." He banged his fist on his desk. "Case closed. You three can go."

He shouted for his constables to take the Whitelys and lock them up until they could be sent to the nearest prison.

Maman was near spitting with rage, but she took Pol's elbow when he offered it to her and allowed herself to be escorted from the baron's house.

POL SAW THE ladies back to their cottage. "We should leave as soon as possible," he said. "I will arrange a cart for your things, and a post chaise to travel in. How long will it take you to pack?"

Oscar was going to hear that his henchmen had been arrested, and he was not going to be happy. Indeed, Lady Riese would probably hear first, and from Lord Barton. Pol had no idea what they might do then, but he did not want Madame and Jackie to be here once they decided their revenge.

"What about your grandmother?" Madame Haricot asked.

He had been thinking about that. "I'll have to come back for her after the Rieses have left for London. I won't be able to get her out of the dower house without the servants noticing, but they won't stop me. Not before they can get a message to the viscountess."

Madame gave a decisive nod. "We will not go far, then. Perhaps to Alstonebridge?" Alstonebridge was the next town to the east after Civerton.

"That will work," Pol agreed.

The ladies went inside to pack. Pol continued along the road between the village and Civerton. He'd already asked in the village and been told there was not a chaise available, nor any cart, either. But in the town, where the influence of the Rieses was less pervasive, he hoped to find what he needed.

Still too pervasive, though. Or perhaps he was reading too much into the refusal he got at both inns that catered to travelers. Perhaps there really were no chaises or any other carriages to hire. Perhaps neither place could spare a cart and a horse to draw it.

An hour and a half's ride took him to Alstonebridge. That town was on the main highway north and it boasted six inns. He had no trouble finding the transport he needed. He paid in advance and arranged for the carter and the post rider to meet him at Madame's cottage at nine the following morning.

Since this would be their destination tomorrow, he took the opportunity to ask about accommodation. "I'll need a place for four people to stay for a month. Myself and three ladies, one of whom is frail and elderly," he told the innkeeper from whom he had rented the vehicles. "Can you recommend a quieter inn? Or a boarding house, perhaps?"

"Would a cottage be suitable, sir?" The innkeeper asked. "The thing is, I have one. It's a wee step out of town, mind, in Little Tidbury. Fifteen minutes ride, sir, or an hour's walk."

"That would not be a problem," Pol assured him. "How do you come to have a spare cottage?"

"Well, sir, this is how it is. My uncle owns the inn, but he's getting older. He wanted me to come and work for him. Well, sir, I was keen to give it a try, but I've been independent for too long just to move in under his roof, so I took a lease on the cottage for twelve months, to give us time to see how we worked together. Only, my uncle has had an apoplexy and needs his family. We have moved in, my wife and children and I, so the cottage is sitting empty. It would be a weight off my mind to have it lived in."

It sounded too good to be true. "May I go and take a look at it?" Pol asked.

Less than two hours later, he had paid the month's rent and was on his way home. They had transport, and they had a place to stay. And the Whitelys, at least, had been dealt with. It had been a productive day.

HIS FEELINGS OF satisfaction lasted until he arrived at the steward's house, to find his belongings on the doorstep. Ah. The Rieses had heard about his involvement in the complaint to the magistrate, had they?

The steward must have been watching from the parlor, for he came to the door.

"I'm sorry, lad, but I have been told that I cannot let you in," he said. "I heard you had the Whitely boys arrested. What possessed you to accuse Lord Riese?"

"Only two of the Whitelys," Pol corrected. "Riese paid them to kidnap Miss Haricot."

The steward shook his head. "I don't doubt it, Pol. But you must have known that Lord Barton would never hold Riese to account unless you caught him in the act of committing a crime."

"And even then, he'd find a reason to blame the victim," grumbled Pol, still annoyed at how the magistrate had spoken about Jackie.

His old friend looked deeply distressed. "I have been instructed to tell you to take your things and leave the estate. You are dismissed and you are no longer welcome here. I'm sorry, lad."

"I wonder what Lady Riese will say about that." With Amanda off to London, he supposed he had outlived his usefulness as a music tutor, and she could easily find other people to fill the positions of secretary and under-steward. But she would have no one to send after Oscar when he was in his cups, and that would surely annoy her.

"It was Lady Riese who gave me my instructions," the steward said. "Perhaps, if you apologized…"

Pol shook his head. "It is time and past time for me to leave, sir, and find a place of my own in this world. I cannot be sorry this has happened." Though he would have preferred to wait until after the Rieses had gone to London. Still, he could come back for his Gran, and he would.

The steward sighed. "You are right, my dear boy." He handed Pol a neatly folded envelope with his name on it. "Your salary for the quarter. Also, a reference. From me, I'm sorry to say. Lady Riese said you would get none from her or from her son. Where will you go? No. Best not tell me. If I do not know, I will not have to lie. But perhaps you could send me a letter from time to time? Just to let me know how you are getting on?"

Pol had to swallow a lump in his throat. He had thought he would feel nothing but relief when he left, but in truth, he would miss the steward. Yes, and others on the estate who had been good to him when he was growing up. But especially this man, who had been a teacher and then had become a friend and a colleague. "I will," he promised. "I can never repay you for all you have done for me, sir."

To his surprise, the steward blushed. "I have not done enough, Apollo. But if you feel you owe me something, live a good life. That will be reward enough. Live a good life."

Pol nodded. He could not speak for fear he would weep, and

that would embarrass them both. He felt the urge to hug his old friend, but he suppressed it. Perhaps it was the Italian in him—he had grown up with people who hugged and touched and walked arm in arm. But here in England, men were more reserved.

Besides, if Oscar had people watching—and Pol would be prepared to wager that he did—the steward might suffer for such a display.

"I shall write, sir," he repeated. "I shall let you know how I am, and where you can write back. Please say goodbye to the others for me." The steward would know he meant those who had stood his friends during his lonely youth—the butler, the housekeeper, the stable master, and others.

He tucked his small trunk under his arm, shouldered his bag, then walked away from the cottage that had been his home for the past six years and the estate where he had lived for sixteen.

That part of his life was over, and his future—full of possibilities—lay before him. He couldn't help but hope that Jackie would be part of it.

Chapter Eleven

POL SLEPT THE night in Jackie's shack. Or, rather, part of the night. It was cold without the blankets she must have retrieved, but he put on extra socks and covered himself with his greatcoat and managed to catch a few hours' sleep.

He should be honest, if only with himself. It was not the cold that kept him awake, nor the loss of the only home he had known in sixteen years, nor the uncertainty of where he would find work and how soon, nor even worry about Gran.

Perhaps it was a little about the uncertainty of work and quite a bit of worry about Gran. Mostly, though, it was Jackie. She was the daughter of an earl. A French *Comte*, which was the equivalent of an English earl. Dispossessed and dead, to be sure. But still, how could the baseborn offspring of a viscount's exiled son and his Italian mistress dare to court such as she? She had the breeding and—beyond a doubt—the training of a grand lady. She was beautiful, intelligent, brave, intrepid, and altogether wonderful.

All she lacked was money, and he did not have enough to make up for his deficiencies. Except he wanted her. Was he in love? He didn't know—he had seen little of the emotion in his years at Riese Hall. But he admired her, he desired her, he couldn't stop thinking about her.

When he had heard her call out and had burst through the

bushes to see Whitely pinning her down, he had been filled with an incandescent rage. He hoped he would have leapt to the defense of any woman in such a situation, but the red-hot fury that surged to the beat of the words "mine, mine, mine" was something primitive he'd never before experienced.

As was the possessive surge of desire he'd felt after Whitely was subdued. It was as well her mother was there, or he might have embarrassed himself and distressed her further by kissing her witless.

He hadn't wanted to let her out of his sight. When Lord Barton insulted her, it was all he could do to keep from punching him. Only with deep reluctance had he left her so he could go to Alstonebridge and secure her safety.

He had to court her. He could not imagine ever feeling for another woman what he felt for her, and without her, his future would be bleak indeed. Whether or not she accepted him was up to her, but he would do his best to persuade her.

He must have drifted off when he had made that decision, for the next thing he knew, the dawn light was filtering in through the single window. He rose, washed as best he could in the rain barrel, and dressed for travel. The vehicles he had hired would be leaving Alstonebridge about now and would be here in two hours. Too early to visit the ladies, then. He sat on the bench just outside of the shack, pulled out a notebook and a pencil, and began a list of ideas for finding a new position.

MAMAN WAS UP at dawn. They had finished packing all her fabrics and notions the previous evening, as well as their clothes and personal belongings, the kitchenware that they owned, and their pictures and ornaments. Everything was crowded into the parlor, taking up the middle of the floor. They'd pushed the furniture that had come with the cottage up against the walls.

"Hurry, Jacqueline," Maman said, giving her shoulder a gentle shake. "We have the whole house to clean before we leave."

Jackie thought about arguing. When they had arrived the place was dusty, dirty, and uncared for. They had cleaned for three days straight and had kept it clean ever since.

But there was no point in saying anything. Though they'd been here for years, Jackie was old enough to remember the frequent moves when her father had been alive. Every single time, Maman insisted on cleaning everything until it gleamed before she would leave their old place. Sometimes, when the move was urgent, because Papa had upset someone, she would clean all night. "I will not have some woman moving in here and thinking it has been a home for pigs," she always said.

Then, when they arrived at a new home, she did it all again. No place they moved into was up to Maman's standards. Jackie sighed and resigned herself to more cleaning, both here and later in Little Tidbury.

By the time she was dressed, Maman had brioches and coffee ready, and they were soon washing down walls and scrubbing floors. "It will not take long," Maman commented. "We should be ready by the time the transports arrive."

At that moment, someone knocked on the door. Not a simple rat-a-tat-tat, either, but pounding, on and on, as if the person outside wanted to batter the door down.

Jackie guessed who it was before the hated voice shouted, "Let us in before we break down the door!" Lord Riese, his words slurred and stumbling.

"He has been drinking," Maman commented, calmly, then shouted back, "Go away, Lord Riese. We have paid the rent. If you break into our home, you will be committing a crime."

"Gonna throw the bitches out," said another voice. "Pay them back for having Bill Whitely put in prison. No skirt gets to do that to my mate."

"Tha's right," Riese roared. "Tried to get me in trouble with Lord Barton. Upset my mother."

Maman had opened her trunk and was searching around under her clothes with one hand. She pulled out the *espingole* that Jackie's father had bought for her many years ago during their escape from France.

It was a gun like those the mail-coach guards used, but shorter, its barrel just over two feet long and flared at the tip—for easy loading, Maman had told Jackie, and so that the six lead balls with which it was loaded could more quickly diverge. The gun was designed to stop a group of attackers, which was why the English equivalent, the blunderbuss, was a favorite on the mail runs.

Her hand had dived into the clothes again and come out with a leather bag from which she was loading the gun with quick efficient movements. "We will back up against this wall, *cherie*," she said, calmly. "If they break down the door, I shall wait until they are all through the doorway and then shoot."

"Yes, Maman," Jackie said, looking around for something she could use as a weapon. The fire tools had been packed, but she retrieved the poker. Maman nodded with approval. "And the kitchen knives, Jacqueline. They are on the table in their box. Fetch and set them ready to our hands."

Jackie obeyed, taking the opportunity to make sure that the back door was locked and barred. The kitchen window was too small for anyone to climb through, even if they managed to break out the wooden supports that held the little panes of glass. The windows in the bedroom and the main room were larger, but of the same type. If they came in that way, they'd be vulnerable to her poker, and she wouldn't hesitate to use it.

She put the knife case near Maman, open so the knives were within easy reach, and stationed herself where she could easily reach any of the windows in a few paces.

The men outside were making so much noise that surely the neighbors must have heard, even though the nearest was two hundred feet or more away. But the neighbors were all tenants of Lord Riese. What could they do against four inebriated men, one of them the landlord?

Jackie could pick out at least four voices, all clearly drunk. Two were singing. Jackie could not make out all the words, but enough of them to know it was about vile things the singer wanted to do to a series of girls known only by the name of their city, with a typical chorus line being, "…until the virgin of York is a virgin no more."

The other two, one of them the viscount, were arguing about whether to ram the door with a log or chop it down with an axe.

"Go home, Lord Riese," shouted Maman again. "We are armed, and will protect ourselves against anyone who enters."

A new voice entered the fray. "I would listen to her if I was you." Pol! He sounded almost bored, but Jackie could picture him—tall, lean, and alert, perhaps with his pistols in his hands.

"You traitor," Riese screeched. "You tried to have me arrested."

"You sent the Whitelys to abduct Miss Haricot," Pol answered. "I was only just in time to stop Bill Whitely from raping her."

"You bastard," Riese shouted. "You lie. You want her for yourself." He addressed his friends. "He always wants what I have," he whined. "He makes up to the servants and the tenants so they like him. The steward likes him better than me. Even my own mother says I should be more like the Italian half-breed."

"He won't shoot you, Riese," said one of his inebriated mates. "He's your cousin."

"He'd like to shoot me, wouldn't you, Polly? You'd like to be viscount instead of me. You think you'd make a better viscount than me. Well, I've got the title, and you can't have it! Finders keepers!"

"He can't have the title, Riese," said another friend. "He's a bastard."

The viscount sounded confused when he said, "Yes." But then, more firmly, he added, "Yes, of course, he is." He hushed his voice so that Jackie could barely hear. "Never tell anybody. It's a secret."

"Go home, Oscar," Pol said. "You're drunk. Go home and sleep it off."

"Maybe we had better do what he says," one of the friends offered.

Jackie held her breath until Oscar shouted, "Madame Dressmaker! I want you out by Saturday! There's no place for you on my estates. And you can take your bitch of a daughter with you. Come on, fellows. The cow isn't worth it."

Except the word he used was not cow, but another word intended as an insult. Jackie had heard it around the stables but was not entirely certain about what it meant. No matter. He was going away, and soon, so would they.

Jackie and her mother stood, stiff and anxious, until a firm knock on the door. "They have gone, Madame Haricot." Jackie sagged as the tension went out of her, and Maman crossed the room quickly to unbar the door and let Pol in.

"Mr. Allegro, good timing," she said.

He took in the *espingole*, which she still had in her right hand. "It looks as if you were ready for him, but given yesterday's fiasco with Lord Barton, it is probably as well not to have to spend the morning explaining the injury or death of the local viscount and his friends."

"I quite agree," said Maman, a slight shake in her voice the only evidence of the tension she had been under. "You are early, Mr. Allegro. I am glad of it."

"I could not sleep," he admitted. "I was thrown off the estate last night, and spent the night in the shack in the woods. Just as well, since otherwise I might not have been here so early. Now. What can I do to help?"

Maman set her gun to one side. "But I shall keep it handy in case they come back." She found Mr. Allegro a broom, and he impressed Maman and Jackie by knowing how to use it. By the time the carriage and cart arrived to take them and their possessions away, the house was clean to Maman's standards, their little flock of chickens had been confined in a series of baskets, and the nearest neighbors had been invited to help themselves to vegetables from the garden and fruit from the trees. "For the rent is paid for the next quarter," Maman said, "so they are my vegetables and fruit to give away."

"We shall stop in the village," Maman decreed, "to say goodbye to the shopkeepers. After all, we no longer need to keep our departure secret from Lord Riese."

"Don't mention where we are going," Pol warned. "I'll tell the post boy and the carter the same."

POL TREATED THE two men from Alstonebridge to an ale at the inn.

"I've heard ye've been dismissed and turned out, sir," the innkeeper said. "I'm sorry for it. This place won't be the same without ye. Have ye somewhere to go?"

"I'll be looking for a new position," Pol told him.

"I wish ye all the best, sir. You've been a fair man to deal with."

That was a surprise. Pol had thought the innkeeper one of Riese's supporters. He had to change his mind about quite a few other people when he left the inn to find a crowd of villagers and a few farmers from the surrounding land waiting to say goodbye to him.

The blacksmith was there. He had a bit more freedom of speech than most, since he owned his own cottage and smithy and provided essential services not just for the village and farms but for the travelers who made the inn and shops prosperous.

"You've kept Riese from ruining this village," he said. "With you gone, he'll have no brakes at all. He'll drive us headlong into disaster. Within years, I reckon. I'll be looking for another place, though my father and his father had the smithy before me."

There were a few nods and some affirmative murmurs, many

stony faces, and no one who denied what the blacksmith had said.

"I hope you are wrong," said Pol. "I wish you all only the best. If I can help, I shall, but I've only ever had a tiny amount of leverage with my cousin and my aunt. And apparently, I've used it up. Will you all let friends who are not here today know that I said goodbye and good luck?"

"And the same to you," said the blacksmith and a chorus of others. On a flood of goodwill, Pol climbed into the post chaise, where Jackie and Madame Haricot were already waiting, and the post rider set the horses into motion.

Chapter Twelve

MADAME HARICOT BROKE the silence in the chaise. "I apologize, *Monsieur*. My daughter and I have brought trouble upon you."

Jackie nodded her agreement. "You lost your position because of me," she said.

"I have lost my position because of Riese," Pol argued. "He is to blame. If he had never set out to force you into his bed, then I would not have had to help, and I would still have a job. But only for a week or so more, remember. I was intending to leave. Madame, your apology is appreciated, but not necessary."

"Your cousin is a horrid man," said the comtesse, "and his mother is unpleasant, also. They have not been a good family to you, have they?"

Not in the least. Indeed, Pol firmly believed that he would have been sent to the parish workhouse the day he arrived had he not been delivered to the door by a man his aunt did not wish to annoy. "I was sent to England when my mother died." His Italian grandparents must have resented being left with the evidence of their daughter's mistake, and keen to pass him on to his English family.

No need to mention that to the ladies. "My Italian family had an English friend who brought me to England. But before I arrived here, my father's brother—my uncle—died. His wife was not at all pleased when I arrived at her door. Looking back, I must suppose she was grieving. It must have been a hard time for her."

For the next few years, the man had visited every few months, often without warning. Had that been why Lady Riese had allowed Pol to stay? Or had it been Grandmother's intervention? Probably both.

"What did Lord Riese mean about you being viscount instead of him?" Jackie asked. "Finders keepers? It makes no sense."

Pol had been wondering about that, too. "He had been drinking all night," he pointed out. That was it. Pol's parents had not been married, and Oscar's drunken ramblings wouldn't change the situation. "I have no idea what he meant." And that was the truth. Enough about his rather boring and inconsequential life.

"Do you mean to start up again as dressmakers?" he asked. "Perhaps take a shop?"

"We will continue what we have been doing," Madame Haricot said. "So many modistes long to go to London, to open a shop to serve the wealthy. And yes, there are fortunes to be made. Fitting out the ladies of one household for the Season can justify the expense of a London shop and the seamstresses and other servants to run it well. If the dressmaker's bill is paid. But one must acquire the notice of the best sort of customer to achieve success, and meanwhile London rents are high, and many others are struggling to be noticed. Even when one reaches the top, a few unpaid bills can spell disaster."

Pol nodded to show that he was paying attention, and indeed, he was fascinated at the thought she had put into the matter.

"In a village," she continued, "I—we, I should say, for Jackie is even more skilled than I at creating a 'look' that will suit a particular customer—have no rivals. Those who want to dress well, and do not have the time or the skill to make their own garments, must come to me. And it does not hurt that the wives of farmers and merchants pay their bills."

"In our first few years in Tissingham," Jackie commented,

"we were able to easily meet the rent and put away savings, besides. But then Lady Riese discovered how good Maman was and began commissioning her to sew—first a few dresses and then more and more, until at least half of our time was spent on garments for the Rieses. They pay late and always a few shillings short. And that is after beating Maman down on the price in the first place. With the rent going up and the income coming down, it was time for us to leave." She shrugged. "We finished all our current commissions, did we not, Maman?"

Madame Haricot giggled like a schoolgirl. "Most of them," she said, with a look of mischief that made her look as young as her daughter.

"Maman? What have you done?" Jackie asked, frowning.

"We finished and delivered all the garments for which customers would pay," Madame said. "You know full well, *cherie*, that we need not expect timely payment for the two gowns Lady Riese ordered. As for Lord Riese's shirts, he would never have paid for them and does not deserve them, besides! They are in the cart, in a box, all ready to be sold to a man who will pay for our good work. Miss Amanda Riese, she will have her gowns and her redingote. I sent them up to the manor yesterday afternoon, while you were taking the surplus vegetables to the Widow Garrett, Jacqueline. The deposit that Lady Riese paid for the entire order was almost enough to cover the cost of what I have delivered. When I sent the bill from the inn, I wrote on it that I accepted the deposit in settlement of all obligations between us. And Lord Riese can wear his old shirts to London, for all I care."

THE COTTAGE WAS charming. It was one of a row of six that, with other houses and a small cluster of shops around a green, formed a village called Little Tidbury. Pol said it was fifteen-minutes' walk from the town where the inn was, and where the post boy headed with the chaise as soon as they had descended and retrieved their possessions. The carter waited while Pol used the key he had been given, and Maman and Jackie went inside to inspect their new home.

It was somewhat larger than the one they had left, with two parlors, one of which Maman immediately designated as their workroom, as it had large windows and so plenty of light. Upstairs were three bedrooms, but Pol insisted on taking the little bedchamber downstairs. It was off the kitchen, so probably intended for a cook or maid of all work, but Pol said it would be all he needed, and that he hoped his grandmother would soon be able to occupy the other bedroom upstairs.

Everything was so clean that it sparkled, and even Maman could not find fault, and so they began offloading the cart, with Pol and the carter carrying everything heavy, Jackie managing lighter packages, bags and boxes, and Maman directing where things should go.

Before long, the cart was empty, and Jackie settled the little flock of poultry in the coop in the garden, which also had neat rows of vegetables and two fruit trees, one a plum and the other an apple.

Pol and the carter went to return the cart. He came back in a little gig driven by the innkeeper's wife, whose husband held the lease on the cottage.

"I hope you will be very happy here," she told Maman. "I have brought you a game pie, some fresh soup, and a couple of loaves of today's baking, just to show you we are pleased to have you in our village, for we still count the village as our own, though we live in the town, now."

Maman was a little taken aback at the hospitable welcome. "Thank you. That is very kind of you."

After several minutes more conversation, the innkeeper's wife said, "You are very busy, I know," and took herself off, but not before inviting Maman to join the Parish Ladies' Committee for their meeting in two days' time. "Ten o'clock, at the inn in town. Everyone will be so pleased to meet you. Your daughter can come too, of course."

"Well!" said Maman, when she was gone. "I wonder what that was about?"

"This place has a very different atmosphere to that of Tissingham," Pol commented. "People are friendly and welcoming. I think Mrs. Wrexham just wanted to be the first to meet you. And, of course, this was her house. I suppose she wanted to know if nice people would be living here."

"Her house?" Maman said. "She is a good housekeeper, then."

It was Maman's highest praise.

Jackie saw the village for herself the very next day. Maman was arranging the workshop and wanted no assistance and no interruptions, so she ordered Pol and Jackie out of the house, and they walked along a lane to the village green which was surrounded not only by the cottages but by several shops, a small tavern, a smithy, and a church.

There was a grocer's, a baker's, and a draper's, selling fabric by the yard, skeined wool, and sewing notions.

At the baker's, a man introduced himself. "You must be the people who have rented the innkeeper's cottage. I am Samuel Brown, curate of St Asaph's here in Little Tidbury. I live in the house by the church. Welcome to the village.

"We have found it very welcoming so far, sir," Jackie told him.

"I trust you and your husband will be very happy here," he said.

"Oh, he is not my husband," Jackie exclaimed.

The curate was taken aback, and his warm expression chilled as he frowned at Pol. "I am a temporary boarder, sir," Pol explained. "Madame Haricot, Miss Haricot's mother, has been good enough to agree to take care of my grandmother while I work. I came ahead to escort the two ladies and to make certain everything was prepared for her and will return to fetch her within the next week."

The explanation satisfied. "I shall look forward to meeting your mother, Miss Haricot, and your grandmother, Mr. Allegro. The Sunday service is at nine o'clock, but you are most welcome to call at the vicarage at any time."

"If you are walking our way before Sunday, Mr. Brown, please visit. Maman will be delighted to meet you. She will tell you that we are at sixes and sevens, but I assure you she has the whole cottage the way she likes it. She sent me and Mr. Allegro away so she could organize her workshop without being interrupted."

The curate picked up the humor in her voice and smiled. "She and my wife will get on famously, I imagine. What sort of work does your mother do in her workshop, Miss Haricot?"

"My mother and I are dressmakers, sir. My mother, in particular, is very skilled, both at designing and cutting, and at the actual sewing."

"Ah, you shall wish to meet our draper, then. Mrs. Thompson has a fine stock of fabrics, as well as ribbons, laces, and other such things. When you have made your purchase here, come along and I shall introduce you."

Jackie turned to the task of selecting from the baker's fine array. Behind her, the curate turned his inquisition on Pol. "What is your work, Mr. Allegro?"

Pol showed no irritation. "I am looking for a position, sir. In my last job, I spent part of my time as a land steward and part as a gentleman's secretary, so I could do either or both."

"Both, eh? And what was your reason for leaving this last position, if I might ask?"

"My employer and I disagreed," Pol explained. He pressed his lips together and then grimaced. "Given he is not here to defend himself, I am uncomfortable with providing details. Suffice it to say, I try to make sure that my actions are both moral and legal, whether on my own account or under instructions from my employer. After several arguments, we came to a parting of the ways. His steward, who was my direct master, has written me a reference, however."

"Our squire is looking for a secretary. If you wish, I shall give him your name and tell him your circumstances, young man. He will wish to meet you and make his own decision, of course."

"I would be very grateful," Pol said, bowing.

The curate could be forgiven for his busybody questions, Jackie decided, if his purpose was to be helpful. Her opinion of him improved still further when he introduced her to the draper with the words, "Mrs. Thompson, meet Miss Haricot. She and her mother have moved into the cottage the innkeeper owns here in the village. They are dressmakers, and I thought immediately of that idea you had to carry some ready-made garments. Now, you ladies talk to one another, and Mr. Allegro and I shall go for a stroll, for I have just seen the squire at the smithy, and I want him to meet Mr. Allegro. Oh, Mrs. Thompson, this is Mr. Allegro. He, and soon his grandmother once he fetches her from her old home, board with the Haricots."

By the time Jackie left the drapery, she and Mrs. Thompson had agreed that Jackie would come back with her mother and most of the garments Maman had not sent to the Rieses—six white shirts and two fine gowns. Jackie was already planning to make over the other white shirts for Pol. His clothing was downright shabby and did not fit properly. But Jackie and Maman planned to fix that.

"If she likes our work," Jackie told Pol as they began the walk home, "—and she will, because the shirts and gowns are excellently well made—she wants us to make up some more gowns, partly unfinished so they can be fitted to the buyer. The sort of garment a prosperous farmer's wife might purchase, and perhaps shirts for the farmer. She is going to sell on commission but not charge us for the fabric until the sale is made, so I think Maman will agree." She skipped, her satisfaction demanding a physical outlet. The draper was in competition with a larger establishment in Alstonebridge and hoped that Jackie's and

Maman's skills would give her an edge.

"That's wonderful," Pol agreed. "I was somewhat annoyed with Mr. Brown's inquisitive questions, but he is a treasure."

"What of you?" Jackie asked. "Will the squire employ you?"

"For a week, on trial. Then he will give me a week to fetch Gran and see her settled. If he is satisfied with my work, I shall start after that."

It was an excellent start to their stay in this new village.

$$\mathcal{Chapter\ Thirteen}$$

B Y THE TIME Pol left for Riese Hall a week later, he and the squire were well-pleased with one another, and the partnership with the draper was serving the Haricot ladies well. They had already sold six of the shirts, and both gowns were displayed in the shop, drawing a great deal of attention. They were hard at work at several commissions from some of the more prosperous villagers, while still carving out enough time to make the practical garments that the draper had requested.

"Once I have made arrangements to get Gran away from the house, I will return for you," Pol told Madame Haricot. She had promised to come and care for Gran during the journey.

"I shall be ready," the lady promised, "and so will her room."

Pol's borrowed horse made easy work of the distance. The way was becoming familiar. He had made an early start, driven by a sense of dread that had been growing all week. He would not feel easy in his mind until he saw Gran, and knew that she was, at the least, no worse.

He arrived in Tissingham long before most of the gentry would be up, though if the Rieses had kept to their plans, the only one he would need to avoid was Baron Barton. He went straight to Squire Pershing's place, and asked the stable master there if he could leave his horse while he visited his grandmother. The stable master might be able to give him the news he needed, too.

"Have the Rieses gone to London?" he asked.

"Aye, and Lord Barton with them," the man said. "Word is that Lady Riese wanted to stay to give her son time to search for you, but Miss Riese threw a tantrum and Lord Riese refused outright. They didn't want to stay here when they could be in London, going to all the parties and such. But Mr. Allegro, if you are planning to go back to Riese Hall, think again. They've put it about that you stole jewelry and silver when you left, and the magistrate has left instructions you're to be arrested. And shot if you resist arrest."

"It's a lie!" Pol said, indignantly.

"So says the steward. He said you went straight off the estate from his house, and never had the chance, even if you were that sort. But Lord Barton says you must have been planning to leave, since you got away so quickly, so you may have stolen them at any time. He released the Whitelys on the argument that the word of a thief cannot be trusted, and nor can that of a female. Riese has them guarding the estate so you can be caught if you sneak back in."

"Will you tell them?" Pol asked.

"Would I be telling you if I meant to peach on you, Mr. Allegro?" the stable master answered. "The way I see it, Riese is a liar and his mother is worse. You've always been a fair man to deal with, and more of a gentleman than most with a right to the name. And you rescued Miss Jackie from those Whitelys. From Riese, too, for that matter. They say you left here with Miss Jackie and Madame La Blanc. Is all well with them?"

"They are very well. They have entered into an agreement with a local merchant and are very busy."

The stable master grimaced. "The magistrate has a warrant out for their arrest, too. Lady Riese says that they stole two gowns and a dozen shirts from her."

Pol laughed. "They took garments that they still owned, for Lady Riese was refusing to pay for them. In fact, Lady Riese owes them more than ten pounds for previous orders, so if anyone is a thief, it is the person wearing the gowns she has not paid for."

"I thought it might be something like that." The stable master shrugged. "It makes no difference to Lord Barton. Be careful, Mr. Allegro."

"Thank you for the warning," Pol said, sincerely. It changed the way he planned to approach Riese Hall, which he still needed to finish searching. He'd have to go in through the servant passages and wait until a time he knew they would be empty. That meant he needed to go to ground for the afternoon, but he would do so somewhere he could watch the house. Fortunately, he knew just the place.

First, though, he must check on his grandmother.

✦

Chapter Fourteen

T HE WHITELY BROTHERS were, indeed, on guard, if you could call it that. Four of them were sitting beside the front gate lodge, passing around jugs of some sort of alcohol, and the other two were by the back gate lodge, doing likewise.

Pol saw them while he circled the estate, keeping always to cover. They were not guarding the dower house, but Pol soon realized there was no need. Nothing and no one was moving in the vicinity. None of the chimneys were smoking. None of the windows were open. When Pol peered through the windows, much of the furniture was gone and what remained was under dust covers.

He tried all the doors and windows until he found a latch that could be forced and went inside. Sure enough, the house had been abandoned. His Gran's possessions were all gone. When he checked the servants' rooms, all their clothes and personal possessions had been removed.

Had Gran been moved to the main house? Had her illness taken a turn for the worse? Surely, if she had died, the stable master would have known and would have said something?

He needed to talk to the steward. He retreated from the dower house and made his way back to the woods and from there to the wall of the main estate. He crossed the wall where the trees were thick and approached the steward's cottage from the back, having slithered through undergrowth and skulked along hedges to reach it without being seen.

The house was locked. Pol knew where the key was kept, of course. Or where it had been while he lived there. When he felt along the top of the door, it was still in the little hollow above the left top corner of the frame. He let himself in.

His former bedchamber would give him a good view of the house, but the attic would be better. The steward had only the one live-in servant—a cook-housekeeper whose bed chamber was on the ground floor next to the kitchen, so the attic room overlooking the park and the house was bare, with nothing more in it than a couple of tea chests. He pulled one up to the window and sat on it and prepared for a long day.

The maids arrived to clean. He saw them approaching and heard them at their work. The cook-housekeeper came home with a large basket, presumably filled with supplies from the village. No one came up to the attic floor, and Pol was not disturbed.

The environs of the manor were busy, with grooms and gardeners about their work, and occasionally a visit by one or other of the Whitelys, presumably checking to see if the outdoors workers had seen Pol. The house itself appeared to be slumbering. Had the Rieses taken most of the servants with them to London, as they usually did? Pol watched and waited, ignoring his growing sense of urgency.

The steward arrived home as the stable clock was chiming twelve times. Pol waited some more. Unfortunately, it must be a day the steward had meetings, for he left again while the maids remained.

They would do the dishes from dinner, make everything tidy and clean, and leave by the middle of the afternoon, and sure enough, an hour or so later, they walked away toward the gate closest to the village.

He didn't see the cook-housekeeper, which meant she remained here in the cottage.

Nothing else of interest happened all afternoon. Even the gardeners and the grooms had disappeared. Pol waited, fretting about his grandmother, and at last his patience was rewarded when the steward returned.

Alone, thank goodness, but Pol made his way downstairs before someone else arrived to spoil his time with his old friend.

"Apollo," the steward said when he saw him. "I take it you have returned for your grandmother. How can I help?"

"Tell me how she is," Pol said.

"Not well, they say. She has been moved to the main house, and the doctor has been every day. No one has been allowed to see her, except that maid of hers, and she speaks to no one. I'm glad you're here, my boy, but you must be careful. We've been ordered to apprehend you if we see you, and to hand you over to the magistrate."

"I've heard," Pol said. "I will be careful, but I must see her."

⊱≫≪⊰

POL WANTED TO rush to his grandmother immediately, but he waited until it was time for the servants' tea and then entered the manor house through a side door and straight into the warren of hidden passages within the walls.

The servants' passages were dimly lit by narrow slits of windows that were hidden in the decorative stonework of the manor's outside walls or in the plaster adornments of the inside walls. Pol knew the lesser used parts of the warren perhaps better than anyone else alive. He had been traversing them since he was under ten, staying out of the way of Oscar and his aunt. And, for that matter, the butler, his tutor, and anyone else who might be inclined to give him a punch or a kick as he passed.

Several long passages and two steep staircases later, he was able to reach the peep holes that let him see into the various bedchambers, and he soon found Gran's room.

One glance was all it took to see that his concerns were justified. The poor dear lady, looking frailer than ever, was vomiting into a bowl—or at least into the general direction of the bowl. Her so-called maid was out of his view, but he could hear her voice in an endless string of vituperation aimed at Gran, calling her useless and telling her that even her favorite grandson had abandoned her.

Pol had planned to stay in the walls until the nasty shrew abandoned her charge for her tea, for she always took it on a tray in her own room, but seeing Gran suffer and hearing the maid's abuse tried his self-control to the limit.

The last straw was her saying, "The doctor does not know why you are still alive. Just die, you old hag. Nobody cares about you."

Pol could wait no longer. He fumbled for the catch of the hidden door that would let him into the room and opened it. As he stepped out, he saw the door on the other side of the room close behind the nursemaid. Which was probably for the best, though confronting her would have given him some satisfaction.

He had an hour, perhaps two, before the maid came back. Would it be enough? Just to be safe, he turned the key in the lock.

"Frederick?" said Gran's quavering voice. "Is that you?" Apollo sighed. Frederick Riese, his grandfather, was close to twenty years in his grave.

"It is me, Gran. Apollo. I've come to take you somewhere safe."

She waved her hand as if to chase away the thought. Her answer came in short bursts of words, as if speaking, even breathing, was a struggle. "Too late... My dear boy... The doctor says... I am dying... But I shall die... happy for seeing... my Frederick."

Apollo had always thought the doctor was another of Lady Riese's sycophants, a quack who would only attend those who could afford to pay his bills, who bled his patients to the point of death and dosed them with all sorts of questionable nostrums, and who blamed the frequent deaths on "the will of God". It chilled him to think that his beloved Gran was suffering that snake's "care".

Gran's hand, when he took it, shook as much as her voice, and felt like parchment stretched over bone. She was so pale that her skin was translucent—all the skin he could see was criss-crossed with a network of blue veins beneath. What had they done to her? She had been nowhere near as bad as this when he saw her last. He'd returned just in time, he thought. Hopefully.

She had lowered the basin to the bed. That evil crow had not even bothered to collect it and find her a clean one. Pol took it to the washstand, where he was pleased to find that the cupboard held a slop bucket. He emptied the basin, rinsed it out from the jug of water on the top of the stand, and put it where he could easily reach it. He then wet a linen cloth and used it to wash Gran's face and hands, and to wipe up a spill from the bed linen.

"I'm taking you out of here," he insisted. "I'll take you to see another doctor, and if it is your time, Gran, then you will die in a clean bed surrounded by loving care."

Gran nodded. "That would be… nice," she agreed.

"I'll just pack for you," Pol said. He emptied the contents of several drawers into the bag he took down from the top of Gran's armoire and added as many gowns as he could fit. They would be crushed, but it couldn't be helped.

"What else do you need me to take, Gran? Grandfather's miniature? Your jewelry?"

"Louella… took my… jewels," Gran said. "Take… Fred. And… my Bible."

Pol took down the little painting and put it into the bag, then searched for the well-worn Bible, which had been on Gran's bedside table for as long as he could remember but was now tucked into a shelf near the window.

She would need something to wear for her travel. He took a warm woolen coat from a hook on the wall and then retrieved a pair of socks from the bag. "I'll just get you into these, Gran," he said. She nodded but could do little to help as he moved her this way and that to fit her arms into the sleeves and tuck the coat around her. She had been bled. Her arms and legs showed the distinctive scars of recent leech bites, some almost faded and others more recent.

And other bruises, too. Pinch marks, by the looks. Anger surged in him so powerfully that he almost choked on his need to remain gentle in the way he touched her.

How was he going to manage the bag and Gran? And all the dozen or so bottle of medicine, too! Should he take them? He stopped to read a few of the labels, but apart from one which said clearly that it was laudanum, he didn't know what they were for. On one of the armoire's shelves, he found a cloth bag, and on another a couple of towels with which he wrapped the bottles. He'd better take them all.

A dose of laudanum might make the trip easier for her, but from the look of her pinpoint pupils, she had already had plenty. He didn't dare give her more.

"Gran, I'm going to take the bags downstairs and then come back for you," he said. He gave her a kiss on the forehead. "I will be as fast as I can."

It hurt to leave her. He was afraid something would happen to her while he was gone. The nurse would return, or she would simply breathe her last. Almost as bad would be for him to be caught, for if he was unable to take her away today, he feared she would lose all chance of surviving.

But the servants' ways were still deserted, and he made it to the side entrance without seeing anyone. He hid the bags in the shrubs outside the door and hurried back upstairs. The nurse was still absent. Thank God or whoever was listening. It was a fervent prayer. He sent up another that she would stay away until he had Gran safe.

He wrapped Gran in a blanket and lifted her into his arms. She had fallen asleep and didn't wake when he lifted her. She was all skin and bone, and no burden at all, but he needed to be careful not to bang her legs in the narrow passages. The poor dear had bruises enough.

All the time he was negotiating the passages and stairs, he was worrying about his next steps. How was he going to escape the house without being detected? Not once, but twice, because he had to take the bags, as well. As he approached the panel that opened from the servants' passages into the little hall where he had entered the house, his senses were on high alert.

Being primed for action saved him. As he went to step into the hall, he heard the voices beyond the outside door and glanced up to see the handle tilt downwards. He shifted his weight backward and closed the panel, then stepped sideways to the peepholes that allowed a view of the hall.

Chapter Fifteen

IT WAS BILL Whitely and another man with the same shock of pale hair. "It's a waste o' time, Bill," the other man was saying. "The bastard ain't comin' back 'ere. Why should 'e?"

"'Cause 'is old Granny's 'ere, Lord Riese sez. In any case, Pete, the pay's good and so's the grub."

"Can't be a complete villain if he loves 'is Granny," Pete mused. "But yer right about the grub. Dan and Mickey sez today we got meat pies, big ones."

"This is the job for me," Bill commented. "Nuffin' to do but walk around all day and eat as much as we like."

"Boring," said the other. "But I could do with a bit of boring. Nothin' to do and no one shootin' at us. Come along, Bill. Best get to it. Pat and Vince'll be wantin' their turn."

Their voices faded as they turned the corner toward the back of the house. Pol looked down to check his grandmother—she was still sleeping—and opened the panel again. The guards must be taking their dinner in shifts of two. Hopefully the other four were occupied at the lodges, but he would keep an eye out. "Walking around all day," Bill had said.

He carried Gran to the steward's house. The path was sheltered most of the way. A long walk bordered by rose-covered trellises took him half the distance. It ended at a maze, and the tall hedges of the maze hid him until he was within twenty-five paces of the cottage. Since he'd explored the maze for the first time sixteen years ago and knew it well, it was a quick and safe route to take Gran to safety.

Within a few minutes, he was at the door of the steward's cottage—it opened before he could bend low enough to reach the handle while keeping his grandmother steady in his arms.

"You have her!" said the steward. "My dear lady, how are you?"

Gran stirred, and her eyes opened. "Edward," she said. Her smile was tremulous, but it was still there.

The steward smiled back, but when he looked up and his gaze met Pol's, his eyes held both horror and fury. Pol felt the same, but he was taken aback by the strength of the steward's reaction. The man had himself well in hand, however. "Bring her ladyship this way, Apollo," he said. "My lady, we shall soon have you comfortable."

Pol followed him upstairs to a neat bedroom—the one that had been his when he lived here. "Mrs. Finch made up the bed for your grandson, my lady," the steward was saying, "but I can soon make up another for him. You will be safe here."

Gran smiled up at them both. "Safe," she repeated.

"Yes," Pol agreed. "You will be safe here, and tomorrow, I will take you to my new house, where Madame Haricot has agreed to look after you. You will remember her as Madame Le Blanc, the dressmaker."

"The… dressmaker." Gran sighed. "So… tired."

"Sleep a little, Gran," Pol suggested. "I need to go back now and get your bags. I put them outside by the door to the manor."

"Sleep," Gran agreed, and her eyes drifted shut.

Outside her room, the steward whispered, "What is wrong with her, Apollo? She looks as if she has not had a good meal in months!"

"She has been abused. I heard that disgrace of a nursemaid threatening her, and she has bruises everywhere. Leech marks, too. The doctor has bled her to within an inch of her life. I could not leave her there."

The steward shook his head. "No. No, of course you could not. Go and get her bags, dear boy. You and she shall sleep here tonight, and in the morning, we shall take her to Madame Haricot."

Pol had a narrow escape. He had just left the shelter of the roses when the side door of the manor, which was a bare ten yards away, began to open and Bill Whitely stepped out.

Throwing himself backward, Pol thanked his lucky stars that Bill had paused on the doorstep to look back over his shoulder. He and his brother emerged, talking about the pies they'd had and what might be for supper.

"Glad I'm not one of them Turners," said Pete Whitely. "Workin' all night. Gonna be a cold night, too. Wet."

Bill scoffed. "Workin'! Them Turners don't know what work is. Reckon they'll drink half the night and sleep the rest."

"Don't make no difference," Pete said. "Allegro ain't coming back. I reckon…"

What he reckoned was muted by the wall of the house as the Whitely brothers turned the corner of the manor. Pol didn't wait. He raced across the short distance separating himself from the shrubs either side of the door, grabbed the bags, and raced back. Safely out of sight again, he slowed down but kept to a swift walk until he had closed the steward's door behind him and the bags.

AFTER POL LEFT, Maman announced, "We have work to do, *cherie*, preparing the house for an invalid." They washed the already-clean sheets for the dowager viscountess's bed and put out all the other bedding to air. Jackie was not sure what else Maman thought they could do. The whole house sparkled from top to toe.

"We shall make up her room and set a nice chair for her in the parlor, for she might wish to sit there, Jacqueline."

"I heard she was confined to her bed, Maman," Jackie said.

"Poor lady. We shall have to see whether we can do better for her, for I tell you, Jacqueline, I do not trust any nursemaid that woman hired." She stood up from the table. "Can I leave you to clear and do the dishes, *mon ange*? I must look at my medicine chest and see if I have all the supplies I am likely to need."

By early afternoon, Maman was happy with her preparations, though Jackie was sure she'd make further changes several times before their guest arrived. She was not so pleased with her medicine stores, however.

"I shall need to go into town to the apothecary," she mused, looking at the list she'd made. "But I've done no sewing today, and there is the embroidery to be completed on the bodice you pintucked for the squire's daughter. Jacqueline, if I explain exactly what I need, you could do the trip to the apothecary for me."

Jackie nodded enthusiastically. Since Maman had learned about Jack Le Gume, and about the danger to her daughter, she had been reluctant to let Jackie out of her sight. Jackie understood. She even treasured the evidence that her mother, who was usually more inclined to a criticism than a compliment, was frightened for her.

But Jackie was accustomed to more freedom than most girls, and besides, to be in Maman's company all day every day was oppressive. Jackie loved her mother, and she knew Maman loved her, though the lady had never been demonstrative. She sometimes watched other mothers and wished hers could be warmer, but she would settle for Maman trusting her more and criticizing her less. A trip to the nearby town, on her own, would be wonderful.

"It will be safe," Maman muttered to herself. "That devil Riese does not know where we are." She fixed Jackie with a glare. "You will go straight to the apothecary and back here. I shall worry every moment you are away."

Jackie kissed her cheek. "I shall be careful, Maman," she promised.

"*Hmmph.*" Mama's snort was disbelieving. "Be sure that you are."

Of course she would be careful. She always was. She was still here, was she not? Sometimes more by good luck than good management, but there was no reason to believe she was about to be deserted by her good luck—or her holy angels, as Maman would have it.

Being out of the house without Maman at her elbow was as wonderful as she expected, even if she did have to wear a bonnet that prevented her from a clear view to each side unless she turned her head. However, she did not dare take it off. Quite apart from the fact that it provided a small measure of anonymity, someone might mention to her mother that she had been seen walking bareheaded.

She took her time walking to town, and went by the foot-paths through the fields, rather than by the road. In the village, they had suggested the paths, because they were less dusty and less traveled, and so it proved to be.

As advised, she kept an eye out for riders, who also used the paths, but nobody was out and about but Jackie and the animals who lived in the fields. Sheep, cows, a gaggle of geese who contested her right-of-way but desisted when she flapped her skirts at them, hawks flying overhead, a cat that kept pace with her for a field or two when she passed close to a barn, a flock of swallows, an elderly cart horse who ambled over to see whether she was interesting and left after a scratch of his withers, which she could barely reach, he was so tall.

It was marvelous. She was sorry to see the town—first the spire of the church, then some taller houses, and finally the first few cottages as the path ended at a style that let into a lane. Her quiet walk was over, but she could look forward to returning the same way.

To reach the Main Street of the town took several more

minutes, and was interesting in its own way, as cottages gave way to large houses in extensive grounds, then to townhouses, and then to the usual jumble of buildings typical in a town—rows of houses, many of which had shops on the ground floor, the occasional warehouse or larger shop, and workshops and manufactories of one kind or another.

Finally, she came out into the town square, with its market building, town hall, church, and more shops. One of them was a modiste, with a fashionable evening gown on display in the multipaned bow window. Jackie was very tempted to go inside, to spy on the opposition. But she had promised to go straight to the apothecary, who had a shop, she had been told, in a small lane to the right of the town hall.

And there it was, tucked between a townhouse on one side and a bookshop on the other. Jackie walked slowly past the bookshop, wondering what kinds of books they sold, but the window was an old-fashioned one with multiple panes of crown glass that let in the light but distorted the view. "I promised. Straight to the apothecary and straight home," she reminded herself.

She opened the door to the apothecary's shop and set a bell tinkling, so that a man came through a door behind the tall counter and smiled a greeting. He was tall, thin, and slightly stooped, with a receding hairline and watery blue eyes.

"May I help you, Miss?"

"I have a list," Jackie said. She had her head bent over her reticule, looking for the list, when the bell tinkled again. A man brushed past her. "Apothecary! My master needs one pint spirit of lavender, one half-pint double distilled cardamon, two bottles of Steers Elixir, two bottles of laudanum, and half a pound of arsenic trioxide."

The apothecary looked at Jackie, saying, "This lady was first." But Jackie had caught a glimpse of the man's face and recognized him. He was from Tissingham and was the doctor's servant. She waved a dismissive hand, lowered her head so that her bonnet hid her face, and turned away. Making her voice hoarse, she said, "Please serve the gentleman," hoping that he would not behave like a gentleman and insist on her taking first turn.

He didn't. Jackie bent to examine the shelves, which displayed bottles of various sizes with different colored liquids or lozenges. She occupied herself pretending to read the labels to keep her face hidden.

The apothecary must have begun making up the man's order, for nothing further was said for a few minutes. "Did I not sell you arsenic trioxide just two months ago? What is your master using it for?"

"Face powder," the man said, glibly. "But he spoiled a batch. Hurry up, can't you? He expects me back, and I shall be blamed if I am late."

Arsenic? Just a few months ago, the newspapers had been full of a case where people had died after eating sweets that had been made using arsenic by mistake for gypsum to mix with the sugar. Apparently the two substances looked the same, but one was a relatively harmless adulterant to make the expensive sugar go further and the other was poison! Jackie didn't believe for a moment that the doctor was making cosmetics, but if the arsenic was for a legitimate use, why lie about it?

"Here you go, then," said the apothecary. "That'll be one pound, two shillings and six pence."

A short time later, the bell tinkled again, and the door shut behind the doctor's servant. Jackie gave her own list to the apothecary. She hoped the servant really was heading straight back to Tissingham. She certainly did not want to encounter him!

Chapter Sixteen

THEY BROUGHT THE steward's cook-housekeeper into the secret. The steward assured Pol that Mrs. Finch would be sympathetic to Gran and would tell no one. Pol agreed. They needed a woman to wash Gran and make her comfortable in a clean night rail, and Pol knew Mrs. Finch to be a kind woman and a good one.

Since she was the steward's only servant and they were making extra work for her, Pol volunteered to bring up heated water and do anything she needed in the kitchen, after he stripped off the clothes he was wearing. Gran had vomited twice while he was carrying her, and had suffered a flux, dirtying his trousers.

After he'd washed and changed in the cottage's little laundry shed, he put the clothes he'd been wearing in to soak, dressed in some old clothes of his own that Mrs. Finch had found in the attic and then went through to the kitchen to peel some extra vegetables for dinner, since the maids had only prepared enough for Mrs. Finch and the steward.

It gave him something to do while Mrs. Finch was with Gran and helped to keep him from peering out the windows to see if the servants were out hunting for Gran, for he had expected the nurse to set up a hue and cry long before this. He also had to resist hurrying upstairs every few minutes to ask how Gran was.

She was so weak, so gaunt, so sick.

"You're a good lad," Mrs. Finch said approvingly, when she came downstairs and saw what he had done. "And the kettle's hot, too!"

"I thought you might need a cup of tea," Pol told her. "Gran, too. How is she?"

"Asleep, poor dear. Keith is sitting with her for a few minutes. I expect you'll want to go up, but I just wanted to talk to you first, Mr. Allegro."

"Sit down," Pol suggested. "I'll make that tea."

She protested, but without much spirit, and was easily convinced to sit while he poured the boiling water into the prepared tea pot. He took a seat opposite her. "Now tell me," he said.

"Her ladyship is in a bad way," the housekeeper told him. "I don't know all that is wrong with her. She is more than half-starved, and they have been dosing her with laudanum. All sorts of other things, too, but it is the laudanum that makes her forgetful and confused."

She frowned. "I don't like the way she's vomiting, and that's a fact. Could be one of those elixirs, or it could be that quack of a doctor took too much blood, for that he did. She is bruised all over, from the leeches and from being pinched or hit. You were right to take her out of there, Mr. Allegro. They were killing her, between them."

She poured her tea. "This was kind of you, sir," she said.

"A way of showing how much I appreciate your kindness to my Gran," Pol replied.

"She is a great lady, sir. We should have noticed what was happening, and that is a fact."

"I should have noticed," Pol told her. "Though I think she is much worse than she was when I last saw her, nearly two weeks ago."

The housekeeper nodded. "Likely. Whatever they have been doing, they had to be careful when you were visiting nearly every day."

"I should have taken her with me when I left." Though how he could have done so when he was turned off the estate with nowhere to go, he did not know.

"You are here now, sir. One of us must sit with her through the night. I'll give you a jug of barley water. We'll need to get as much of it into her as we can. My Mam always said that if liquid came out, liquid had to go in, and she nursed three of us through typhoid fever."

"You think Gran has typhoid?" Pol asked, alarmed.

"I don't see how. She goes nowhere and sees no one. And I've not heard of typhoid in the village or on the estate. Besides, she has no fever. I wish I knew how long she has been sick."

"Gran might know," Pol suggested. "When will she be well enough to travel?"

The housekeeper didn't know that, either, but when Pol went upstairs with the jug of barley water, the steward said it didn't matter. "We can't keep her here," he said. "Sooner or later, they'll search this cottage, Allegro. The pair of you will have to leave. In the morning, I'll ride into town and organize a carriage."

"I daresay there'll be a hue and cry as soon as the maid returns to Gran's room," Pol admitted.

"I'm the steward," his old friend pointed out. "In the absence of the Rieses, I can keep the Whitelys and other servants out until someone thinks to go to the magistrate in town to get authority to search."

He went off downstairs, leaving Pol to take his turn watching Gran. Pol roused Gran enough to drink some of the barley water through an invalid's cup that the housekeeper had found, but she fell back into a deep sleep as soon as he allowed her to lie back on the pillow.

Darkness had fallen. Pol could see the lights of the house beyond the hedges of the maze. Not too many lights. With the family away, most of the life in the building would be below stairs. He could not see Gran's window from here, but at any moment, he expected to see the house light up as people hurried from room to room, looking for her.

It didn't happen. Perhaps he still had an opportunity. After catching Jackie in the study, he'd searched it for something that might incriminate Oscar, and then he'd searched Oscar's chambers. Predictably, Oscar was not the sort to keep paperwork or souvenirs. Both searches gave Pol zero ammunition.

Lady Riese's suite of chambers had been beyond his reach, however. If she was not in them, her maid was or was likely to return at any time. But not now. Not this evening, when Lady Riese was in London and so was her maid.

He couldn't leave Gran, of course, until the steward or his housekeeper took over the watch. It was, in any case, too early to make his foray into the manor house. Later. When the servants were all asleep.

That is, if Gran's nursemaid—her keeper, more like—didn't set the whole house stirring like an ant nest by announcing that Gran was missing, and she would, of course. Something had delayed her return to Gran's bedroom, but as soon as she went back, she would have every servant on the estate out looking for the missing dowager countess.

As the night deepened, candlelight shone through the attic windows of the rooms where the maids slept. The servants were going to bed. Still no alarm. Perhaps the nursemaid had no intention of seeing Gran again tonight, in which case, Lady Riese's bedchambers might be within his reach.

Gran shifted restlessly as she slept, but didn't wake even when he fed her more barley water. He sat watching her, but his mind was miles away, in Little Tidbury, with Jackie. It would please her, he was certain, if he found something in Lady Riese's rooms that could be used against the awful pair. He had no idea what sort of thing he might find, but the thought of Jackie's reaction made him determined to take the risk.

Jackie. It had seemed like a good plan, back when he proposed it, for the three of them—four, with Gran—to share a cottage. And financially it made sense. He had not considered what it would be like to live in the same house as a woman he desired. A woman with whom, if he was going to be honest with himself, he was falling in love.

Not so much the falling, either. He'd spent a week in close quarters, and his head and heart were full of her. Her smile over the breakfast table, her greeting when he arrived home from work, her conversation over dinner, her sweet face bent intently over her sewing while he read out loud of an evening, her on his arm as he escorted her and her mother to Sunday services.

He wanted more. He wanted the right to live with her for a lifetime, to wake up next to her every morning, to kiss her in greeting when he came home, to follow her up the stairs and join her in their bed every night.

Yet, all his earlier doubts were still justified. He was a poor man without a permanent job. He could not offer her the kind of life to which she should have been accustomed. He was base born. No lady—for she was a lady, even if she had to work for a living—would consider marriage to such as him.

It didn't matter next to the truth that he loved her. If Pol could persuade her to marry him, he would spend his life making certain that she never regretted it. Whether searching Lady Riese's rooms would help, he did not know. But he was going to do it.

The steward rejoined him. "I'll watch your grandmother, Allegro. You should get some sleep."

"Not quite yet," Pol said. "First, I want to search Lady Riese's rooms. There must be some evidence that I can use to stop Oscar and his mother from exploiting and tormenting the people around here, but I've already searched Oscar's room and the study and found nothing."

He waited for the steward to tell him not to go, though Pol didn't think the man would actively try to stop him. However, the steward surprised him. "Look for the family Bible," he said. "It went missing some time ago. Lady Riese may have taken it to London, but if it is still in the house, it must be in her rooms."

"The family Bible?" Pol asked. "Why would she hide it?"

"I cannot be certain," the steward said. "I think it records your parents' marriage and your birth, but I only had one glimpse, when it was brought out to write Amanda's name sixteen years ago. Lady Riese saw me looking and sent me on an errand, and the Bible was gone from its place when I looked for it later. I never saw it prominently displayed again. I don't know where she put it."

"My parents' *marriage?*" Pol's head reeled as he absorbed the steward's words and the room seemed to recede around him, leaving him remote from everything except the steward's voice. If his parents were married when he was born, that changed everything.

"Look for that and anything else that might show you are the true viscount," the steward advised. "Marriage lines, letters to your grandfather."

"She might have destroyed them all," Pol recovered enough from his shock to point that out. If she had stolen his heritage, then destroying the evidence made sense. But then, in fact, if he was a threat to her and her son, why had she kept him at all? She could have had him killed or sold him to a chimney sweep—which would have amounted to the same thing.

"I've worked for the Rieses for a long time," the steward said. "One thing we can say about your aunt is that she always has a backup plan. If I am right about you being legitimate, then you were Lady Riese's backup plan in case something happened to her son."

It made a sort of sense. "Why have you never mentioned this to me before?" Pol asked.

"Back then, I was not certain," the steward said, "and I did not think there was much a boy of your age and a man like me, with no powerful friends, could do against Lady Riese. All I would do, I thought, was get you killed and me dismissed. I should have said something when you turned twenty-one. But your cousin had already been confirmed as viscount, and the

House of Lords does not like admitting it has made a mistake. I was too much of a coward to say anything when there was no chance of it making a difference."

"It would have made a difference to me," Pol told him, his building anger at the steward deflected by the man's admission of cowardice. He had to remember that the man had been his good friend for this last decade. He was a good man, if timid.

As to his news, if Pol's father had loved his mother enough to marry her... It didn't change anything, and yet, it changed everything. "If I can prove that Lady Riese deliberately hid the truth, will the House of Lords put right the injustice?" he asked.

The steward shrugged. "I do not know, Allegro. A lawyer might be able to advise you. Look for the evidence. If you can find something to prove you should be viscount, something that warrants an inquiry, then you can decide your next steps."

Pol had no fear of being caught. On a wet night like tonight, the guards would be tucked up in the lodges, drinking. In the unlikely event they bothered to look out a window, they would see nothing because of the rain. In the house, the servants would be asleep. He would have all the rest of the night to search Lady Riese's chambers.

Chapter Seventeen

A ND SO, IT proved to be. He was tired and a little frustrated, but still alert when they left the steward's house the following morning. It was after sunrise, but the heavy cloud cover meant they were moving in the gloom. The steward had, in the end, borrowed a carriage from the squire, who was more likely to be silent about it than the innkeeper.

"I thought I might have to get him out of bed," the steward said, "but he was in the stables. He'd been up early with a foaling mare. He said I could take it and be welcome and even sent his stable master to drive the carriage."

In the carriage, while Gran slept and the miles between them and the doctor in Alstonebridge grew shorter with each turn of the wheels, Pol explained what he had found out.

"Gran's maid was in her own room, fast asleep and stinking of liquor," he told the steward. "I doubt she'll be getting up for some time. If anyone else tries Gran's door and finds it locked, I'm counting on them assuming it was the maid who locked it. We will be clean away before any alarm is sounded, or so I hope."

"Did you find the Bible?" the steward asked.

"Yes," said Pol. "Tucked into a drawer of her desk. But the family record pages were not all there. The page with the most recent additions had been torn out. Which is suggestive but proves nothing. I left the Bible there. The only other thing that might be useful were some letters from my father to his father, in which he talks about his wife and baby son. He refers to me as my grandfather's heir. It sounds as if you were right."

"Do you have them with you? It might be enough to justify an inquiry."

Pol patted his pocket. "Safe and sound. But who is to say at this stage that they were truly from my father? Or that what is in them is true? It is good to know that I am legitimate, but there's not enough to prove that Oscar and his mother are usurpers."

The steward looked disappointed, but then he rallied and said, "I am glad you know the truth, Allegro. Or should I say, 'Riese'?"

Pol shuddered. "I'm not sure that I want anything to do with that name. If it were not for the people of the village and the estate,"—and his desire to be worthy of the daughter of a French *Comte*— "I'd forget the whole thing."

⤜⤜⤜✕⤛⤛⤛

POL CAME BACK with his Gran in a coach driven by the stable master from Tissingham. He was accompanied by the Riese's steward. Pol lifted the old dowager, Lady Riese, out of the carriage and Jackie had her first sight of the poor lady. She looked as if a gentle breeze would carry her away.

Maman gave a distressed cry at the sight of her and hurried to Pol's side. "Follow me, Mr. Allegro. I will show you to Lady Riese's room."

"Gran, you know Madame de Haricot du Charmont, do you not? And this is her daughter, Mademoiselle Jacqueline de Haricot du Charmont."

"Madame… La Blanc…?" the old lady asked.

"My working name, Madame," Maman explained. "You have been ill, I see. Let me get you settled in your room, and we shall find something for you to eat and drink. A cup of hot tea, and perhaps some chicken soup."

The dowager viscountess managed to smile and nod. To Pol, she said, "My... medicine...?"

"I will take you to your room, Gran," Pol told her. "Then I will go for the doctor."

"Doctor... says... I am... old..."

"We shall see what the doctor here says." Pol climbed the stairs behind Maman and followed her into the room they had prepared. He set his grandmother on the bed. "I shall leave you with Madame Haricot," he told her. "She will make sure you are comfortable, Gran."

Jackie followed Pol back downstairs. She had a nasty feeling about old Lady Riese's condition. "Pol, I overheard a conversation at the apothecary. The doctor from Tissingham had sent his servant to buy laudanum and arsenic. He told the apothecary that the doctor uses it to make face powder."

"That can't be right," Pol said. "Wait. You think Gran...?"

"I don't know," Jackie told him. "But I think it is possible."

"Lady Riese has been poisoning my grandmother," Pol said. "I must go, Jackie."

"Your friend the steward and the stable master from the squire's are in the kitchen. I told them I'd make them a cup of tea and a bite to eat before they head back to Tissingham. Perhaps the stable master will take you into town to get the doctor while I put a meal together."

Pol's expression lightened. "Thank you. That's a good idea. Let's go and ask him."

The stable master agreed, and in no time, the doctor came back with Pol, his horse tied on behind the carriage. Maman stayed with Gran while the doctor examined her, but they sent Pol downstairs to wait. Jackie was in the kitchen feeding the stable master and the steward, and tried to get him to eat something, but he was not hungry.

"I've told him about the arsenic," he said. "He says it can be hard to detect, but he is pleased to be aware of the possibility."

"Arsenic?" the stable master asked.

Jackie explained what she had heard, and the stable master and steward were suitably horrified. Not surprised, though, Jackie realized. *Five people have heard about the arsenic now, and four of us know the viscount's mother. None of us four think it impossible, or even unlikely, that she has been poisoning her mother-in-law.*

"My housekeeper reads the broadsheets," the steward said. "There was a case recently where a woman was poisoned with arsenic. Apparently, if a person is given it over time in moderate doses, it can mimic a disease of the gut, so when the dose is increased to a fatal level, the authorities are unlikely to suspect foul play."

"Aye, I heard summat about that," the stable master commented. "Her husband, wasn't it. He got caught because his first wife had died the same way, and her daughter was suspicious."

They were silent for a moment while they considered the implications.

"What if I was too late?" Pol asked.

"You couldn't have known," Jackie said, but Pol shook his head, his eyes bleak.

"I left her there, with them," he said.

The steward gripped his shoulder. "If you had stayed, you would have been arrested. Miss Haricot, too, and who knows what might have happened to her. You couldn't have helped your Gran or Miss Haricot from a prison cell."

The two men from Tissingham had finished the lunch she had prepared for them. "I'll make a cup of tea," she decided. "Will you have a cup before you get on your way?"

But both men asked if they could stay until they heard what the doctor had to say, and so the four of them sat around the kitchen table, drinking tea, until they heard him come down the stairs.

"Go and talk to him in the parlor, Pol," Jackie said. "Then come and tell us what you think we should know."

POL MET THE doctor at the bottom of the stairs and ushered him into the parlor. "How is she, doctor?"

"Your grandmother is extremely fragile, Mr. Allegro. I could wish you discovered your dissatisfaction with your previous physician before he bled her to within an inch of her life. Add to that the stomach complaint, which has further weakened her, and the laudanum addiction." He shook his head. "I must caution you against too much hope."

Pol, who had prepared himself to be told that Gran was dying, received the news with a slight lift of his spirits. "There is *some* hope?"

"She is alive," said the doctor, unwilling to commit himself further. "I have instructed Madame Haricot to throw out all her old medicines, in case your fears of poisoning have substance. I have taken some samples for a few experiments and have provided a new bottle of laudanum. Apart from that... Careful nursing, plenty of fluids, an invalid diet, if she can tolerate it. It is the best we can do. As to whether it is enough, we shall just have to wait and see."

"More laudanum?" Pol asked. *Surely it would be better to throw that out with the rest?*

"She has had the drug habitually, Mr. Allegro. Stopping it abruptly has been known to kill even a relatively healthy habitue. If she recovers, it will be time enough to taper the laudanum doses. Even then, I caution that haste will be risky. You have removed her from the custody of other relatives, you said?"

"I have, sir. As soon as I saw her condition." Pol only wished he had done so earlier. He should have seen what was going on!

The doctor nodded. "If she survives, you will have saved her life." His stern mien softened into a smile. "I will call again tomorrow. If she takes a turn for the worst, send for me immediately. I have told Madame Haricot the symptoms to look for."

"I cannot thank you enough, sir," Pol said. He took his purse from his pocket. "May I make a contribution to your work?" Physicians were gentlemen, and—in theory—did not ask payment for their services. However, a gift was certainly expected from patients and their families.

"That certainly goes some way toward thanking me," the doctor commented, dryly. "Five shillings would be a most appreciated contribution."

Ouch. If they paid that every day, they would soon run through Pol's ready cash. Though, he consoled himself, not the extra stash of coins he'd liberated from Oscar's goose the previous night.

"A weekly contribution," the doctor clarified. "I imagine I shall be a regular visitor for at least the next fortnight."

Five shillings a week was reasonable. "Thank you again," Pol said.

After he'd shown the doctor out, he went through to the kitchen and told Jackie and the others the gist of what the doctor had to say.

"We shall be praying for her, lad," the steward said, "Mrs. Finch and I."

"Aye," said the stable master. "I remember her from when I was a boy. A good lady, your grandmother. I wish her well, Mr. Allegro. Send news, if you can without those monsters finding out where you are."

"Yes," the steward agreed. "Perhaps a note to the squire?"

Repeating their good wishes, the pair of them went on their way back to Tissingham.

"Right," said Jackie. "Sit down and have something to eat." She gestured to the table, where food and drink waited for him. "You will wish to see your grandmother. I shall check with Maman and come and fetch you."

He watched her go. His worry for Gran was somewhat lightened by Jackie's care for him. *What a woman. What a wonderful wife she will make.* To someone. The revelation about his birth had removed one of the barriers between them, but Pol still had to find a position that would allow him to support a family before he could ask her to be his bride. Tomorrow, he would return to work at the local squire's.

Chapter Eighteen

THE DOWAGER LADY Riese lingered on the edge of eternity for two days and nights. She was no longer vomiting or soiling herself, but she still slept most of the time and was too weak to lift her head when she was awake.

Maman was reluctant to leave her bedside, allowing Pol or Jackie to sit with the dowager for no more than a few minutes while Maman saw to her own needs, and an hour or two while she slept. She fed the lady frequent small sips of barley water or warm milk, gave her a measured dose of laudanum every few hours, kept her clean and comfortable, and talked to her in French and in English.

"She needs to hear a friendly voice, *cherie*," Maman told Jackie. "She sleeps better if she can hear that she is among friends."

Since Jackie was only needed for an hour here or there to sit with Lady Riese, she undertook more of the sewing and called on the draper to assure her they would deliver the garments they'd promised, even if they were a day or two late.

Pol was working mornings at the squire's, but when he noticed how busy Jackie was, he took over the care of the house and proved that he could cook. He even made a thin chicken soup and strained it so Lady Riese could sip it easily from the invalid cup that Maman was using for other drinks.

Jackie, who had admired him from the first, tumbled even further in love.

The doctor visited each morning, approved what Maman was doing, and left again. And then, three days after he had seen her first, he declared that her heartbeat was stronger and her color better. "Keep doing what you are doing," he said. "I make no promises, but she appears to be improving. Mr. Allegro, may I have a private word?"

Pol took the doctor to the parlor. He came to the kitchen after escorting the doctor to his horse. "Jackie, the doctor fed some of Gran's medicines to some rats. Two lots died." Pol looked a little green, as if he had not believed the wickedness of his aunt until now. "He wants to know what I am going to do about bringing the perpetrators to justice."

"But how?" Jackie asked. "Your aunt will deny everything. She will blame the maid, or the doctor, or just insist that none of it is true and you put the poison in the medicines yourself."

"The doctor has suggested we hire someone to investigate. He knows some people in London who might be able to help." Pol frowned, looking more worried than uncertain. "A Mr. and Mrs. Wakefield. Maybe…" He trailed off, biting his lip.

"I have not spent all the money you gave me for the rent," Jackie offered. "I'm sure Maman would agree we should spend it on your investigators. Perhaps they can find out enough to put the bad Lady Riese and her son behind bars."

Pol shook his head. "It isn't the money. Depending on what they charge, I can pay for it." He chuckled. "Or Oscar can, actually. I robbed the goose while I was back at the Hall." He frowned again. "It is just that I was wondering if it would be worth asking them to look into whether I should be viscount, and whether or not the viscountess knows it."

Jackie's heart sank. If Pol was a viscount, he was out of her reach. Oh, her birth was appropriate enough. The daughter of a French *Comte* was the social equivalent of an English earl. But long before Papa had died, the family had lived on the tattered fringes of respectability, and now she was nothing more than a seamstress and sometimes groom.

But her own selfish romantic fantasies didn't matter here. Pol, if he was indeed the viscount, deserved a wife who moved in the Ton and could raise his status among his peers. "That is a good idea," she said. "Will you write? Or go to see them?"

"It would be best to see them, do you not think? I will go to London on the mail coach once I know that Gran is well again."

Ah, how Jackie wished that she could go, too.

AFTER THOSE FIRST few days, Gran improved day by day. The leech wounds had almost healed and the bruises from the nurse's pinches were fading. She began to spend longer and longer awake, and even to sit up—at first in her bed, and then in a chair by the window, while Madame de Haricot du Charmont sat in the facing chair with her sewing.

The two older women were so absorbed with one another that Pol and Jackie might have been alone in the house. Pol constantly fought the temptation to touch his beloved, to kiss her. More than that, he would not do until they were wed, or at least until she had accepted the proposal he had not yet made. With his future so uncertain, it would be unfair, possibly even dangerous. He shuddered to think what Oscar might do to Pol's wife. That is, if he had been told that Pol was the rightful heir to their grandfather.

Should he kiss her, though? She was attracted to him, he was certain. He was not the rake his cousin was, nor was he a complete innocent. She wanted him, unless he was imagining the signs of her desire—the way her body tilted toward his, the husky tone when they were alone and she spoke to him, her habit of touching her tongue to her lips, her enlarged pupils.

As for him, he yearned to hold her, to kiss her, and everything that followed. In his dreams, they enjoyed the greatest of intimacies. He slept restlessly and woke hard and aching. Would kisses make it all worse?

Surely not. He had learned self-control in a hard school. He could kiss her and do no more. Day by day, he became more certain that a private kiss or two would do no harm. More than that, it felt inevitable.

In the end, though, there was no question. He stepped out of his little bedchamber off the kitchen just as she hurried past, and suddenly she was in his arms. He made no conscious decision to lower his head and press a kiss to her lips. One tender but gentle kiss became another, the heat building in him as she responded.

"Jackie," he murmured.

"Pol," she replied, or he assumed that was the word she intended, for as soon as she opened her mouth after pronouncing the "P", he slipped his tongue past her lips to explore her mouth. It was clear she'd never been kissed before, but she was a fast learner, as he might have guessed she would be. Everything he did to her, she did in return to him, stroking his tongue with her own, brushing her tongue along the inside of his cheeks and pressing it far into his mouth and then retreating so that his tongue followed hers into the warm cavern of her mouth.

They were pressed together as tightly as two people could be with clothes on, he with one hand on her buttock and one in the middle of her back, and she exploring his chest and his back with hands that stroked and caressed.

His own hands stayed where they were, though it took every ounce of self-control he still possessed not to use them to shape her breasts, to reach for her feminine core. Not here. Not yet. Not in the kitchen where her mother might appear at any moment.

The thought was enough to slightly temper his ardor, but rather than step away, he backed into his bedchamber, bringing her with him. He wouldn't close the door, because even in his current state—especially in his current state—he didn't think it wise to be kissing Jackie in a room with a bed in it.

"Beloved," he said to his dear delight. "Jackie, my heart, my love. You cannot know how much I want you."

"Perhaps nearly as much as I want you," she replied, which made him chuckle. Trust Jackie to challenge him.

"I've no right to ask you to marry me when my future is so uncertain," he admitted, taking the leap toward his heart's desire—if only part way.

But half a leap was never going to satisfy his intrepid darling. "The future is never certain, Pol. I've learned that. Anything can happen. We should snatch what happiness we can."

"Then you will promise to marry me?"

"Pol, I can't. If you are a viscount…" she began.

He pressed another kiss to her lips as a prelude to arguing with her, but the sound of feet on the stairs had them springing apart.

Pol stepped into the kitchen and closed the door, leaving Jackie to tidy and compose herself. *I can't. Not I won't.* He would have to convince her, but in words, not in the heat of passionate kisses, and he supposed he'd better speak to her mother first.

In fact, here was Jackie's mother now. "Ah, Pol, there you are. And where is my daughter?"

Was he blushing? He hoped not. "She was here a minute ago," he said. "Would you like me to tell her that you need her?"

Madame shook her head. "No need. I see she has prepared the tray I came down to fetch." There it was on the kitchen table, covered by a cloth.

"I shall carry it up for you," Pol offered, seizing the chance to get his darling's mother out of the kitchen so Jackie could leave his room.

But apparently the *Comtesse* had seen more than Pol thought, for she looked directly at Pol's bedroom door, smiled, and called out, "Come out when you are ready, *cherie*. And when you do, take that basket of petticoats to the drapers." She smiled a satisfied cat-in-the-cream smile then and said, "Bring the tray, Pol, and after I have served your grandmother, you and I shall have a little talk."

Chapter Nineteen

GRAN HAD PROGRESSED to feeding herself. Jackie had prepared a fragrant chicken soup which was much more substantial than the thin broth that was all Gran had been able to stomach when she'd first arrived. By now, it had barley, carrots and peas in it, as well as pieces of chicken meat. With it were thin slices of buttered bread, a pot of tea, and a slice of cake. The cook at the squire's often sent Pol home with a basket of food, and the Haricot ladies were happy to trade sewing for items the household needed.

"Sit and entertain your grandmother while she eats," Madame de Haricot du Charmont ordered Pol. "Tell her what you are up to."

Pol obeyed, at least in so far as he sat in the chair opposite the elderly lady. "How are you, Gran?" he asked.

"Better than I have been in a long time, my dear boy. Well, enough to know what you have not been telling me. I understand you have removed me from Louella's grasp, and that she was giving me something to make me ill. How bad was it, Apollo? Did she intend to kill me?"

Pol, who had been prepared for an interrogation about his intentions toward Jackie, was taken by surprise. What should he tell her? He examined her face as he thought about it.

The Gran who faced him with one eyebrow lifted in question was not the frail confused elderly lady he had visited daily in recent years. Frail, yes, but recovering strength day by day. Elderly, of course, but the blue eyes that met his were clear and determined. And they held the wisdom formed by a lifetime of experience. She would not be easily fooled or placated.

The truth, then.

"I believe so, Gran. I think she has been giving you laudanum for a long time, though I do not know why. We think she added something worse to your medicines recently. Arsenic, we think. Jackie—Miss Haricot, I mean—overheard her doctor's servant ordering arsenic at the apothecary. The doctor here says arsenic fits the symptoms."

Gran nodded. "Louella is a wicked woman. I would not be at all surprised to find out that she poisoned me. I know too much, you see."

Pol opened his mouth to ask what Gran knew, but she surprised him again by asking, "And what are your intentions toward Miss Haricot? She is a lady, Apollo, I hope you remember."

"I know she is, Gran," Pol replied, managing with a struggle not to look at Madame de Haricot du Charmont, where she sat by the window with her sewing, probably listening to their conversation. "I have spoken to her of marriage, but I have not yet proposed." He risked a glance. Madame was bent over the fabric on her lap, but her needle was still. "I must first approach her mother to ask for her blessing," he said.

"See, Eloise," said Gran. "I *told* you he was a good boy."

"Handsome is as handsome does," Madame de Haricot du Charmont replied, her voice heavy with irony. She looked him in the eye then. "Why do you wish to marry my girl, Apollo Allegro? And how will you support her?"

"He is the real viscount, Eloise," Gran said. "Once he has reclaimed his title and the estate, he will easily be able to support a wife."

"It's true, then? I should be the viscount?" Pol asked. "That is,

I think my parents were married, but is it true?"

But before Gran could answer, Jackie came clattering up the stairs and hurried into the room without hesitating. Her eyes were wide and her face pale. "Oscar's men are in the village. I saw Bill Whitely. The draper says they have been asking for a man and his old sick grandmother, new to the village. Two other women might be with them, they say. An older one and a pretty young one, both seamstresses. They say they have the law on their side, and the man and the young woman are both wanted for theft."

Bother. With that description, Oscar's men would be on the doorstep at any time.

But Jackie hadn't finished. "She says they have been throwing their weight around, insulting people and breaking things. So, the villagers have closed ranks against them."

"That will only last until threats or bribery causes one of the villagers to send them our way," Pol commented, and the women all nodded.

"We should all go to London," Jackie said.

"London?" Madame de Haricot frowned. "Why should we go to London?"

"The enquiry agents that the doctor recommended are in London," Pol told them. "I have been thinking of going to talk to them—about investigating not just Gran's poisoning, but also my claim to the viscountcy. Since we must leave this village, I'd also like to seek more substantial employment there. I've seen advertisements in the papers from London employment agencies. I should visit one of those. I need to find a position that will support us all, and working part time for the squire is not enough."

"Jacqueline and I can support ourselves," Madame de Haricot du Charmont said, sharply.

"Your work is superb, Maman," Jackie acknowledged. "But would there not be a greater market for it in London? We do not need to open an expensive shop, but perhaps we can find work the same way we did here, through a draper?"

From the arrested look on Madame's face, her daughter had the right strategy to persuade her. Gran also made a telling point, when she suggested that her friends from her days in Society would be in London for the Season. "We were close, once," she said. "I have lost touch in recent years, but I am sure one or more of them will help me and my grandson if I ask."

Even so, it took another fifteen minutes before alternative plans had been proposed and rejected.

"London it shall be, then," said Madame de Haricot du Charmont. "And as soon as possible." She stood. "I'll start cleaning for our departure right away."

"We will leave tonight," Pol suggested. "I shall hire a post chaise in Alstonebridge. Would the draper consent to store anything you cannot fit in your luggage, to be sent for once we have dealt with this nonsense of the theft charges?"

"I think so," Jackie said.

"Then this is what I think we must do…"

THEY TRAVELED UNDER aliases: Mrs. and Mr. Remington, a lady and her grandson, and Mrs. and Miss Harper, a lady and her daughter. Remington was Gran's maiden name, and Harper was an alias Maman and Jackie had used before, back in the days when Papa had occasionally needed them to pretend to another identity to escape persistent creditors.

They had stuck close to the truth in deciding their story. Mr. Remington was accompanying his grandmother, his betrothed and the mother of his betrothed to London. If anyone asked, Pol had legal and business matters to deal with—likely in a young man approaching marriage—and Jackie needed bride clothes.

"Almost true," Maman said, "though I have not said that I would approve this marriage, and he has not asked."

Jackie still doubted that the marriage was in Pol's best interests, but everyone else seemed so certain it was going to happen that she did not argue. Perhaps in London he would see how unsuitable she was for a viscount. Meanwhile, she would enjoy being his pretend betrothed.

On their first night away from Little Tidbury, Maman and Gran—as she'd asked Jackie to call her—were leafing through a copy of Debrett's that they'd found at the inn where they were staying that night.

They were using it to confirm names and addresses for the letters Gran wished to write. Gran had apparently kept up a voluminous correspondence with dozens of Society ladies until she became sunk in poppy dreams. Amongst Gran's friends were a duchess, a marchioness, and several countesses, all of whom might be in London for Parliament and the Season, though presumably they must be close to Gran's age, so nearly seventy. Some of her friends had died, and some had remarried.

"Would you care for a walk, Jackie?" Pol asked. "I need one after being cooped up in the carriage all day."

"Do not go too far," Maman scolded, not taking her eyes off the pages she was perusing.

Jackie was only too pleased to escape downstairs, and soon they were walking along the street. The inn was on the outskirts of a small town, and a few minutes' walk brought them to a path alongside a canal, peaceful in the evening light.

"I hope Gran is not disappointed," Pol commented. "Perhaps none of her friends come to London anymore."

"The copy is a year old, so probably there have been further deaths," Jackie said. "Perhaps they no longer wished to acknowledge the past friendship, for she has not written in years. But I hope she is as fondly remembered by them as they are by her."

"Your mother is wonderful with her," Pol said.

Maman had agreed to care for Gran for the sake of the money Pol had promised, but they had rapidly become warm friends, though Gran was old enough to be Maman's mother.

"Maman admires your grandmother, Pol. She has suffered greatly and retains enormous dignity."

"The same applies to your mother, my dearest love. What must I do to gain her permission to our marriage, Jackie?"

Jackie frowned. "Pol, you are a viscount. I am a seamstress. You need a wife suitable to your station."

"Whether I turn out to be a viscount or not, I need a wife who loves me, Jackie. One whom I love more than life. More than the world and all that is in it. You are a *comte's* daughter. Your mother is a lady to her fingertips and has raised you to be the same. If I am not a viscount, then I'm no fit husband for your parent's daughter, and that has held me back from telling you how much I love you."

Jackie was taken aback by his admission that he thought he was not good enough for her. "But Pol, someone who knows the Ton could help you in your new role." Someone who loved him to distraction would surely be even better, though. Someone who would stand beside him every day, whatever life threw at them.

"No one else will do for me, Jackie," he said. "Will your mother agree, do you think?"

The last of her doubts dissolved. "You do not require her permission, Pol. Only mine. I am of age. You need to ask *my* permission."

Pol stopped. Since she was holding his arm, she stopped, too, and found herself looking down on him as he closed his hand around hers and dropped to one knee. "Jacqueline de Haricot du Charmont, will you be my wife? Will you take me to husband? I have nothing to offer you except myself, but I will work for you every day of my life to give you the best life that I can. I love you, Jackie, and I can be twice the man I am with you by my side."

"Yes," Jackie replied. "Yes, Pol." Those were the only words she could manage, though no doubt she'd think of some clever answer later. Something about him being enough, and her standing beside him forever. But the thoughts would not form into speech, and apparently her "yes" was enough, for she was in his arms, and his lips were on hers, and she was betrothed, whether Maman approved or not.

The last of the sun had set and the moon had come up before they made their way back to the inn, reluctant to walk away from the magic they had been making on the canal path, but conscious that Maman would be worried.

Sure enough, Maman complained about how long they had been outside. "I thought you had been taken by those fiends," she scolded.

Jackie made an instant decision. "Pol asked me to marry him, Maman, and I said yes." She braced herself for her mother's disapproval.

"Excellent," said Maman. "Come and give me a kiss, *cherie*. You, too, Apollo. It did not take you very long at all."

"But you said you would not approve," Jackie said, confused at her mother's about face.

"You are of age, Jaqueline. My approval or disapproval should not matter to a young man in love. Is this not good news, Clara?"

Jackie exchanged a glance with Pol. *I doubt if I shall ever under-stand my mother.*

Chapter Twenty

J ACKIE WAITED WHILE Pol paid off the post chaise at an inn in London. Maman supported Gran into the inn. They had shortened their travel time each day, for Gran's sake, and had crowded three to the backward facing seat so she could sleep, but still the four days of travel had been hard on her.

"At the very least, they shall find me a place where she can sit while they prepare us a room," Maman said, as she left Jackie with the luggage.

Pol finished with the post rider and shouldered the largest of the trunks.

"Carry your bags, sir?" said a somewhat weedy-looking individual, touching his cap.

Pol looked him up and down, but before he could decide another man rushed up, this one in livery. "Be off with you, or I'll have a constable on you," he said, and the first man scurried off.

"I'm sorry, sir. We're a bit rushed at this time of night. Someone should have been outside to chase off scoundrels like that. They look for people who are laden with bags, offer to help with some of them, and then scarper with whatever they are carrying."

Pol shot a glance at Jackie and grinned. "He'd have been sorry if he'd tried to carry off one of our bags," he commented. "This dear lady would have been onto him in a moment."

Jackie was not so confident. Not in these skirts. But she grinned back.

"Anyone in this livery can be trusted, sir," the liveried man was saying, as he picked up most of their luggage and waved for someone else to take the smaller trunk and the bag that Jackie was carrying.

"Does Sir require a room for Madam and himself?" The first man was walking rapidly into the inn, even though he must be carrying nearly his own weight in bags.

"One room for Mrs. Remington and Mrs. and Miss Harper, and a second for me," Pol said.

The rooms were opposite one another on an upper floor. Both rooms would be noisy—the smaller one looked out over the coach yard, and the larger over the busy street. The rooms were clean enough and nicely appointed, and the bed in the larger room was large enough for Maman and Gran to share. A maid was already setting up a truckle bed for Jackie, and another appeared with a jug of hot water for them to wash.

Maman helped Gran to a comfortable chair and began unpacking the bag that held their nightclothes.

"Will that be all, Ma'am?" one of the maids asked Maman, who said, "For the moment. I shall ring if we require anything."

An early task would be to send one of the inn's servants to post the letters that Gran had written to her friends. Pol had said that sending the letters would probably have to wait until the morning, so they would be here at least for tonight.

If no one replied to Gran's letters, Pol had another plan. He would look for rooms they could rent—expensive, in London, or so Jackie understood. But still cheaper than staying in an inn.

Not only would the cost of a London inn quickly deplete the resources liberated from Oscar's goose, but rented rooms, perhaps giving Jackie her own bedroom, would, she hoped, be both quieter and more comfortable.

There was a knock on the door, and Jackie answered it. Pol waited in the passage outside. "May I come in, Miss Harper?"

She stepped aside, and he entered the room. "Ladies, I have asked the manager, and there is no private parlor available. Would it be acceptable if dinner was served to us in this room?"

He left again once he had their assent, promising to return in forty-five minutes, at which time the meal would also arrive.

Maman and Jackie washed and changed for dinner, as they always did, whether they had spent all day traveling or all day sewing—changing for dinner was part of what Maman called maintaining standards. Then Maman assisted Gran to wash and change, though in Gran's case, Maman was content to see Gran into her nightgown, slippers, and a voluminous house coat that buttoned from her neck to the bottom.

"There, Clara," Maman said. "You may eat at the table with us if you choose, but I believe you shall be more comfortable in bed, where you may rest your head against the pillows."

Gran chose the bed, and Maman helped her up the steps and saw her pillows arranged to ensure that she was comfortable. "Thank you, Eloise," said Gran.

The next knock on the door was a pair of footmen with a heavy tray each, which they put down on the sideboard. One then spread a tablecloth on the room's table, and another set out cutlery and glassware. Pol arrived while they were busy, and one of them stopped to tell him what the dishes contained, clearly believing that the man of the party was the proper person to address, rather than any of the women.

They were to start with cream soup, followed by a *haricot de mouton* and vegetable pie, with piccalilli. For dessert, there were little cakes and lemon custard.

"We shall serve ourselves," Maman announced. The footman who had been describing the dinner glanced from her to Pol, as if checking that he approved of the lady's decision.

Pol nodded, ushered the two footmen to the door, and slipped each of them a coin. "We shall call when we wish you to clear," he said, then returned to move the chairs out of the way. "Let's set the table at the foot of the bed so that we can all eat together," he said, and Jackie helped him to lift and move it. He rearranged three of the chairs around the table, so they were facing Gran, and Jackie moved the place settings to match the chairs.

Soon, they were enjoying the soup, which was rich in vegetables and fragrant with herbs. "I gave your letters to the inn manager, Gran," Pol told her. "He said he would send runners with them this evening, so perhaps you might have some replies tomorrow morning. He was most impressed with the names on the envelopes."

"Clara used to move in the highest levels of fashionable Society," said Maman.

"Not the highest," Gran objected. "Frederick used to be friendly with the royal princes, and especially with the Prince of Wales, but their parties were not quite the thing, you know. Not for a faithful wife."

They were just about to clear the second course and begin on the dessert when someone knocked on the door again.

"I'll see who it is," Pol said, and went to the door.

"Good evening," said the unseen caller. "Am I at the correct room for Lady Riese?"

"And you are?" Pol asked.

"Drew Winderfield. I have been sent by my stepmother, the Duchess of Winshire, in response to a letter from Lady Riese."

"Eleanor!" Gran said, sitting up straighter in the bed, her face aglow with pleasure. "Bring him in, Apollo."

Pol stepped back, and in came a tall, dark stranger, beautifully dressed in fashionable gentlemen's evening wear. His eyes scanned the room, and he addressed a pleasant if vague smile toward them all, but he brightened as he saw Gran. "Lady Riese, I presume. Aunt Eleanor sent me to invite you and your party to Winderfield House, my lady. She would have come herself, but she was expected at a ball for one of her goddaughters."

Gran beamed back at him. "Eleanor has more godchildren than anyone else I know," she commented. "We would like to go and stay with the Duchess of Winshire, Apollo, would we not?"

"If you wish, Gran, and if it is not too much trouble."

The young lord—he must be Lord Andrew, a son of the duke—shrugged his eyebrows, still smiling. "The house is enormous, and Aunt Eleanor is beside herself with delight to have rediscovered an old friend."

"But where are my manners?" Gran said. "Eloise, Jacqueline, allow me to make known to you Lord Andrew Winderfield, the fourth son of the Duke of Winshire. Lord Andrew, my friend La *Comtesse de Haricot du Charmont* and her daughter, Mademoiselle de Haricot du Charmont. And this is my grandson, Apollo Riese, rightfully Viscount Riese, Lord Andrew."

Maman had a full repertoire of curtseys, learned for the French court. She'd taught them to Jacqueline who drew on them now. Item, one curtsey from a *comtesse* to the younger son of a duke. Item, one curtsey from a *comte's* daughter to the same gentleman. The gentlemen bowed.

"I have interrupted your dinner," Lord Andrew noted. "I beg your pardon. Please, take your time. We can leave whenever you are ready."

"You mean us to go tonight?" Pol asked.

Lord Andrew inclined his head in something between a nod and a bow. "Winshire House will be much quieter and more comfortable for the ladies, and is only a short carriage ride. Lady Riese, you need not even get dressed. My father's carriage is parked in the carriage yard. We can wrap you in a blanket and carry you down, and straight into the carriage. Within twenty minutes, you can be sitting up in bed in the room my father's housekeeper is even now preparing for you."

Gran held out a hand and Maman hurried to take it. "What do you think, Eloise?"

Maman pursed her lips in thought. "I think, if it is a comfortable coach, and the distance is not too far, it will do no harm. Do you wish it?"

"Oh, yes," Gran said.

Pol raised his eyebrows and nodded at Lord Andrew. "The ladies have spoken," he said.

His grin was Lord Andrew's only reply.

"Please be seated, Lord Andrew," said Maman, waving to one of the fireside chairs. She and Jackie resumed their seats at the table.

"Would you care for cake and custard?" Apollo asked the young lord. "We have been given a most generous plateful of cakes and have custard to spare."

"Call me Drew," Lord Andrew invited. "Yes, please. They look delicious."

They were and were soon gone. After that, Drew helped Pol carry the luggage back out into the hall, where she could hear him giving instructions to someone. Pol went downstairs to settle with the innkeeper, and a few minutes later he returned to carry Gran downstairs, wrapped in a soft, warm blanket that one of Drew's servants had brought up from his carriage.

They settled Gran across one capacious seat, and Pol, Maman and Jackie took the other. Drew had a horse waiting. "Did you have any trouble with the innkeeper?" Gran asked Pol.

"None," Pol said. "He was deeply awed that we were going to stay at the house of the Duke and Duchess of Winshire. Besides, I paid for the night's accommodation as well as the dinner, which was only fair, I think."

In no time at all, they arrived at a townhouse that took up all the space from one street corner to the next and dwarfed those around it. Jackie had little time to gawk, for Maman said, "With me, *cherie*," and hurried up the stairs after Pol, who was carrying Gran.

Inside was unbelievable. Jackie had been in a few country houses in her role as seamstress, several of them larger and more elegant than Riese Hall. This was as far above those as Riese Hall was above the cottage they'd rented in Little Tidbury.

The front entry hall soared the height of the house, ending in a cupola far above her, and stairs swept up both sides of the hall, with landings crossing the expansive space on each level. It was a rich interior of marble, polished wood, glittering crystals, bright tapestries and paintings, gleaming ornaments, and more—so much that she could not take in more than the overwhelming impression of wealth and good taste.

She wasn't given much time to look around her, for a woman stepped forward and announced herself as the housekeeper. "Her Grace has instructed that we are to make you comfortable, my ladies, sir. She looks forward to seeing you in the morning. If you would come this way…?"

She led them off up the left-hand stairs with Pol behind her. Drew bowed to Jackie and Maman. "You are in good hands, my ladies. I, too, shall see you in the morning."

❧

Chapter Twenty-One

"ARE YOU WELL?" Pol asked Jackie the next day when he found her in the conservatory that linked the ladies' drawing room to the garden. At this time in the afternoon, the drawing room was empty, and he had gone there looking for a brief escape from all the friendly, active, interesting people who shared this house. From there, he'd glimpsed a shape beyond a bank of flowers, and somehow known it was her.

"They are all so kind and welcoming," Jackie said, "but there are so many of them!"

"Exactly!" He sat down on the bench next to her. "I am used to spending much of every day alone."

"For most of my life," Jackie commented, "it has just been me and Maman. Even before Papa died, when we still had servants, Papa was usually away, and Maman and I were alone in the schoolroom or her parlor. So many people live in this household! Not just the family, although that is large enough, but also the people that came with the duke from beyond the Caspian Sea."

The foreign-looking men and women—Pol had seen more than a score of them—seemed to be not quite family and not quite servants. Jackie was right. Between the family, the foreign retainers and the English servants, there must be close to one hundred people in the house, bustling about on their own business, so no room was still for more than a few moments.

"And they do not leave the children to the servants," Jackie added. "Pol, Lady Sutton had her baby at the breakfast table!" Lord Sutton was the duke's son and heir, and the baby was little Lord Elfingham, the Sutton's first son after several daughters, and the apple of his parents' eyes. "And when Lady Ashford visited, everyone went up to the nursery. Everyone. Even the duke!" Jackie sounded bewildered.

"Yes." Pol did not have a lot of experience of aristocratic houses, but this behavior was unusual, judging from the astonishment on the faces of both Gran and Maman, who had such experience, albeit not recent.

He put that into words for his beloved. "I don't think other households are like this one. Your mother and Gran don't seem to think so, in any case."

"Maman says that the household is very well run, except that children do not stay on the nursery floor," Jackie acknowledged.

Proof of how well the house was run came hurrying into the conservatory and took a seat within sight and out of earshot. A maid, come to play propriety. Although Pol hadn't seen an observer taking note that he and Jackie were alone together, obviously someone had not only seen them but reacted.

A very well-run household indeed.

"I am grateful that you and your mother took my wardrobe in hand," Pol commented. "I might not have clothing as fancy as that worn by the duke and his sons, but at least everything fits properly."

"Maman and I are in despair," Jackie commented. "Maman has always insisted that what we wear is an advertisement for our work, so I need not blush for the gowns I wear, but there are so few of them! I daresay the ladies here do not wear the same gown twice!" She pointed one foot and examined the shoe on it with a frown. "As for my shoes, they are a disgrace."

The shoe that so offended her was neat and clean, and shod a foot so pretty that Pol felt an urgent need to change the subject lest he discomfort the chaperoning maid. "We are fortunate the duchess is in town and remembers Gran fondly."

"She has been very kind," Jackie said.

The duchess had said that Gran had been kind to her when she was a young bride and still finding her feet as a duchess. It was hard to imagine the commanding grand lady had once been unsure of her place. Now, said the duchess, she could return the favor.

"She has been very helpful," said Pol. The four of them had agreed not to disclose the details of why they were in London to anyone but the enquiry agent, and even then, they had intended to be judicious about what they said.

Gran must have forgotten, for within ten minutes of her reunion with the duchess, she was spilling out everything. Her belief that Pol was the real heir to his grandfather and that her daughter-in-law had hidden the truth. The terrible treatment Pol had suffered in what should be his own house. How Oscar and his mother terrorized the neighborhood, with the connivance of the local magistrate. The trumped-up charges against Pol and Jackie. Even her own poisoning.

When Pol, Jackie, and Madame de Haricot du Charmont had joined the two older ladies, Her Grace knew everything. She asked how she could help. "I will, if you have no objection, ask Wakefield and Wakefield to send an enquiry agent to discuss your case. I am familiar with the firm, and agree they are a good choice."

The agency had responded to the duchess's note to say that someone would call as soon as possible. "Do you want to be part of the meeting with the enquiry agent?" Pol asked Jackie. "This affects you as much as it affects me."

"I would like that," Jackie agreed.

Her gaze moved to a point behind Pol's shoulder. He glanced back. A footman was standing a few paces away, waiting to be noticed. "Lord Riese, sir. Mr. Wakefield has called to see you. He is in the Chinese parlor."

"Thank you," said Pol. "Can you show us to the Chinese parlor? Jackie? Are you coming?"

Having a guide was essential. The whole of the first floor of the townhouse was given over to reception rooms of one kind or another. The Chinese parlor must have taken its name from the style of the interior. Everything from the wallpaper and light fittings to the furniture and ornaments was in the chinoiserie style that had been highly fashionable in the middle of the previous century.

The person who was waiting for them did not fit Pol's picture of an enquiry agent. He was expecting some bluff burly character of indeterminate middle age, with a working man's coat and flat cap, and perhaps a flashy waistcoat.

This man was dressed quietly but neatly in a gentleman's morning attire—the kind of garment worn by a solicitor or a physician—or, for that matter, any gentleman with no particular desire to scale the heights of fashion.

In appearance, nothing about him stood out. Dark hair, hazel eyes, medium height and build. He was notable only for the smile he was addressing to the other occupant of the room.

The other occupant was a surprise. The Duchess of Winshire sat with the enquiry agent, engaged in warm conversation. She stood when she saw Pol and Jackie, and the man rose, too.

"There you are. Miss de Haricot du Charmont, Lord Riese, allow me to make known to you Mr. Wakefield." She put an arm on Mr. Wakefield's arm. "David, dear, do give my love to Prue. And let Antonia know that I was very proud of her last night."

Mr. Wakefield bent for the peck of a kiss she placed on his check. "I will leave you to business," she said, and sailed out of the room.

"Her Grace is godmother to my eldest daughter, who is currently enjoying her first Season," Mr. Wakefield explained. He shuddered. "Unlike her poor Papa."

Pol rearranged his assumptions about Mr. Wakefield's social status up another couple of notches.

"Shall we be seated?" the enquiry agent suggested. "I take it the matter you wish to have investigated affects you both?"

Jackie took the seat that Her Grace had vacated, and Pol and Mr. Wakefield both sat when she did. Mr. Wakefield took a leather case out of his inside jacket pocket and opened it to reveal a notebook and a pencil. He set these on his lap and settled back in his seat.

"Pol," Jackie said, her eyes on his notebook, "you explain."

Pol did so, starting with his personal history, and then explaining what had happened in the past couple of months to cause them to consult with Mr. Wakefield.

"There are three key issues," Pol said, finally, "but a tangle of complicating factors. First, I need to find evidence that my grandmother was deliberately poisoned with arsenic, and proof of who did it, why, and for how long. Second, I want to know whether my parents were married before I was born, and if so, whether my aunt by marriage knew that to be true when she had her son declared viscount. Third, if possible, I want evidence that my cousin—and perhaps his mother—are involved in criminal acts."

Mr. Wakefield's only reaction was the uplift of a single eyebrow. "I can see how there might be complicating factors," he commented.

He steepled his hands, and bumped his lips with his forefingers, then lowered them to say, "I will need to know more, of course. To take the first case, what makes you believe that your grandmother was poisoned with arsenic?"

Slowly, over the next hour, he questioned Pol—and Jackie, too, when she offered a comment. He had a way of drawing information out of a person and combining it with another answer to create a new set of questions, taking notes occasionally as things appeared pertinent to him.

Pol found himself telling Mr. Wakefield things he didn't know he remembered—discrepancies he had never consciously noted, both in his grandmother's health and in the way the Rieses treated him. "They gave me a gentleman landowner's education, but had me cleaning silver in my spare time," he commented.

Mr. Wakefield did not appear to be concerned about the accusations of theft against both Pol and Jackie. "In theory," he said, "Lord Riese and his mother could pursue the two cases here in London, but there's a question about whether any warrant is going to be valid so far away from the village where it was issued. Added to that, you are staying in the house of a duke. Any thief taker is going to want to have a strong case before they'd risk annoying the aristocracy. Even so, it might pay to keep a low profile."

Jackie appeared amused. "I don't think anyone is likely to be inviting us to balls and dinner parties," she said.

"You might be surprised," said Mr. Wakefield. "You are staying with the Duke and Duchess of Winshire, after all. However, if, despite all, Lord Riese and his mother discover you are in London and manage to talk some thief taker into attempting to arrest you before we've resolved who, out of you and them, is the criminal, our best strategy would probably be to ask Aunt Eleanor to introduce you in polite Society. I very much doubt your relatives will want the kind of public attention that would ensue under those circumstances."

With that, he put his notebook back into the leather case from which he'd taken both notebook and pencil. "I'd like to speak with your grandmother, Mr. Riese, on both the poisoning and your legitimacy. I understand she has been in poor health, and must be tired after her recent travel, so that can wait a couple of days, if necessary."

"I'll tell her, and let you know when would suit, Mr. Wakefield," Pol said.

Mr. Wakefield nodded. "On the poisoning, I shall have someone make enquiries in Little Tidbury, and interview the doctor that suggested the investigation. They can investigate what is being said about the claimed thefts, as well, and what locals understood about your legitimacy when you first arrived. I can see if any marriage was registered here in England, and also whether a will was registered for probate. Your grandfather's, your uncle's, or your father's. If your grandmother can give me a direction, I'll also write to Italy, but it may take some time to obtain a reply."

Pol nodded. That made sense. "Thank you," he said.

"One possibly fruitful area of investigation is old gossip. With your permission, I will ask Her Grace to talk to her friends and see if anyone was in correspondence with your father. Again, your grandmother might have an idea of who his friends were, and whether he had aunts or a godmother with whom he might have kept in touch."

Jackie raised her eyebrows even as she nodded. Pol would certainly never have thought of that.

"Yes, please do that," he said.

Mr. Wakefield rose. "I shall make weekly reports. More frequently if I discover something of particular interest. Please contact me if you have any further information."

"So now we do what?" Jackie asked, after Mr. Wakefield had left. "Sit and wait?"

"I suppose I should be visiting employment agencies looking for work as a steward or a secretary."

Jackie nodded. "And Maman and I need to find a place to sell our gowns and other garments, but surely one day more or less will not make a great deal of difference. We are in London! I have always wanted to see Hyde Park!"

Pol grinned. "The Tower of London."

"The British Museum!" Jackie said, smiling.

"London Bridge."

"St Paul's and Westminster Abbey."

"The royal parks and palaces."

"A day of sightseeing?" Jackie asked, and Pol nodded. It was too late today, and in any case, they needed to report to Gran and Madame Haricot. But tomorrow, they would go out to see the sights of London.

WHEN POL AND Jackie went up to the little sitting room between Gran's bedchamber and Maman's, Maman was flustered. Her Grace had visited Gran while Jackie and Pol were with Mr. Wakefield, and had mentioned expecting them all for dinner, though Gran was excused if she did not feel well enough.

"But what will we wear that is suitable for dinner in the house of a duke?" Maman asked Jackie. It was, of course, a rhetorical question, and Jackie knew better than to imagine otherwise. Maman was already undertaking a mental pillaging of their wardrobes to decide what might be suitable.

"You must come with me this minute, Jacqueline. I think the ivory silk might be made to do, but perhaps we may wish to retrim it. Apollo, you will stay with your grandmother, yes?"

"But Maman, we wished to tell you about our meeting with Mr. Wakefield, the enquiry agent," Jackie protested.

It was swiftly accomplished. Gran agreed that she would see Mr. Wakefield the following day and answer his questions. Maman, with her mind on what to wear for dinner said that Pol might take Jackie to see the sights without her along as chaperone, as long as they were accompanied by a maid.

"You, are, after all, betrothed," she commented. "Now come along, Jackie." And the rest of the afternoon was spent retrimming the ivory silk and making sure it was pressed after being packed for travel more than once.

Jackie was nervous about eating dinner at a duke's table, since she had never been to a formal dinner except on a Sunday, when her mother insisted on them dining in splendor. She required full table settings and formal manners suitable for a noble—or even a royal—table, even if dinner was nothing more than a potato and leek soup and stick bread cooked over the fire.

The first hint that Jackie need not have worried came when the company gathered in the drawing room before dinner. Those in attendance included adults of all ages—even the duchess's ward, Frances Grenford, who had not yet made her debut, and several of the foreign retainers, who proved to be on first name terms with the duke, his duchess, and his children.

Jackie's manners were more than adequate to the meal. Indeed, though the dinner was not as informal as luncheon had been, it was very much a family meal, with people speaking across the table and younger members of the household cheerfully joining in the conversation.

Her appearance was up to standard, too, as was Maman's. They had done one another's hair and had paraded for Gran before leaving her to the company of the maid who had been sent to sit with her. When the ladies retreated to the drawing room after dinner, Lady Sutton, the duke's daughter-in-law, complimented Jackie and asked where she had purchased her gown.

"Maman designs all our gowns," Jackie replied, "and we both sew them." Then she caught sight of Maman's frown and wondered if she should have brushed off the question. Ladies, after all, did not work for a living, or so Maman had always said. But since she insisted that she and Jackie were ladies, despite that, Jackie had not taken her seriously.

It was very confusing.

In any case, Lady Sutton seemed to see nothing wrong with Jackie sewing her own gowns and continued to be lavish in her praise.

One of the other ladies asked what Jackie planned to do while she was in London, and she mentioned her desire to see some of London's sights. "It will be unexceptional for you to do so with your betrothed," the duchess declared. "Though I can send a maid to be chaperone if your mother wishes. I think we have Mr. Phillip's guidebook, *Picture of London* in the library. I shall ask Miss Pomfritt to find it for you."

Miss Pomfritt, who was the duchess's secretary, smiled and nodded. "Of course, Your Grace," she said.

That prompted others to suggest places Jackie and Pol should go, and the ladies were still discussing the matter when the gentlemen joined them.

After that, the company dispersed. Most of them had social engagements for the evening. Pol, Jackie, and Maman retreated to Gran's suite, to discuss the day and their plans for the next. Jackie's heart lifted at the thought she would have a day of leisure seeing the sights of London with the man she loved.

Time enough after that to get back to the business of making a living.

❦

Chapter Twenty-Two

THE FOLLOWING MORNING, the duchess provided not just the guidebook and a maid, but also a carriage and a driver, waving off protests and thanks. "There is no need for thanks, Apollo, Jacqueline. My dear Clara was a Godsend in the early days of my marriage. I have no idea how I would have survived without her. I am only too happy to be able to repay her many kindnesses."

Nor would she hear of them seeking work just yet. "I know I am being selfish, dear children, but I am not willing to give Clara up so soon. However—it is foolish, I know, but people will have these ideas—you cannot run a dressmaking business from my husband's house, Jacqueline, and Apollo, you must not abandon your grandmother and your betrothed for a new position already. Surely it cannot hurt to just take a holiday for a week or two. While David Wakefield looks into your problems."

How could they argue when she presented it as a favor to her? Not to mention that a week or maybe two of holiday was enormously appealing, especially when they expected to spend it together.

It was a glorious day. Just the day to be out and about in London in a sociable, or two-bodied phaeton, with the maid and driver up before and Jackie and Pol in the seat behind, the whole of London at their feet.

Their first goal on the first morning of their London adventure was Westminster Abbey. "It was built by the order of Henry the Third," said Jackie, reading from the guidebook. "Or rebuilt, rather. There has been a church and abbey here for more than a thousand years."

"Henry the Third is… what? Six hundred years past?" Pol commented. "It is certainly a magnificent building!"

"Breathtaking," Jackie agreed, and insisted on seeing the choir where kings of England were crowned, each of the chapels, and dozens of tombs, including those in Poet's Corner. Pol, who was taking a turn with the guidebook, read, "It says, 'never could a place be named with more propriety'." They spent perhaps fifteen minutes reading the epitaphs of luminaries such as Chaucer, Spencer, Shakespeare and Milton.

For sixpence each, they were allowed to climb nearly three hundred steps to the top of one of the western towers to look out over London. The maid was offered the chance to accompany them but looked so alarmed at the prospect that Pol suggested she make her way back to the carriage and gave her a couple of pennies to purchase tea or ale from a street vendor.

They were not alone on the tower, however. A kindly verger explained the vista spread before them: the Banqueting House at Whitehall, St. James's Park, with the Parade and Horse Guards, Carleton House where the Prince of Wales had his principal residence, the gardens of the Queen's Palace, the Green Park, the western end of Piccadilly, and Hyde Park, with the Serpentine curling amongst the green trees and lawns. Looking toward the Thames, they could see both Westminster and Blackfriars bridges, with the river spread between them. Beyond, St Paul's Cathedral, with the sun falling on, was exquisitely beautiful.

"We shall go there, shall we not, Pol?" Jackie said.

And they did. They visited St Paul's Cathedral, drove past Queen's Palace and Carleton House, and through Green Park and Hyde Park, all before the fashionable hour.

They returned to Winshire House to describe the sights they'd seen to Gran and Maman, and to read out what the guidebook had to say about the Tower of London, which was to be their first stop the following day.

And Pol managed to find an unused parlor after dinner, as they made their way upstairs to bed, so Jackie finished the day thoroughly kissed, and went to sleep dreaming of more. It was a perfect day.

On the following day, they spent the entire morning at the Tower. Jackie was intrigued by the grim history of the place, but less enamored of the animals in the Royal menagerie. "They all seem so sad, Pol," she said.

"Trapped, far away from their homes and families," he replied, and she guessed he was thinking of his own exile from Italy to the colder climes and even colder hearts of Riese Hall. She slipped her hand around his arm, and he put his hand over hers. They left the menagerie, in one mind on this, as on so much else.

THE AFTERNOON WAS given over to the Levarian Museum, a private collection of curiosities and art objects, open to the public for the princely sum of one shilling apiece. "Well worth it," Pol declared, after they had torn themselves away from the room of Roman and medieval artifacts, the Sandwich room with its collection of objects from the Sandwich Islands, where Captain Cook had met with his end, gowns from the time of Charles the Second, and a large collection of stuffed monkeys, posed in groups.

Even the maid, who had trailed behind them with her mouth wide open, nodded at Pol's statement. They drove back across Blackfriars Bridge, chatting about the things they had seen. Pol had found the first room the most compelling, with its evidence of earlier times. Jackie had been fascinated by the gowns.

"The monkeys made me shudder," she said, and shuddered again, to prove it. "Poor little things."

Pol agreed. The slightly worn stuffed animals, no matter how artfully posed, had been more pitiful than interesting.

Suddenly, Jackie put her hand on his arm. "That man…"

"Where?" Pol stared in the same direction as her, but no one appeared to be looking their way.

"He's gone," she said, the tension going out of her. "Pol, I'm sure it is the same man I have seen before. At Westminster Abbey, and before that at one of the inns on the way to London."

"Do you know him?" Pol asked. "Is it one of the Whitelys?"

She shook her head. "Not one of the Whitelys. And no, I do not recognize him. Yet, I feel that I ought to. There is something familiar about him." She grimaced. "It has only been a glimpse each time. When he sees me looking, he disappears. What do you think it means?"

Pol had no idea, but he would discuss it with Drew. Perhaps it would be wise to stop their excursions, or to take a guard with them.

OVER THE NEXT three days, Jackie saw the man twice more—once in the bookshop known as the Temple of the Muses, and once in the street outside the Winshire townhouse as they came down to join their carriage one morning. Both times, he was out of sight before she could point him out to Pol or to one of the two retainers Drew had sent to attend them.

From the glimpses she had of him, he was a man in his middle years, of slightly above medium height and of average build. She had not seen him hatless, so could not make a guess at his hair color, and he had never been close enough for her to get more than an impression of dark eyes. The sense that he was somehow known to her did not abate, but nor did she receive any enlightenment about who he was.

The visit to the Temple of the Muses resulted in an unexpected addition to their party. She and Pol were waiting outside for their carriage, strolling up and down as they talked. Jackie stopped at a sound.

"Do you hear that?" Whimpering came from the narrow alley that ran between two buildings.

Pol's brows drew together in an expression of puzzlement. "Hear what?" he asked.

Jackie let go of his arm and took a couple of paces toward the alley, one of the guards moving swiftly to reach it first.

"Miss de Haricot is correct, bey," the man said to Pol. "An animal is in pain."

"Let me see," Jackie insisted, and they all entered the alley, with the retainer in the lead, then Jackie, followed by Pol—the gap was too narrow for them to walk shoulder to shoulder.

It was Jackie who discovered the sack—a grimy flour bag, tied tight at the top by a scrap of rope, more than half sunk in a water trough. The sack jerked and flopped as whatever was inside it struggled to keep its head above water.

Pol lifted the sack from the water. The retainer used a knife from his boot to cut the rope. The creature that emerged was a mid-sized, and very wet, dog of indeterminate breed and color. It seemed to believe it owed its rescue to Pol, for it wriggled on its belly to lick his boot, whimpering all the while, and wagging its tail so vigorously that its entire bottom swayed to and fro in the dust of the ally.

They couldn't leave it there, of course. The dog went home with them, sitting on the floor of the carriage, occasionally attempting to put its paws up on Pol's leg but subsiding when he ordered it, "Down, Scruffy."

"Scruffy" was a good name for the disreputable creature, with its shaggy coat, matted with dirt. By the time they arrived back at Winshire House, both Pol's trousers and Jackie's gown were marred by streaks of muck flicked from the beast's eager tail. "I had better take him to the stables and see if someone will give him a bath," Pol said, and followed the carriage and horsemen into the mews while Jackie entered by the front door and went up to see Gran and Maman.

⁂

BY THE TIME the dog—who proved to be a she, not a he—had been washed in two separate baths, Pol was wet to the skin and Scruffy was a creamy white rather than a muddy grey. The stable master produced some dry rags, and Scruffy accepted a toweling with blissful enthusiasm. Dried, or rather, dryer, her long coat tended to curl, suggesting that poodle played a part in her makeup, though Pol guessed at some spaniel and perhaps a couple of other breeds as well.

The stable master did not have a place for a dog, but agreed to keep Scruffy until Pol could make other arrangements. Scruffy, though, was not happy. In the end, to stop her from following him, they had to shut her in the harness room, and he could hear her whining and then howling as he walked away.

An hour later, he had had a bath of his own and changed into clean clothes, and was describing the dog, as it was now, to Jackie, Gran, and Madame when the door opened and he heard a gasp.

Why was the maid attempting to juggle the tray as she crossed the threshold into the room? The answer to the mystery was shooting across the carpet on her belly, her tail wagging ninety to the dozen. She arrived at Pol's feet, flopped two paws and a nose onto his boots, and gave a deep sigh.

"This, I take it," said Madame, her voice bubbling with suppressed laughter, "is Scruffy."

"I'm sorry," said Pol to the ladies, and repeated the apology to the maid, who had managed to keep everything on the tray, "Though not all the milk remained in the jug, my lady," she apologized to Gran. But the cake was still on its plate, and the biscuits, which had not been so fortunate, did not appear to have suffered from their minor encounter with the spilt milk.

"It is fortunate that the footman had the teapot," Gran commented. "Had that spilt, someone might have been injured. Perhaps you could let the stables know that the beast has found its way up here?"

"I'll take her back down," Pol said, standing. "Come along, Scruffy."

This time, they tied her in the stables. An hour and a half later, after the family and guests had sat down to dinner, she appeared again, a sudden weight against Pol's legs under the table, and with the same contented sigh. A brief examination showed she had chewed through her lead.

Nothing they did deterred her for long. She managed to materialize in Pol's room that night, sleeping on the rug beside the bed and not being discovered until Pol put one foot on her in the morning. That time, she had escaped both rope and shut room, and even managed to get into a shut bedchamber, though no one admitted to opening the door for her.

Indeed, it appeared the dog was some kind of magician, as she escaped again after breakfast and followed the carriage in which Pol, Jackie and the ubiquitous maid were going for an early drive. They were already in Hyde Park when she caught up to the carriage, leaping aboard and greeting Pol with a happy yap before settling at his feet.

"She does not like being separated from you," Jackie pointed out, no longer surprised by the dog's unexpected appearances.

"She is happy for an hour or so," said one of their outriders. "But then she becomes restless and before long, she disappears. The stable hands have a betting pool for how long it will take for her to escape and find you, sir."

Pol didn't know what to do. "I can hardly have her with me inside someone else's house," he said.

But Gran applied to the duchess, who said, "She is a well-mannered dog, and will be no trouble." So, Pol gave up trying to keep her out of the house. Once he found she would wait happily in his room if he gave her a boot or a glove and told her to guard it, it was easier. He no longer had to lead her slinking out of the dining room or one of parlors, her tail between her legs and her head hanging so low that the long hairs of her chin trailed on the ground. And so, the little dog became a part of their formed family.

Mr. Wakefield had little to report at the end of the first week. "Continue as you are," he recommended. So, Pol and Jackie continued to go out each morning, but as Gran recovered, she and Madame decided that it was time for Jackie to have a larger wardrobe, and so all three were spending part of each afternoon sewing.

At first at a loose end, Pol discovered the training sessions held for the duke, his sons, his retainers, and any footmen who wished to join them. He joined in with enthusiasm, believing himself to be fit. After all, he was no stranger to hard work, often joining the tenant farmers and other in the fields and the stables.

These exercises were different, and deadly serious. He finished the first session bruised in places he didn't know he had but fronted up the next afternoon determined to improve. After that session, he didn't miss an afternoon.

On most evenings, they attended the Winshire family dinner, and twice, they were guests at a formal dinner with guests outside of the family. On the first occasion, Pol, seated between Jackie and her mother, found it safest to follow their example. While he had been taught formal manners, he had had no opportunity to practice them.

When he mentioned to Jackie how out of place he felt, Drew and his sister Ruth, Lady Ashford, overheard. They both chuckled and began telling stories of their own experiences. They had arrived in England eight years ago, the half-Persian children of the exiled third son of the former duke, who had unexpectedly inherited the ducal coronet.

Ruth spoke of her horror that women ate at the same table as men, and Drew had been flabbergasted that most of the duke's guard were excluded from a formal dinner. "What the English upper classes regard as a sign of good breeding would be the height of ill manners in other parts of the world," they agreed.

"Just be yourself," Drew advised. "Most people will understand that any blame for your lack of experience with the Ton belongs to your aunt, if blame is even the right word."

Ruth was more scathing about those who thought manners matter. "People worth knowing will care about the quality of your character rather than whether or not you know how to use a citrus fork," she said. She inclined her head toward Lady Sutton, her sister-in-law. "Sophia—who is a Belvoir by birth and so whose blood is bluer than blue—told me once that some people espouse a set of rules that they call manners merely so that they can exclude others. But real manners are merely a matter of behaving in a way that makes other people comfortable. And you do that without thinking about it, Pol. Because you are a gentleman."

Later, as Pol and Jackie hid in a quiet alcove just off the stairs, she said to him, "I know what you mean about dinner, Pol. Maman and I—we practiced, but it is not the same as actually being at a dinner with two dukes, two duchesses, a marchioness, several earls and countesses, not including Maman, two viscounts—three if you are included—a baron, four knights of the realm, two people that Drew described as captains of industry… and all the wives. It was somewhat overwhelming."

An understatement, but also a reminder. If he was a viscount, dinners like this might become a common part of his future. That would be a good thing if he could just sit there and listen, as he did when the ladies withdrew, and when ideas on politics, science, engineering, business, and even morality were passed as generously as the port. He had never known a dinner like it.

The second dinner was easier. Perhaps, if he attended another sixty or so, Pol decided he might even start to enjoy them.

At least he had suitable clothing. Drew had taken him aside

one day and asked if he would be offended to be offered a coat Drew no longer wore, and before Pol knew quite how it happened, Maman's nimble fingers were altering several coats and waistcoats to his measure, and two sets of evening breeches.

As for shoes and stockings, Pol dug into the money he had taken from the goose to outfit himself and Jackie both. Gran and Maman insisted that they were already suitably shod.

One day toward the end of their second week at Winshire House, a footman arrived just as he joined the afternoon practice session to tell him that Mr. Wakefield had called to see him.

When Pol joined the enquiry agent in the Chinese parlor, he soon discovered that this meeting would be different. Wakefield had found Crawford, Gran's disreputable maid, and the doctor's complicit servant. "The stand-in magistrate has them both in custody," he told Pol, "And both have given evidence that is enough to arrest the doctor for attempted murder. He has taken to his heels, but we found arsenic when we searched his house. I've people looking for him. If we can catch him, and if he will implicate Lady Riese, we'll have reason to arrest her, too. I'd like to get her for her husband's murder, but I'd have trouble proving it at this late stage. Apparently, however, his final illness was very similar to the illness your grandmother had."

That was a shock. "What of my grandfather," Pol asked. "I am told he died while I was still in Italy, but I am not certain when, only that it was before my uncle. My grandmother would know more about exactly how much before."

"A good question." Wakefield made a note.

"On the matter of the theft, I was unable to find the names of the witnesses to your supposed thefts, but the items described by Lady Riese in her accusations against the de Haricot ladies are those detailed in the bill that Madame de Haricot showed me. Squire Pershing has dismissed the charges."

Excellent news. "The ladies will be pleased," Pol commented.

"The question of your legitimacy and your right to the title was the easiest of the three to solve," Wakefield said next. "They told me at the Hall about a man who used to come to visit you. A friend of your father's who delivered you to England. Do you remember him?"

"Uncle Toby," Pol said. "I remember his visits. Lady Riese insisted I must call her 'Aunt Louella' in his presence and tell him what I was learning and how happy I was."

Wakefield nodded. "Tobias Carver, Viscount Fuller. He is here in London and remembers you. He has someone staying with him at the moment who would like to meet you again, too. One Signor Giuseppe Allegro."

Pol started as his heart leapt. He recognized the name, and besides, Wakefield had said "again." It was someone who had once known him. Pol had thought he'd been abandoned by a family who no longer cared about him. Yet…how was this possible? "My uncle? My uncle is here in England?"

"Yes. Your mother's brother, with whom you lived until Fuller brought you to England. Both men were present at your parents' wedding, both men met you within a few hours of your birth, and Fuller can swear that the boy he brought to England and the boy he watched growing up at Riese Hall are the same person. Between the two of them we have all the proof we need that you are Viscount Riese."

Pol sat back, feeling as if all the breath had been knocked out of him. As simple as that? Two weeks of investigation, and Wakefield had the answers. "I don't know what to say. How can I ever thank you?"

"It isn't over," Wakefield warned. "You'll need to apply to the House of Lords, and you'll need a good lawyer to make sure that every 'I' is dotted and every 'T' crossed. But it has fallen into place far more easily than I expected. The Rieses are not clever criminals."

He handed over two cards. "Here is the direction of Lord Fuller, and this card has the name and address of a solicitor who handled a similar case of a stolen title last year."

After Wakefield left, Pol stood in the hall with the two cards, turning over all that he had believed and fitting it into what he knew now. He would send a message to Fortescue, the solicitor, asking for an appointment, and to Lord Fuller asking to call on him and Giuseppe Allegro tomorrow. And then he would find Jackie and tell her what Wakefield had discovered.

✦

Chapter Twenty-Three

G RAN WAS OVERJOYED as was Maman. Jackie could tell Pol had conflicting feelings. She drew him into the corner for a private conversation while the two older ladies were excitedly making plans for a wedding at Riese Hall. "It is good news, is it not?" she asked. "And we do not have to fall in with their plans, if you want a quiet wedding, or one in town…" She tried to meet his eyes, but he was gazing out of the window. "We have announced nothing, if this changes matters for you."

That drew his attention. He faced her and cupped her cheek with a gentle hand. "It does not change how I feel about you in the least, my love. I am having trouble seeing myself as a viscount, but at least I will have you at my side. I will, will I not? You won't condemn me to take up this role without you?"

"I love you, Pol," Jackie told him. "Steward, secretary, viscount? It doesn't matter to me, as long as I am with you. You will be a superb viscount, I am certain. You already know the Riese Hall estate, and you will quickly learn about all the other properties you own."

Pol grimaced. "The dinners this week have brought it home to me that I know nothing about the social and political side of the role, though."

Nor did Jackie, but such things could surely be learned. "We will learn together," she said, with more confidence than she felt.

Perhaps he saw the uncertainty she was trying to hide. "If I am a gentleman, beloved, then you are certainly a lady in every sense that matters. We will learn together." He grinned. "At least I do not have to go hunting around the employment agencies for a job."

Maman and Gran had fallen silent, and when Jackie turned to look, they were watching. "A wedding at Riese Hall, then?" Maman asked. "It is your wedding, *mes enfants*. What would you prefer?"

"A wedding by license within the week, so no one can take Jackie away from me," Pol replied. He grimaced, even as Jackie was about to agree. "But… there is much to be said for a wedding as a good way to start our life at Riese Hall as its viscount and viscountess. It will mark a sea change—a new start, not just for us but for our neighbors and our tenants."

Pol was better at this politics business than he thought. As soon as she heard him, Jackie knew he was right. "How long will it take to confirm the viscountcy?" she asked. "For I do not want to wait longer than the time it takes for the banns to be called. If that."

"Come with me to see the solicitor and my father's friend, Lord Fuller," Pol suggested. "They may be able to tell us what happens next."

"The duke may know," said Maman. "He had to prove his right to be duke when his father died, for there was another challenger."

But Gran did not agree. "His place was not questioned, Eloise. His enemies wanted to deny the legitimacy of his children, but he was able to provide all the evidence needed to show that he and his first wife had been married by an ordained minister of the Church of England."

"Mr. Fortescue will be able to advise us," Pol said.

"Fortescue," corrected Maman. "You are a viscount, Pol. You do not need to call him mister. He is not your equal."

"I will continue to treat others with respect," Pol said firmly. And that attitude and determination was one of the many reasons why Jackie loved him.

⇥≫×≪⇤

A FOOTMAN FOUND Pol in the sitting room Gran shared with Madame de Haricot du Charmont. "Lord Riese, you have visitors." He held out a salver, with two cards.

Pol held them so Jackie could read. Giuseppi Allegro, Patrizio, said one. Tobias Carver, Viscount Fuller, the other. "My uncle and his friend," Pol said, unnecessarily. They must have come over as soon as they received Pol's note.

"Do you wish me to come with you?" Jackie asked.

He nodded. "Please." He had the sense he was stepping off a cliff into the unknown, but Jackie would anchor him.

The two gentlemen who stood when Pol and Jackie entered the Chinese parlor were both familiar, though Uncle Giuseppi had changed more than Uncle Toby. But then Pol had not seen Uncle Giuseppi since he left Italy sixteen years ago, and Uncle Toby had continued to visit until he was eighteen.

Both were tall, elegantly dressed, and had dark eyes and dark curly hair that was going grey over the ears. Until seeing him again, Pol had forgotten Uncle Toby, like Pol, had had an Italian mother.

In the next moment, Uncle Giuseppe strode forward and flung his arms around Pol. "Apollo, *mio nipote*."

Pol found himself hugging the man back, disoriented by the sense that time had rolled backward, and he was safe again in the arms of his mother's brother. "*Zio Giuseppe*." His uncle still used the same shaving water—cedar and an array of spices, but though the smell was right, the dimensions were wrong. His uncle had broadened with the passing of time, and Pol was ten inches taller and at least sixty pounds heavier than the nine-year-old who had left Tuscany.

Uncle Giuseppe rattled off a sentence in Italian. Pol blinked. He'd caught a word or two of the language he'd been raised in. "I have not spoken Italian in many years, *Zio*," he apologized. "That was too fast for me."

"You did not write, Apollo," his uncle complained. "Your aunt and your cousins—we have all missed you."

"I missed you," Pol replied. What an understatement! He had yearned for his family and his home and had written long letters that Lady Riese grudgingly agreed to post. "I wrote," he said. "No one ever replied. In the end, I gave up." How could he have believed he had been sent away and forgotten? But how could he have thought anything else?

Uncle Giuseppe jumped to the same conclusion as Pol. "This aunt, your uncle's wife. The one who stole your title. She took your letters, and those we wrote to you."

"That would be my guess," Pol said.

"I suppose," said Uncle Toby, "that you did not write to me when you were eighteen to tell me I no longer needed to visit you."

"That is why you stopped visiting?" Pol asked.

"No," answered Uncle Toby. "It was the follow-up letter that stopped my visits. It said you had fallen in a hunt and broken your neck."

Pol turned to exchange glances with Jackie, who was still standing just inside the door. "It should not surprise me," he told her.

"Nothing that evil woman is accused of would surprise me," Jackie replied, "but to keep his family's letters from a grieving boy! How cruel!"

The two gentlemen were regarding Jackie with interest and appreciation. Pol realized he had been rude. "I apologize for my lapse in manners, my love," he said. "Please allow me to make known to you my uncles, Patrizio Giuseppe Allegro, my mother's brother, and Lord Fuller, my father's dearest friend. Gentlemen, this beautiful lady is my betrothed, Mademoiselle Jacqueline de Haricot du Charmont."

"I shall ring for tea," Jackie announced, when the greetings and compliments were over. "Or would you gentlemen prefer coffee? Or a glass of wine?"

"The coffee is exceptional," Pol offered.

With a servant dispatched to see to refreshments, Jackie invited them all to sit, for all the world as if she played hostess to a viscount and an Italian noble every day of the week. Pol could not have been prouder.

Tea and coffee were served while Pol was explaining about his life at Riese Hall, as an unwanted and illegitimate cousin. Uncle Giuseppe kept swearing in Italian and then apologizing to Jackie. Uncle Toby repeated, over and over, "I had no idea."

"Why did you not say something when I visited?" he asked at one point.

"I did not know you would care," Pol pointed out. "Lady Riese—Mrs. Riese, I suppose I should call her—assured me you were only carrying out an obligation and were only too happy to wash your hands of me. Complaining would do me no good, and she would punish me, besides."

More swearing from Uncle Giuseppe. Italian was feeling more familiar to Pol by the minute.

And so was the long-buried history of his childhood, as Uncle Giuseppe's presence aroused flashes of memory. Meals with the whole family, Uncle Giuseppe at the head of the table, Aunt Margurita at the foot. Outings in a cavalcade of carriages. Sitting up beside Uncle Giuseppe and learning to drive—with his cousin Marco. How could he have forgotten Marco? They had been the best of friends, only a year apart in age and inseparable.

Once his story was up to the present, he said, "Now tell me about my cousins, and Zia Margurita and the other aunts."

"It can hardly be of interest to Signorita de Haricot," Uncle Giuseppe demurred.

"Call me Jackie, please," his beloved replied, "and yes, please tell us how the years have treated your family. They shall be my family, too, one day soon."

How was it she always knew the right thing to say? Pol smiled at her and squeezed her hand.

The cousins were mostly grown and many of them were married with children of their own. In Pol's memory they were still children, and it was odd to think of, for example, Francesca, who was perennially seven in his mind's eye, having three babies of her own.

Pol had never felt the lack of brothers and sisters until he left Italy, for he had grown up as just another boy in a pack of boys and girls. Uncle Giuseppe was the patriarch of a family of brothers and sisters, all of who were married with children and all of who lived on the Allegro estate or in the nearby town of Volterra. To hear their names and little anecdotes about them was to be immersed again in the love of a large family. His head was spinning.

Another surprise was that Uncle Toby had married Pol's youngest aunt, his mother's sister Maria. All this time he believed himself to be alone in the world except for the aunt and cousin who despised him, the Fullers had been living here in England and grieving him as dead.

Marco was also here in England, traveling with his father. "He is eager to meet you again," Uncle Giuseppe said as the two men were leaving.

"Will you and Jackie come to dinner tonight?" Uncle Toby asked. "Come early, and you can meet your youngest cousins in the nursery."

Pol and Jackie escorted the pair to the door, where Pol was engulfed in another Italian hug, and Jackie, too. "I thank the good God for bringing you back to us, *mio nipote*," Uncle Giuseppe said.

By the time Pol and Jackie had seen their guests out, Gran had shared the news of Wakefield's findings with the Duchess of Winshire. Since she had, from the first, insisted on the Winshire household addressing Pol as "Lord Riese", she took in her stride the confirmation that he was the true viscount.

"Perhaps it is time for Society to meet the true Lord Riese," she suggested.

Jackie pointed out that Wakefield had warned them to keep a low profile. The duchess felt the time for secrecy was past. Pol was in two minds. On the one hand, something in him was jumping with glee at the idea of confronting the two people who had done their best to make his youth miserable. On the other, he was reluctant to test his social skills in public.

"Talk to your solicitor, Apollo," said the duchess. "See what he thinks."

THE CAT WAS already out of the bag, as Jackie and Pol discovered at the Fullers's that evening. Marco had had an encounter with Oscar the previous night, after Wakefield's visit to Uncle Giuseppe the previous day.

"I'm sorry, 'Pollo," he said. "He was just so annoying. A blaggard and a cheat. When I pointed out the card up his sleeve, he told the others at the table that he was an Englishman and a viscount, and that I was an Italian liar."

"So, my son informed him that he was not a viscount at all, but just a thief who had stolen his cousin's title," Uncle Giuseppe explained, with a sigh.

"It is true," Marco sighed. "He made me so cross, *cugino*. I told the other men there that I was Marco Allegro, and that my cousin Apollo Riese had been robbed of his place by this piece of rubbish, but he was taking it back!"

Done was done. Pol told Marco that it had to happen soon, in any case. "I wonder what Oscar and his mother will do in response," he said to Jackie.

The answer came the next day. He and Jackie arrived back at Winshire House after visiting the solicitor to discover they had missed an obnoxious visitor.

"Your neighbor, Baron Barton, arrived with your cousin and two constables," Drew told them. "They demanded to see you, and when informed you were not in, refused to believe it. They demanded that our servants hand you over, as you were both felons. Among other things, you are accused of kidnapping Clara Lady Riese."

"What rubbish!" Jackie said.

"Indeed. That is very close to what Lady Riese told them. She informed the constables that she had been rescued, not kid-napped, for her daughter-in-law had been poisoning her, and charges would soon be laid to that effect. She told your cousin that he was a disgrace to the name Riese, that his accusations against you, Pol, were false, and that you would soon be taking your proper place as viscount. Aunt Eleanor then informed Barton that his warrant was not valid in London and would be suspect anywhere else in England, since the entire country would be informed of his illicit relationship with the widow Riese if he attempted to execute the warrant."

Jackie chuckled. "The widow Riese," she repeated. "I doubt she will enjoy that."

The duchess dismissed Barton and Oscar with a few choice words. "Stupid men. They have no power in my London and are too ignorant to know it. Apollo, you and your betrothed shall attend the Campion ball this evening. It is time for Society to meet the true Lord Riese."

"Tonight?" Pol asked, quailing at the thought of all those eyes. And judgmental minds. "We do not have invitations."

"But you do," Her Grace insisted. "I have been in touch with Sally, Lady Campion, and she has sent invitations for all four of you, Clara and Eloise, too. Your aunt Louella and cousin Oscar will also be guests tonight. You will attend as members of my party—mine and the duke's, if he is home from Lords in time."

Pol's first instinct was to refuse, to hide. *That is what you have been doing for sixteen years,* he scolded himself. *No more hiding.*

Wakefield had said that, if the Rieses tried to have them arrested, they should allow the duchess to introduce them to the Ton.

"We will have to see them sooner or later," he said to Jackie.

Her smile did not touch her eyes, but she said, "Tonight, then." She curtseyed to the duchess. "Thank you, Your Grace."

Chapter Twenty-Four

JACKIE'S GOWN WAS new, finished only that morning. It was a design of her own, made from a light lavender-colored silk figured with cream vertical stripes. Puffed sleeves at the shoulder finished in long sheer sleeves in the same lavender, trimmed with matching satin ribbon which also finished the square neckline. The hem was adorned with five rows of festoon flounces made of net and trimmed with the ribbon.

Maman had covered a pair of dancing slippers to match. The duchess's own dresser had been sent down to do Jackie's hair, through which she threaded lavender and cream ribbon. When Jackie saw the finished effect in the large standing mirror, she was amazed.

Is that really me? The boys in the stables at Squire Pershing's would never believe it. The point was, though, what would Pol think? Jackie couldn't wait to find out.

Maman and Gran were also looking very fine, both in gowns of the latest fashion, one in figured satin of a deep wine, the hem trimmed with clusters of roses, and one in deep blue with two flounces of net, each woman with dyed ostrich feathers in her hair.

They came down the stairs together, to where Pol waited to escort them to the carriage that had been assigned to them for the night. He was talking to Lord Thomas, the duke's youngest son, but Lord Thomas saw them coming and must have said something, for Pol turned and looked up.

His jaw dropped, and then he beamed up at her, stepping closer to the foot of the stairs and holding up his hand to assist her down the last few steps. "Beloved, you look magnificent," he said, and the heat in his eyes sent other messages, more private messages. Messages that made Jackie ache in places she was only just beginning to discover.

"Gran and Maman also look lovely," she told him, hoping to avoid the blush she could feel building, and he blinked as if he had forgotten they were not alone.

He rose to the occasion, however. "Gran, you shall outshine all the other dowagers, and Madame, what can I say? You and Jackie could be sisters."

"Rogue," Maman said, with a pleased smile and a light tap of her fan to his shoulder.

"His grandfather had a silver tongue," Gran commented, with a sigh.

"Ah." The Duchess of Winshire paused on the landing above them. "You are all here." She descended on her husband's arm. "You all look splendid," she said, approvingly. "Jacqueline, my dear, that gown is very becoming."

The ducal couple led the way out to the carriages, as various others of the Winderfield family joined the crowd in the lobby. The plan was that Pol and his ladies would enter with the duke and duchess, but their children would also be present at the event to lend their support if needed.

It was a short carriage ride, but something of a wait at the venue. But at last, their carriage reached the carpet that had been spread down the steps of the house and across the footpath to the road.

Pol helped Jackie to descend, and then Gran and Maman. Drew and Thomas materialized to each offer an elbow, one to Gran and one to Maman. The duke and duchess were waiting just inside the foyer, and together they joined the queue for the reception line.

Jackie knew that people were talking about the four of them, from the covert glances and outright stares, and the way people kept an eye on them while speaking behind a gloved hand or their fans. "Ignore them," Maman said, not bothering to whisper. "Their ill-breeding does not excuse yours."

"People are naturally interested in strangers," Pol pointed out. "Especially those sponsored by such an illustrious couple."

The duchess cast him an amused smile. "Just so," she agreed, "but Eloise's advice is also pertinent."

The line moved quickly, and they were soon in front of Lord and Lady Campion and their debutante daughter. The duchess introduced them. "Clara, my dear, do you remember Lady Campion? She was Sally Albright when you were last in Society. And this is her husband, and their daughter Frederika. Clara, Lady Riese, my dears. Also, the *Comtesse de Haricot du Charmont*, her daughter, and Lord Riese, who is betrothed to Mademoiselle de Haricot du Charmont, and is the grandson of Clara Lady Riese."

Jackie curtseyed as her mother had taught her, and the hostess's eyes lit with approval. "Charming," she pronounced.

Lord Campion, though, reacted to Pol's name. "Any relation to Viscount Riese and his mother, Lady Riese?" he asked.

"An interesting story," the duke replied. "My young friend here is the true Viscount Riese. He inherited the title on the death of his father, older brother to the young man claiming to be Viscount Riese. I had an enlightening discussion today with Sir Isaac Heard, the Garter Principal King of Arms. Apparently, his office was notified some twenty years ago that young Lord Riese had died in Italy. I assured him that news of the boy's death had been much exaggerated."

Jackie hadn't heard that, and from his hastily concealed look of surprise, neither had Pol. Other ball-goers close enough to hear the conversation—and the duke had pitched his voice to carry— were leaning forward in their eagerness not to miss a word.

"But we must not hold up the reception line," the duchess commented. "No doubt the full facts of the matter will be established in the coming week. Come along, my dears."

And she took her husband's arm again and led them into the ballroom, where a servant announced their names and titles.

Apollo Lord Riese. When it was said in the servant's ringing voice, Pol flinched—a small involuntary movement that Jackie only detected because she had her hand on his arm. The words set off a muttering around the ballroom, which the duke and duchess ignored, leading the party across the room to a group of chairs. Each of the Winderfield gentlemen conducted the lady on their arm to a chair.

"They reported me dead?" Pol asked the duke, who nodded.

"Apparently so. You were the heir apparent from the moment your father died, and the viscount as soon as your grandfather died, when you were six. Your uncle took your title, Pol, and passed it on to his son, because you were understood to be dead. Since you are alive, the title is still yours, though under the circumstances, that will have to be confirmed by the Committee for Privileges. The Garter is preparing a report for the Committee, and I have made a request for an appointment with the chair. Given the evidence from your uncles and your grandmother, however, I see no difficulties in proving your case."

Pol had placed his hand over Jackie's, and during the duke's explanation, his fingers had stiffened around hers, but all he said was, "Thank you, Your Grace." His words and tone were courteous, but Jackie knew him well enough to know he was shaken.

The orchestra was tuning up in preparation for the first dance. "Apollo and Jacqueline," the duchess said, "since you are betrothed, you may dance together three times in the course of the evening. I suggest the first set, the supper set, and the final set of the evening. For other dances, I shall introduce suitable partners—to you both."

"May I have the pleasure of this dance, my love?" Pol asked

Jackie, obedient to the duchess's command. He still looked slightly stunned, as if the duke's words had been a bludgeon to the head.

Jackie nodded and allowed him to lead her onto the floor.

They had only a few minutes to speak during the set, since the orchestra had started the evening with a vigorous quadrille. Jackie said, "It is good news, is it not? What the duke said?"

"Everything is changing so fast," he answered, the poleaxed expression fading a little as he spoke. "Less than a month ago, I was hoping my position as secretary would work out, so I could support my three ladies. And today, I am being announced at a Society ball." He chuckled, but there was little humor in it. "I feel as if a fairy godmother has granted me a wish to change my life, and I cannot quite work out whether the new life is the one I wanted."

"Whatever happens," Jackie said, "we shall face it together."

They were needed back in the patterns of the dance again, and Pol had only time for a brief reply. "That, beloved, is what is keeping me sane."

Jackie understood his sense of unreality. Maman had talked for many years of Society balls and of the pair of them being restored to what Maman called "Our proper place." But Jackie had never expected it to happen.

She danced with Drew next, then with Thomas, and after that, other men presented to her by the duchess. It was while she was dancing with Lord Sutton, the oldest of the Winderfield brothers, that she saw Oscar, stalking along the edge of the dance floor with his mother on his arm. Both were scanning the dancers, and both looked furious.

For a moment, Jackie lost the pattern of the dance, but Lord Sutton compensated and helped her to finish the figure, which took them to the edge of the dance floor, near to where the Duke and Duchess of Winshire stood watching the dancers.

"Is something wrong?" Lord Sutton asked her. His eyes widened as he saw Oscar stomping toward the ducal couple, ignoring the dancers, his face flushed with rage.

"Duke!" he bellowed. "I don't know who that female claims to be, but she is an imposter." The way he slurred the word 'imposter' hinted that some of his high color came from drink.

"Get yourself together, man," the duke said, sharply. "You are embarrassing yourself."

"Not me," Oscar insisted. "Her. She is a seamstress, a thief, and my whore."

Jackie could not tell whether the hiss from those around condemned her or Oscar, but before she could tell Oscar to go and put his head in a bucket three times and pull it out twice, the duke thundered. "You, sir, are no gentleman."

Oscar blinked in confusion. "No, Your Grace. Tha's wrong. I'm Viscount Riese. Very old famb… fambly… fa-mi-ly."

"On the contrary, you dolt," the duke declared, his voice so cold that Jackie could have sworn the temperature in the room dropped. Certainly, several of those nearest shivered at the tone. The dancers had stopped dancing, the orchestra was no longer playing, and those around had given up all pretense of ignoring the commotion in their midst and were watching, avidly, with perhaps more decorum but certainly no less fascination than villagers at a wrestling match.

"Assure you—" Oscar began, sticking his nose in the air and grasping each of his lapels in a fist.

The duke spoke over the top of him. "Your imposture has been discovered, Mr. Riese. Also, some of your other crimes. It is you who are the thief. Not this lady, who is a guest in my house and the daughter of my wife's dear friend, the *Comtesse de Haricot du Charmont*. And not the real Viscount Riese, this lady's husband-to-be, son of your father's older brother. Ah! Lord Riese. There you are."

Sure enough, Pol was coming through the cluster of dancers, Her Grace the Duchess of Haverford on his arm. And right behind them came the Duke of Haverford, escorting his mother, the Duchess of Winshire.

Oscar looked from one to another as it slowly dawned on him that his attempted ambush of Jackie had turned into a complete rout.

He blinked at Pol, shook his head to clear it, and said to the duke. "I am the viscount, not Polly. Polly is my secretary. I didn't want him, but Mama said we had to be kind to the family bastard."

His face cleared as he noticed his mother making her own way through the onlookers. "Mama, tell the duke. I am the viscount, right?"

She scowled.

"It's over, Aunt Louella," Pol told her. "I met today with Lord Fuller and *Patrizone* Allegro. They were both at my parents' wedding and met me shortly after my birth more than a year later. I am the only son of Richmond Riese and his lawfully wedded wife. And Richmond Riese was the son and heir of Frederick, Viscount Riese."

The woman opened her mouth, her lip curled. Jackie was ready to hear a denial and probably threats and scurrilous lies. But at that moment, Maman and Gran joined the group, and Gran said, "Louella Riese, you have been a very naughty girl."

The villainess went white, and her mouth dropped open. Then she drew herself up and spoke to her son. "Oscar. Fetch your sister. We are leaving."

Without another word, she strode off through the crowd, apparently creating a path merely by the force of her glare.

Oscar looked from one to another of those gathered and then scurried after her.

WITH OSCAR'S DEPARTURE, the spectacle was over, but conversations within Pol's earshot—and presumably beyond it—reached fever pitch as those with a good view rehashed the entire scene for those who had missed it, and even for those who had seen just as well as them.

In the little group on the edge of the floor, the Duke of Winshire sent his wife a questioning look. "Are you satisfied, Eleanor?"

"Quite," said the duchess. "By the time those who weren't here break their fast tomorrow, the entire Polite World will know that Mrs. Riese and her son are fakes, and our Lord Riese is the real one."

Well. That was one way to look at it. Had the duchess intended this all along?

The orchestra's conductor banged his baton on his music stand, and a hush drifted out from the stage on which he stood, the hostess, Lady Campion, beside him. Her eyes were glowing with delight that such a delicious scandal had erupted right on her dance floor.

"My dear friends, no doubt we all look forward to hearing more about the new Lord Riese, and where he has been all these years. Right now, we have a ball to enjoy. Gentlemen, please find your partners for the supper waltz."

Pol had learnt the waltz along with other dances thanks to Amanda, whose inability to hear music made dancing problematic. Lady—no, Louella Riese had decreed that he was to learn with her, so she had a partner to practice with every day.

The waltz as it was now danced in high Society was a relatively new import from the Continent. It was highly fashionable, but still frowned on in some circles, since it required the dancers to remain with a single partner, to focus intently on that partner, and—most alarming of all—to touch.

The criticism had seemed over the top. Even dancing at the occasional village assembly did not change Pol's mind, though some of the village girls were fun to dance with. It was very different moving to music with Jackie in his arms, her hands touching him, her body brushing his as they executed a turn.

Apparently waltzing with one's love was on a completely

separate plane to attempting to circle a room with one's sixteen-year-old cousin while couching her in a whisper, *left foot back, slide right foot back and to the side, bring left foot to right foot. Right foot back…* And so on, for an entire dance.

And why was he thinking of Amanda when he could give himself over to the music and his beloved? Every step a promise made, every touch the closest to an embrace they could come in a ballroom full of people. Not that he thought about the people, except to keep his partner safe from collisions as the two of them moved like one being, with four legs but a single will driven by the music and their love.

They didn't speak, but they didn't need to. Her heart was in her eyes and his answered it, in a conversation that needed no words, in a dialogue comprising music, movement, and love.

When the music ended and those around them began to move through to supper, Pol and Jackie moved with them, slowly emerging from the dream, until one of the other guests woke them thoroughly by asking when the wedding would be.

So it went through the supper—people walking up to their table, asking Lady Sutton to introduce them, and then asking about Pol and Jackie's romance, the crimes of Pol's aunt and cousin, Pol's origins, Jackie's origins, their plans for the viscount-cy, and more.

Some questions were so intrusive that Lady Sutton rebuked the questioner, but for the most part, she left Pol and Jackie to answer. "Your story will be all over London with the breakfast trays," she told them during a lull in the traffic. "This is your opportunity to make sure that the truth you want to have heard circulates along with the inevitable nonsense."

When they rejoined the rest of the family after supper, they discovered that Gran and Madame de Haricot du Charmont had also been besieged at the table where they sat with the Winshires, until her grace put a stop to the questions by declaring that Clara Lady Riese was tiring and would take no more questions.

Given that Gran had been close to death less than a month

ago, it was surprising she had managed the ball at all, let alone staying up so late. It was well after midnight. Pol opened his mouth to suggest that he and Jackie could escort Gran home, but the duchess forestalled him. "Indeed, I think we might go home after supper, my dears. What is your opinion, Duke?"

"As always, dear Duchess, you have marshalled your troops and overrun the enemy position. By all means, let us go home."

Jackie looked relieved. She was probably imagining, as Pol was, several more dances, this time with inquisitive strangers seeking to gain an advantage in the gossip stakes. And so, they gave their hostess their thanks and farewell and left the ball. "We shall take one carriage," the duchess decreed, and leave the others for the rest of our party." For Lord and Lady Sutton, the duke's younger sons and others of the household were remaining to enjoy the rest of the evening.

While they were outside waiting for the others to enter the carriage, Jackie asked, "What will your aunt and cousin do now, do you think?"

She kept her voice low and private, and Pol answered the same way. "Run, if they have any sense. Louella must realize she has lost and will face the hangman if she remains in England. I wonder if they will take Amanda with them?" Poor Amanda. She was not a particularly nice person, but Pol pitied her, nonetheless. She had not been responsible for anything that had happened to Pol or Gran or Jackie, but she would suffer for it, nonetheless.

"I had forgotten about Miss Amanda. They won't leave her, surely?"

"I don't know, my love. I would not put it past Louella, and I doubt Oscar would think twice about leaving her if he thinks she will slow him down."

Jackie proved once again how wonderful she was. "She will need us, if that happens. Poor Amanda. We will be her only remaining family, you, me, and Gran."

Back at Winshire House, they parted for their own rooms, but Pol felt too restless to sleep, even though it was close to two in the morning. Every time he managed to wrench his mind away from the scene with Oscar, he found himself going over the events and revelations of the past few days, and all the time his mind replayed the sensations of dancing with Jackie, of kissing Jackie, of touching her—not just in the way he had but in the way he longed to do.

Scruffy whined, and Pol grinned. Even when his emotions were in turmoil and his life had just changed forever, some things remained the same. "Yes, girl," he said. "I will take you out."

Chapter Twenty-Five

A T FIRST, NO one had any idea that Pol was missing. Jackie assumed he must have either gone for an early ride with most of the other men, or slept in. Even when Drew and the others joined them for breakfast, she wasn't worried. Until Drew couldn't answer when she asked if Pol was coming.

Then it got scary. Drew said he had not come riding that morning, nor to combat practice. They soon discovered that no one had seen Pol that day and he was not anywhere in the house. Neither was Scruffy.

Questions to the servants and the retainers established only that he had gone out into the garden with the dog in the early hours of the morning. Jackie joined Drew and several of the retainers as they hurried outside. The gardens, though extensive for a London townhouse, were soon searched. No sign of Pol.

"Over here!" The voice was by the gate into the lane that led along the side of the garden to the mews at the back. One of the retainers had opened the gate, and—wasn't that Scruffy? Poor dog. She looked nearly as bad as she had when Pol and Jackie rescued her—bedraggled and covered in muck. On seeing Jackie, she bolted into the garden, evading the retainer who tried to catch her.

She was limping as she ran, one hind leg dragging. She still made a valiant effort to jump up on Jackie but subsided at Jackie's skirts with a whimper. "Who hurt you, girl?" Jackie asked. "Where is Pol?"

The dog whined, then half-walked, half-hopped a few paces away, turned back to look at Jackie, and whined again. "You want us to follow you?" Jackie guessed, and sure enough, when she took a few steps toward the dog, it set off back to the gate and waited for her.

The retainers exchanged a few words in a language Jackie didn't know, and then a couple of them joined her, following the dog out into the mews and east along the little lane, garden walls on one side and stables on the other.

Before they reached the street that cut across the mouth of the mews, Drew joined them at a jog with his friend Jamir, whose mother Patience was governess to the household's children and whose father was some sort of aide-de-camp to the duke. Drew handed Jackie a bonnet and a shawl, and commented to the others, "The dog seems to know where it is going."

The dog was limping along the street, heading north now, but it stopped and waited until their little group started walking again. "It could be showing us where the cat went that it chased," one of the retainers said, dryly.

"You have a better idea, Jamir?" Drew asked.

Jamir was looking around. "A crossing boy," he said, obscurely, and broke into another jog to talk to the boy. The rest of them continued following the dog. Jamir caught up with them after a minute or two.

"The boy sleeps in that area, on damp nights like last night," he explained. "I thought the heat might have kept him awake, and we were in luck. He saw the dog following a carriage," he reported. "Green, with red wheels, and a near-matched team of bays, one with a white sock on the rear offside. He was fairly certain of the colors, even in the lamp light. Also, a crest that included, and I quote, 'one of them crown things above, a lion on one side, a weird beast on the other, and a shield with three patterns. Half with blue stripes on an angle, then the other half with three lions on the top and flowers on the bottom'. The boy was most distressed about the flowers. He felt they were unmanly."

Jackie had a sinking feeling. "I don't know the carriage or team, but the crest is that of Oscar Riese," she said.

"What an amateur," commented Jamir in a disgusted tone. "Who kidnaps someone using their own carriage? With a crest, for goodness' sake!"

The dog led them farther along the street, around a corner, and then past several more streets. Eventually, she turned a corner and stopped a few yards farther along, sat in the street, put her nose to the sky, and howled. A passing hack skirted the beast, the driver sending her a string of oaths and a flick with his whip, which fortunately missed.

"Is this where you lost him, girl?" Jackie asked, as they came up to the dog. Another driver, swinging wide to avoid them, shouted, "Gerrof the road."

"Come on, Scruff," Jackie said to the dog, but one of the men had to pick her up before they could move her from the spot where she had lost her deity.

"Any idea where they might have gone?" Drew asked.

"Possibly to the Riese townhouse?" Jackie suggested. "I do not know where that is, but Clara Lady Riese will." The dog whimpered, and Jackie rubbed behind its ears. "Yes, dog, you have done well. Good girl. Good girl."

"Yours, is she?" The speaker was a man lounging against the side of a building—a workman of some kind, from the look of him.

"She belongs to my betrothed," Jackie told him. "He went out with the dog, and only the dog came back. We think he may have been abducted."

"Did you see the dog here, very very early?" Drew asked. "Perhaps at about three in the morning? It would have been following a carriage."

The man's eyes shifted from side to side and then narrowed at Drew. His lips thinned. Jackie feared he was about to refuse to help.

"Anything you can tell us," she coaxed. "I fear for his life, for the owner of the carriage is heir to my beloved's estates."

The man examined her as if looking for evidence she spoke the truth and then sighed. "I don't hold with kidnapping, nor with murder. The carriage was green, with red wheels and a crest on the door," the man said. "Team of bays. Came along with the dog barking behind. Carriage got stopped behind a dray. Dog attacked the door. He was whining and scratching to get in. Footman jumped down and kicked the poor beast. The carriage moved off and the footman left the dog and got up again. Dog must have been knocked silly for a minute, because it didn't duck the next team to come by. Yelped like nobody's business. Then it limped off back the way it came."

Drew thanked him and passed him a coin. "Thankee, sir," the man said, and then, to Jackie, "Hope you get him back, miss."

So did Jackie. The man faded back into the shadows of a nearby alley.

"What was he doing here at three in the morning?" Jackie wondered aloud.

"Something criminal, or at least nefarious," Drew suggested. "Surveillance of some kind would make sense. We should have had men like him watching Oscar's house."

He then spoke to Jamir. "Hail a hackney, please, Jamir. Ask him if he knows where Viscount Riese lives." He said to the man holding the dog. "Take the hackney back to Winshire House and let my father know what has happened. Arrange for Achmed to check the dog for injuries, then bring some horses and join us at the address the hackney driver gives us."

"Yes, bey," the man said. "But if the hackney driver does not know the address?"

"Then we keep asking till we find the place, Akbar, and you can ask Clara Lady Riese for the address and come and find us."

"Yes, bey," the man repeated.

Jamir had stopped a hackney. The driver looked alarmed to be approached by a party of five tall strong men, three of them in foreign robes, but resolved to be helpful when Jamir handed him a couple of coins and told him there would be more once he had answered a question and agreed to take the injured animal and the man holding it to Winshire House.

A few minutes later, Akbar was on his way, and Jackie was striding to keep up with Drew, Jamir and the other two men. They had an address, and it was only a few streets away.

"Oscar Riese would have to be remarkably stupid to have Apollo kidnapped and taken to the Riese townhouse," Drew commented.

Jackie was hurrying too fast to have much breath left to argue, but she said, "The point you fail to understand, however, is that Oscar *is* remarkably stupid."

POL WAS FURIOUS with himself. He had been stupid. He should never have followed Scruffy out of the gate. He'd no sooner stepped out into the mews than someone unseen had hit him on the head. When he came around, he was gagged, bound, and had a sack over his head. He could tell he was in a carriage, but he had no idea whose, or where he was going.

Even now, when he had reached his captor's destination, he had no answers. He'd been carried inside and upstairs, then they'd loosened the bindings on his wrists. By the time he'd freed his hands and removed the sack and the gag, he was alone. Whoever had brought him had left the room.

It had been dark, then, but the sun had risen hours ago, and since then he had explored every inch of the space. The room must once have been the nursery, by the bars on the windows. It was wider than it was deep, with a locked door on one long wall, two banks of windows on the opposite long wall, and little rooms opening into the main room on the two shorter side walls, one on one side and two on the other.

The arrangement at Riese Hall was similar—a day nursery in the center, with a night nursery on one side and bedchambers for nursemaids or older children on the other.

The side rooms were empty now, and the main room nearly so, save for the narrow bed on which he had been deposited, a cupboard containing a chamber pot, with a wash bowl, a jug of water, and a towel on top, and a table containing another jug of water and a tumbler.

The bed's mattress had no sheet, no pillow, and no blanket.

It had to be the Rieses. Or possibly the man Jackie had seen several times, but his interest seemed to be reserved for Jackie. Pol wondered whether he had been missed yet. He wondered what he could do to improve the chances that he would be rescued.

Jackie would not leave any stone unturned to find him. Would she be able to track the carriage? What about Scruffy? What happened to Scruffy? He had heard a dog barking while he was in the carriage. It had sounded like the little mutt he had rescued, but there must have been ten thousand dogs in London that sounded similar.

The search would be a lot easier if he was in Beddington House, the Riese property in London. It seemed unlikely, though. It was too obvious. Since he had never been to Beddington House, he couldn't tell.

From the windows of the main room and the largest of the three small rooms, he could see a garden. It was perhaps a third of the size of the one at Winshire House, being both narrower and shorter. Beyond the wall on one side was the garden of the neighboring house. He could see what looked like stables over the wall at the bottom, except where the view was obscured by a pigeon loft in the conical roof of a narrow tower halfway down the garden. Presumably this row of houses followed the common pattern of having a mews lane behind.

It was the same on the other side of the garden—a wall, farther away than he might have expected. The garden appeared to be wider than the house, and when he checked in the little side bedchambers, it was. The house must be the end one of the row, for it had, as far as he could see with his face up against the glass, a narrow-paved walk between the house and the side wall. Paved, that was, except for a tree which grew taller than his window and obscured the view from the other bedchamber. From the first bedchamber, he could glimpse a lane, but he could not see any people. Nor, thanks to the wall at the bottom of the garden, could he see people in the mews, or even the mews lane itself.

If you could see anybody, Pol, he lectured himself, *what could you do? Play charades until they guessed you were locked up? And if you did, I daresay they would think you were out of your head, and in need of locking up.*

On the other hand, he thought he could count on those at the duke's house to search for him. He didn't know how easy it would be to find where he had been taken, but if they could narrow it down to this house, it would help if they could see evidence he was here.

Surely there must be something he could do? Yet the room offered little scope.

He tried the windows, but they had been nailed shut, so he didn't even have the option of shouting to attract attention.

Wait a minute, though. The rooms had been stripped of most furniture, probably for some time, but either there had been a previous occupant who needed warmth to survive, or they had warmed the room in preparation for his arrival, for there were ashes in the fireplace.

After some experimentation, Pol managed to make a paste of ashes and water that was thick enough to stick on the glass. Carefully, he went into the room with the window that could be seen from the side lane and wrote on the glass panes of the window. He hoped the printing wouldn't be noticed by his kidnappers, or if it was, that it would just look like random patterns in the dirt. The need to write in reverse so it would make sense from the other side might stand him in good stead in that respect.

"I am here. A." And the picture of a sun, to reference his name. Even if it was seen, he could hope his jailers might think it was a legacy of the children who once lived here, while the hoped-for rescuers understood it as a message to them.

Now all he could do was wait and pray.

❧❧❧

Chapter Twenty-Six

"WHAT IS YOUR plan?" Jackie asked, once Beddington House was in sight.

Drew clearly favored the bold approach, for he proposed to knock on the door and ask to see Oscar Riese himself. "He will deny all knowledge of the abduction, of course, but his reaction will be interesting. Jamir, go round the back to the mews and see if you can see the carriage. Miss de Haricot, I suggest you stay out of sight. You are safe with us but let us not complicate matters."

There was a lane down one side of the house, which was the end house in a row. Jamir headed down it to check the carriage house in the mews, and Jackie went with him as far as the lane. She stopped in a place where a tall tree obscured any view from the house, and Jamir went on without her.

Drew's plan was for the best. He was right that the sight of her would put Oscar on guard. But she hated being shoved to one side. She edged past the tree to gaze up at the house. Only a fool would have a man kidnapped and brought to his own house, but Oscar was a fool. Perhaps Pol was inside even now.

A movement in one of the upper windows caught her eye, and she stepped back under the tree, but as she did, the afternoon sun on the window highlighted markings that she had missed on first glance.

Surely no one in the house could possibly recognize her, with her bonnet casting her face deeper into shadow? She leaned forward just enough to see that the words on the window. "I am here. A." And then a circle surrounded by radiating lines. A sun? Apollo!

"Careful, Miss," said the foreign retainer who had been left to guard her. "Best stay under the tree."

The man Jackie had seen was no longer at the window, but surely the message meant Pol was in that room? "Pol is up there," she told the man. "See? He has written on the window."

Jamir joined them as they gazed upward. "Pol is there," she said.

"The carriage isn't," Jamir replied, "but the grooms described the same vehicle and team that the street sweeper saw. They say the master's friends had it out, and then, when it arrived back half an hour ago, the master and his mother took it out again."

"So, it must be Pol up there," Jackie declared.

"The grooms deny seeing anyone except the master's friends," Jamir told her.

A few minutes later, Drew and the rest of the men came round the house and joined them under the tree.

"Riese isn't at home," Drew reported. "Or so the butler claims, and nor is his mother. The butler clammed up when I asked about visitors, voluntary or involuntary."

Jamir repeated what the grooms had told him, and Jackie pointed out the message on the window. "We have to go and get him," she said.

"We cannot storm the house, Miss de Haricot," Drew told her. "Quite apart from the fact that it would be illegal, we don't know how many men Oscar Riese has. Better to get a magistrate's warrant to search legally. I'll leave a couple of men on watch, and we'll consult with my father. If he lays an information with a magistrate, I'm sure we'll be able to get Pol out—if not today, then tomorrow. If he's there."

"He is there," Jackie insisted. "You can see the sun symbol."

"The grooms didn't see anyone taken into the house from the carriage," Jamir pointed out.

"That message might have been there for years," Drew commented.

Jackie didn't agree, but she could not convince them, and in the end, the horses arrived, with one of Drew's younger brothers in a high-perch phaeton. Jackie had to give up. She clearly would not get far trying to get into the house on her own. However, if Drew's plan of involving a magistrate didn't work, she was going to do something on her own. And she had an idea.

Meanwhile, she accepted a ride in the phaeton, and returned to Winshire House, surrounded by handsome horsemen. If she had not been so worried about Pol it would have been fun.

NO ONE OPENED the locked door to the room as the day dragged on. Since he had nothing to do, Pol stood by the window until he judged himself tired enough to sleep, then lay down on the mattress.

Sleep would not come. His mind wanted to indulge in an endless tumble of if-onlys and what-ifs. *If only I had not followed the dog out of the gate. What if I had asked a footman to take Scruffy out. If only I had something with which to pick the lock. What if they have forgotten I am here.*

All pointless. He corralled it into thinking about Jackie instead. She would be looking for him, and so would the duke's men. He could be certain of that. If he could do nothing to rescue himself, he could trust her to bring the reserves and get him out of here.

Unless they moved him somewhere else. By now, Lady Riese—Louella Riese—must be aware of the idiotic stunt her son's henchmen had pulled. She would realize, even if Oscar didn't, that the duke's men would leave no stone unturned.

Someone must have seen the carriage leaving the lane by

Winshire House, even at that early hour. And if that was Scruffy he had heard, then someone must have seen a dog chasing the carriage.

But what if they arrived too late? His mind shied away from one interpretation of that remark. After all, he could do nothing to stop them from killing him except point out the futility of it. Killing him wasn't going to save the Rieses now he had evidence of their theft of the title.

On the other hand, since they had not balked at one murder, another would hardly bother them. However, what if they ran and took him with them? He should leave a message for Jackie— he had no doubt she would be with the rescuers.

On the windows, again? No. On the wall inside the room where he'd written on the window. Sunlight streamed in from two sides via the windows, so there wasn't a dark corner in the room. He'd be able to see to create his message. A love letter on a wall.

He had finished and was regarding his handiwork when he heard the key in the lock. As swiftly and silently as he could, he hurried back into the main room and lowered himself to the mattress.

Just in time, for the door opened and half a dozen men—all Whitelys to judge from their resemblance to the two among them he'd already met—strutted inside, two of them pointing guns at him.

"Stay there, Allegro," one of them growled.

Pol didn't bother answering. After all, it wasn't as if he had anything to say to them.

Then Louella Riese entered, Oscar at her heels.

She glared at Pol, her eyes narrowed, but her remark when it came was addressed to Oscar. "You should have left him where he was, my son. This will be the first place they search."

"He has got to pay, Mama," Oscar whined. "He is spoiling everything."

"Oscar, I do not ask you to think, do I, dear? Thinking hurts your head, you know it does. Let me do the thinking. Do I not always say that? Haven't we done very well with me doing the thinking?"

"But I am the viscount, Mama," Oscar grumbled. "He's a bastard. You told me!"

"Actually," said Pol, "I *am* the viscount. You are an imposter whose father and mother stole my title."

"Rubbish," said Louella. "Do not listen to him, Oscar."

That was interesting. It sounded as if Oscar had been kept in the dark about the lies and the switch.

"Your father told everyone my father had no legitimate heirs and took my title," Pol told his cousin. "Then my uncle wrote to say my mother had died, and I was coming to England." Pol was guessing, but from Louella's aghast expression, every word was spot on. "Your mother killed your father before I arrived because he was prepared to steal my title while I was far away in Italy and had no idea I was a viscount but was too honorable to kill me or to lie to me about my parents' marriage. She may have killed our grandfather, too. She is certainly the one who had arsenic fed to our grandmother."

"She should have killed you, too," Oscar said, and took a pace forward. "I'll do it." Clearly no help from Oscar, then. Not that Pol had expected any.

Louella came out of the trance his recital had thrown her into and put a hand on her son's arm. "Not yet, Oscar. We may need to barter him against our escape. Once we are safe, then we can kill him."

"Our escape, Mama? What do you mean?"

Louella rolled her eyes and sighed. "We will be arrested if we do not leave England. Do you want to hang, Oscar? For I do not. You heard your despicable cousin. I killed to make you the viscount. If he knows, then others will know. We must waste no time. Go and pack everything valuable that you have."

"I didn't kill my father," Oscar argued. "I don't see why I have to go. I like London. I have an appointment tomorrow to meet some friends at Tattersalls."

His mother raised both eyes to the ceiling, as if seeking divine inspiration, though Pol figured her spiritual allies were below, not above. Way below. "Oscar, you are *not* the viscount. You have no money. You cannot afford new horses. You cannot afford to live in London. Everything you have belongs to Allegro."

"To Polly?" Oscar looked as if he might cry, until his face transformed into the ugly mask of rage that presaged a killing fury. "Not if he's dead," he growled, and took another step toward Pol.

Pol braced himself for a fight, but, at a nod from Louella, two of the Whitelys stepped forward, one on each side of him, and wrapped themselves around his arms.

"Come along, Oscar. We need to pack and leave. You can kill your cousin later."

The rage died from Oscar's eyes at the promise, and he allowed himself to be led to the door. "Where are we going?" he asked.

"To Burnwood House," said Louella. Burnwood House was an estate entailed to the Viscounts Riese. Just an hour's drive from Mayfair, it had been used by successive viscounts and their families for weekends out of London during the Parliamentary season and house parties in the summer. Pol had corresponded with its butler and its steward but had never been there.

He could still hear Louella talking as she walked down the passage. "I cleaned out the safe before I left Riese Hall, but there is jewelry and cash at Burnwood." The remaining Whitelys filed out of the house behind her, the two with guns going last and backward. Before they closed and locked the door, Pol heard a snippet more from Lady Riese. "Then, who knows. Perhaps to Amer…"

Right. Pol needed to amend his letter to Jackie before they came back to get him. He wanted them caught even if he didn't survive this.

It was as well he made another mix of the paste and wrote his message immediately, for it could not have been more than an hour later that the Whitelys came for him and took him away.

They bound his arms to his sides and once more gagged him, then threw a cloak over him, head and torso, so the bindings and gag were hidden. They took him down successive flights of stairs, with a Whitely on either side to guide and hurry him. Then came a short passage and a doorstep. The feel of the space changed, and the temperature.

Sound, too, somewhat muffled by the cloak. Distant hoof-beats, the rumble of carriage wheels, a singing bird, the rustle of leaves. He was outside, walking down an uneven path, tripping a little on the edges of cobbles or flagstones.

"Wot we stoppin' 'ere for, Pete?" asked one of the Whitelys. Another voice told him, "Shut yer gob," even as a door creaked open.

Pol tripped on another flagstone, and only the grips on his arms kept him from falling. The surface underfoot had changed. The door creaked again, and the outdoor noises faded.

Someone pulled the cloak off him. He was, as he'd thought, inside again, in a round windowless room walled with planks. The pigeon tower, he guessed. The only light came from the open door. A ladder led up into the gloom above. Four of the Whitelys were with him.

Pol tried to speak past the gag, to ask them to take it off. Two of the men giggled at the noise he made, but one of them dragged the kerchief that bound the gag off over Pol's head—Pol thought it might be Bill, but the brothers all resembled one another, with only the two youngest distinguished by their youth, being shorter and scrawnier.

Pol spat out the rag in his mouth. "Thank you," he said.

"If'n ye yell, it'll go on again," his benefactor grumbled.

"May I have the bindings off, please?" Pol asked.

Bill, if it was Bill, stared at him and said, "Not yet," while another brother jeeringly repeated Pol's words, making a poor attempt to round his vowels and sharpen his consonants like an aristocrat. The others found that hilarious, and fell about laughing, so the would-be mimic said it again, which fetched him a cuff over the side of the head from the man who'd removed the gag.

"Knock it orf, Bill."

"Awww, Pete!" Bill protested. "Wotcher do that for? Wot're we doin' here, anyways?"

So, it was Pete who had removed the gag, and clearly Pete who was in charge. He was the eldest of the brothers, from what Pol remembered, and had only recently arrived back in Tissingham after serving with the army. Perhaps he was the smartest, for he was regarding Pol with narrowed eyes. "You lot keep yer mouths shut," he ordered his brothers. "I'm gunna talk to 'is lordship 'ere, and you ain't gunna say nothin' about it to anyone. Get it?"

"Aw, Pete," whined Bill. "Wha' about Lord Riese?"

Pete's response was a growl. "'Specially not Oscar Riese. You 'eard 'is Ma. Them lot is scarperin' and oo'll be left be'ind? Oo'll be goin' to prison and maybe 'anged? I'll tell ye who. You, Bill. You and Dan, and maybe the lot of us'n."

"Lord Riese'll protect us." Bill smirked. "Magistrate is in 'is Ma's pocket. Or in her muff, more like." He snickered at his own crude joke.

Pete rolled his eyes and shook his head. "Listen up, idiots. *This* Lord Riese—" he waved a hand toward Pol—"'as a duke on 'is side, and who knows how many magistrates a bloody duke 'as in '*is* pocket?"

Interesting. It sounded as if Pete planned to change sides. Pol did his best to keep his face blank and his body still while the brothers argued. He did not doubt that Pete would prevail.

Pete had no doubt either. He poked Bill with a finger. "*Your* Lord Riese wants to kill 'is own cousin. And 'is Ma killed 'er 'usband and had a go at killing 'is Gran. He don't care about that. Think 'e's gonna care what 'appens to ye? Don't make me larf! So shut yer mouf. And keep it shut."

He turned his attention to Pol. "If I 'elp ye escape, Lord Riese, will ye forgive me and me bruvvers for our part?"

Pol considered the offer. It was probably the best chance he had, but it went against the grain to let Bill go. Pol had nothing much against Pete, who had been away in the army for years and seemed to be sorting his family out now that he was home. But Bill was a bully and a layabout, and Dan was following down the same path.

Perhaps Pete followed his thoughts, for he said, "What yer folks did, cheatin' ye and lyin' about ye. It sits wrong wiv me. This lot—they can be dumb as bricks, and Bill's picked up some bad ways workin' fer yer cousin. But the thing is, they're mine. Family stands fer family, and I stand fer me bruvvers. So, if ye're gunna come after any o' them, I gotta take ye where Riese said and let 'im do ye in. And I don't want to, 'cause it's wrong."

"Did you help abduct me, Pete Whitely?" Pol asked.

The man shook his head. "No, sir. I didn't."

Pol held Pete's gaze and waited to see if he would add anything. The man remained silent but Bill and another of the brothers squirmed. Pol turned his head to stare straight at each of them and then looked back at Pete.

The choice was easy. Take what Pete offered or be handed over to Oscar. "Yes. I agree. I'll not seek to have Bill or any of the rest of you arrested for crimes against me. I can only promise for myself, though. Not for anyone else in Tissingham or elsewhere that they've bullied, terrorized, or assaulted, whether on their own account or on Oscar's."

Pete grimaced. "Fair enough. Ye'll take note that we're tenants of your'n? Keepin' yon Oscar happy—well, it kept 'im off Ma and the girls." He was behind Pol now, moving the rope at Pol's back—presumably undoing the knots.

"I'll keep that in mind," Pol promised.

Pete came back into view, even though the coil of rope still restricted Pol's arms.

"What is the plan for my escape?" Pol asked.

"Well, me lord, we're goin' to go now, we Whitelys. We'll take the carriage like Riese told us. 'E'll think ye're with us."

"But what about when Riese finds out?" Bill objected. "'E'll kill us."

Pete grinned. "Oi've a plan, young Bill. Don't ye worry. Way I reckon, the Riese carriages be your'n, me lord, right?"

"I suppose they are," Pol said.

"Then if we was to take a carriage back to Riese 'All, we won't be breaking no laws, right?" Pete grinned. "It'll be one of me bruvvers driving," he explained.

Pol grinned back. "Good man," he commented.

"If'n ye climb the ladder, me lord, ye'll be able to see when yer cousin and 'is Ma leave, and the house is quiet. Ye can just come down then and go back to yer duke friend."

Pol had been shifting his shoulders and arms to loosen the rope and it finally slipped down his body. He stepped out of it and held out his hand to Pete. "I'll remember this, Whitely. I owe you my life." Pete looked surprised to be offered a handshake, but he held out his own and gripped Pol's firmly.

"If yer a fair lord to us, me lord, we'll serve ye well," Pete said. He felt in the pocket of the loose coat he wore. "'Ere. This'll be useful." He handed over a metal box, then picked up the cloak he had taken from Pol and tossed it over one of the brothers. "Here, Caleb, ye can wear this. Grasp him like 'e's a prisoner, you two."

The Whitelys left, hustling Caleb with them, muffled in the cloak. Pol opened the box, found a candle and a flint, and managed to set light to the wick of the candle before the closing door left him in darkness. By the light of the candle, he found the ladder, climbing one-handed and using his shoulder to open the trapdoor at the top.

The trapdoor opened into the conical roof space of the little tower. It was lined with tier upon tier of open-fronted boxes, except at floor level, where a foot of wall was broken by six pigeon-sized doors, all of them shut and barred. The pigeon loft was not in use, then, and had been left clean, though layers of dust and cobwebs hinted that the cleaning was years in the past.

Pol put the candle on the floor and set about unbarring the doors, both so he could see out and to let the daylight in. The crash of the trapdoor closing took him by surprise. It was followed by the sound of metal rasping against metal and a harsh voice, saying, "Take that, Allegro. Stay there an' rot till me mate Oscar comes for ye."

Bill Riese. Pol could hear him continuing to mutter as he moved away—descending the ladder, presumably. "Take that, bloody Pete. Ye ain't the boss of me."

IT TOOK LONGER to gain a magistrate's warrant than Jackie liked. She waited, if impatiently, until the sun was setting, and she could wait no longer. Even with the dusk in her favor, she didn't manage to leave the duke's mansion without being seen. Two of the duke's men materialized out of the shadows as she unlatched the garden gate into the lane. "Miss de Haricot du Charmont?" one said. "May we escort you somewhere?"

Jackie, who had dressed for her expedition in the boy's clothes she had packed at the bottom of her trunk, was surprised he had recognized her. She recognized him, too. Akbar, the one who had taken Scruffy back to the house. "I am just going for a walk, Akbar," she said.

He exchanged glances with his companion, then announced. "I shall come with you." It was not a request, and she did not think he would obey an order to remain behind.

"There is no need," she told him.

"You are the guest of our *patyşa*," he said. "There is need. I shall come."

At least he was not trying to stop her from leaving. She gave a single nod and strode off down the street, trying to remember to move like a man. Akbar followed a few paces behind, asking no questions. She did her best to ignore him.

The streets were full of carriages, as the people of the Ton moved from one entertainment to another, but not many people were walking. Jackie had to cross the street several times to go around a cluster of people making their way into a house where there must have been a dinner, for it was too early for balls to have started. Otherwise, the walk was an easy one, and they soon came to Beddington House.

Here, another retainer emerged from the gloom of the area steps and addressed her silent escort in the language they used among themselves. Jackie examined the building, which showed no lights except in the window at the base of the area stairs. All the better if everyone was out or asleep.

The clip clop of horseshoes had her turning to see Lord Thomas, the duke's youngest son, arriving on one of the magnificent horses of which the Winderfields were so proud. He waved to her and joined the other two men.

She would not let him stop her. She headed toward the lane and the tree she had noticed during the afternoon. Akbar caught up and spoke for the first time since they left Winshire House. "Miss de Haricot, the ladies from the house left nearly an hour ago, in a traveling coach with another coach for all their baggage. Most of the servants are gone, too. Traveling with the lady and her daughter, or dismissed. One carriage took men who were guarding someone hidden under a cloak."

Dear God, no. She was too late. Lord Thomas had also come after her, and he reassured her. "Some of our men followed them. A message has been sent to my brother Drew. They will not escape us, Miss de Haricot, and we shall get Lord Riese back."

Jackie had not slowed down. "I am going to check the room in which he was imprisoned, to see if he left a message," she explained, as she opened the gate to the garden.

Akbar and Lord Thomas didn't try to prevent her as she walked to the tree, clasped a branch just above her head, and walked her feet up the trunk until she was able to clamber onto a stout limb. Thomas swung up behind her and followed her as she climbed higher.

"You do not have to come," she pointed out to him.

The sound he made in response was both derisive and expressive. Clearly, he was neither going to argue nor desist.

The trickiest part of the climb was edging out along a branch to the barred window next to the one with the message. It bent slightly under her weight, but it must have grown up to the house and been trimmed back multiple times, for it was thick, stubby, and strong.

The bars on the window were solid, however, and the window would not shift.

She could feel and hear the branches shift as Thomas climbed higher. There was a groaning sound, as if wood was scraping on wood, and a moment later he came back to her level. "A window is open on the next floor," he reported. Jackie waited for him to say more, but apparently, he was leaving any decisions to her.

"I'll go in that way," she decided, and once again led the way up.

The branch at this level was less sturdy than the first, and slightly off to one side of the window, but Jackie clasped the sill and dragged herself inside, forcing the window up a little more with the same groan she had heard a short while ago. Thomas must have pushed it up before he came back for her.

The room was dark, and it took a moment for her eyes to adjust. In that moment, Thomas landed beside her. "It is a servant's bedroom, I think," she told him. "But not used."

He moved past her to open the door and peered into the space beyond, then stepped back and waved at her to pass him. It was dark in the passage that appeared to run in both directions. Jackie made a decision and turned right, walking carefully into the darkness with one hand on the wall.

A door at the end of the passage opened to a narrow stairwell, barely lit by the occasional window. The stairs were steep, and she had to go slowly, feeling with her leading foot for each step, but she soon reached a small landing and opened the door to a wider passage, which had light coming from some source part way along, so that it was not as black as the one above.

The barred windows must be to her left at the other end. She headed in that direction. The light source proved to be a large multistory window beyond a staircase that led down through the house.

She paused on the gallery to look down at the entrance hall, four flights below her before she continued into the passage on the other side of the stairwell. A couple of the doors on the left should open to the rooms with the barred windows, but the first two she opened let onto empty rooms whose windows had no bars.

"Light," said Thomas, looking back over his shoulder toward the stairs. Sure enough, some source of light in the stairwell was growing larger—or coming nearer. Thomas moved between her and the stairs and indicated the room she had just inspected. "Into this room, Miss de Haricot. Perhaps whoever it is will not see us."

But a voice shouted, "Miss de Haricot!"

Thomas's whole stance relaxed. "Drew," he informed her, and shouted back, "We are here!"

The light bobbed into view beyond the doorway to the stairs—a lamp. Drew was carrying it, and Jamir and Akbar were with him. "Miss de Haricot, good evening."

"I needed to see if Pol had left another message," Jackie blurted defiantly, expecting him to scold her for climbing into the house.

"I have a warrant to search the house," Drew said, peaceably. "Apparently our birds have flown the nest, but we might as well search anyway. The servants in the basement let me in. Apparently, the only ones left have no place else to go. I've told them to carry on until the true master returns to take up residence."

"He will, will he not?" Jackie said. "We shall find him?"

The perceptive man answered the question she did not ask.

"He was alive when he left here, Miss de Haricot. That is hopeful, is it not?"

"We are looking for the rooms with barred windows," Thomas said.

Drew nodded. "A nursery, I expect. Try the end of the passage. Here. Take my lamp. Jamir and I will check the other rooms."

They came to find her a few minutes later. Thomas was holding the lamp to illuminate the message writ large on the wall beside the door in one of the rooms, and Jackie was reading it. When Drew and Jamir joined her, she threw them a triumphant glance. "I knew he would leave a message if he could," she said, and turned back to finish reading it.

It was clearly a second effort, for the first, on the other side of the door, had been scribbled over, though she could still decipher a few words. *Kidnapped. Whitely. Unhurt.*

The second read:

Jackie my darling

Oscar ordered me kidnapped. I told his mother I knew who I was and what she did to Oscar's father and tried to do to Gran. She is going to take whatever money and steal whatever valuable property she can and then make for overseas. She mentioned America. I am to be insurance in case they need to bargain for their freedom. She won't let me be killed, at least not until they feel safe.

We are going to Burnwood House to rob that of money and treasures. Then to the coast to find a ship.

Whatever happens, know I love you with all my heart.

Pol.

"Well done, Miss de Haricot," Drew said. "We know where they are heading. We will be there almost as soon as they are."

"But they are more than an hour ahead of us," Jackie objected.

The men all grinned. "With a carriage and a team that is all show and little substance, Miss de Haricot," said Drew. "We, on the other hand, will be riding our own horses." Turkmen horses, as tame and loyal as dogs to their riders, and fierce independent beasts to everyone else. Jack the stable boy had wished he'd had the pleasure of caring for them. And, Drew claimed that they were the best long-distance horses in the world.

Jackie hoped he was right.

Chapter Twenty-Seven

THE HORSES WERE at full gallop before they were a dozen paces away. Jackie glared after them. Drew had point-blank refused to allow Jackie to ride with them and had ordered Lord Thomas to stay to see to her welfare. "He is my betrothed," she grumbled.

"They will save him," Thomas assured her. "You shall see, Miss de Haricot." He glanced over her shoulder and his eyes widened and then narrowed. "Forgive my impertinence," he said, as he laid an arm over her shoulders. "Please walk out of the lamplight. Not as if you were hurrying, but as if we have nowhere in particular to be. That's it."

She had fallen into step beside him before she had time to question, but now she heard a carriage drawing up behind them.

"Don't look back," he warned, as he used his free hand to try the gate of the area they were just passing. It opened, and he nudged her ahead, following her partway down the area steps to where they could peer from pavement level to see the carriage without being seen.

Oscar stood in the lamplight, arguing with the jarvey of the unprepossessing hackney that stood outside the door of Bedding-ton House. Bill Whitely was with him. As Jackie and the men watched, Bill tugged at Oscar's sleeve and murmured something that made Oscar dig in his pocket for a coin that he threw carelessly at the jarvey. The man snatched the coin from the air and went grumbling back to his seat on the carriage.

Oscar, heading toward Jackie, Bill at his heels, turned off into the lane that led down the side of Beddington House. Jackie hurried back up the stairs as soon as he was out of sight.

Thomas came after her. "I will follow him," he offered. "You stay here, Miss de Haricot."

That suggestions did not warrant an answer. Jackie reached the lane's corner and peered around it. Oscar and Bill were entering the grounds of Beddington House by the gate Jackie had used earlier. Good. They wouldn't see her creeping down the lane, making use of every shadow to keep herself hidden.

Thomas kept up with her, as stealthy as she, and together, they reached the gate and let themselves inside.

"Let me take the lead," Thomas said, his voice little more than a breath.

A shake of the head was answer enough. That and her stride forward. She was tired of being treated like a helpless female. Pol didn't treat her like one, and she was determined that his faith in her—in spite of how every other man, it seemed, regarded her gender—wouldn't be for naught.

She led the way to the back corner of the house and paused. Across a patch of flagstones, a tower rose from the garden, slender but tall, round, windowless, and topped with a conical roof. It was for doves or pigeons. In the twilight, and with the light of a full moon, she could see small arched doorways in the top of the wall, just below the roof.

Bill was dumping a load of wood at the base of the tower. Oscar was not in sight, but someone was breaking something up inside the little building. After Bill had brought two more loads of wood from somewhere out of sight behind the structure, the displaced viscount appeared from the doorway, holding an armload of smaller sticks. No, not sticks. That was dressed wood. He had been breaking up chairs or something similar.

"Here," he told Bill, his voice high-pitched with excitement. "Kindling. Did you see any straw? Or paper?"

He was going to set fire to the dovecote? But why?

Someone else wanted to know, too. "Here! Stop that! What do you mean by it?" Jackie could not see the speaker, but from the direction of his voice, she guessed him to be at the back door. One of the abandoned servants, perhaps?

Oscar peered at him. "Are you still here, Mitchell? I thought Mama had dismissed everyone."

"Nowhere to go, Lord Riese," the servant told him. "Not on such short notice."

Oscar ignored the resentment in his tone. "Make yourself useful, then. Go get a scoop of coal from the kitchen and bring it here. I mean to burn this to the ground."

"Do you have a gun?" Jackie whispered the question to Thomas.

He frowned at her. "I do, but I will not put you at risk for the sake of a pigeon house, Miss de Haricot," he whispered back. "Let him burn it."

"But *why* does he want to?" Jackie couldn't understand. Oscar should be trying to escape, not remaining here in London to burn a little garden folly—for that was all it was, the narrow wooden tower with its pigeon loft.

Perhaps he had hidden papers or some other incriminating evidence inside.

"Let us go and fetch help to arrest these men," Thomas insisted. "Just ten minutes, my lady, and we shall be back."

Jackie hesitated. It was the sensible thing to do.

"Here you are, my lord," said the footman, hurrying toward Oscar from the house, carrying a shovel full of glowing coals.

Oscar took the shovel then stepped back to look up at the pigeon loft. He shouted, "Polly! Oi! Polly!"

Pol? Pol was still here? Jackie started forward and Thomas caught her by the shoulder to keep her in the shadows.

"You've lost the viscountcy, Oscar." Pol's voice came from

the pigeon loft. "It was never yours in the first place. But if you kill me, you'll hang."

"Nobody will ever know," Oscar shouted back. "Even if they find the body, they'll not know it was you. The Whitelys took you away in their carriage. People saw you being taken out."

"I will know," Jackie said, shrugging off Thomas's grip and stepping forward. "And so will Mitchell and Bill. Do you intend to kill us all?"

"You might find Miss de Haricot harder to kill than you might think," Thomas added, stepping up to Jackie's side. He had produced a pistol from somewhere and held it as if he knew how to use it.

Oscar looked wildly around him and then dashed the shovel full of coals onto the fuel that he and Bill had piled around the foot of the tower. Straw caught and flared up even as Oscar ran into the house, followed by Bill.

The doorway was still clear of fire. Jackie raced for it, thankful for her boy's trousers, which allowed her to leap a low hedge and jump over the low steps into the building. Inside, she came to a stop. The inside was wreathed in shadows, but she could see no way up to the pigeon loft. No stair or ladder. No opening far above her head.

Her mind fed her the image of Oscar emerging with his arm full of pieces of kindling. A ladder? He must have broken it into pieces, for Pol had reached the pigeon loft somehow. She had to find some way up! She shouted, "Pol, I am going to look for a ladder!"

His voice came back, muffled by the floor. "Get out of here, Jackie. Don't risk yourself."

Hah! As if I am going to stand back and let him burn! She didn't stop to argue, but leapt out of the door, rushing through the flames at the tower's base.

In the brief time she had been inside, Thomas had found himself a workforce. Servants from the house, perhaps, or men from the stables in the mews. Some had formed a chain to bring buckets of water from farther down the garden. Those at the tower receiving the buckets were throwing them on the walls to damp them down.

Other men were using rakes to pull the wood and straw away from the flames. A third group had large sacks they were throwing over the scattered embers before stamping on them.

Jackie let out a breath she had not known she was holding. Perhaps the tower was not going to burn, after all.

"Is Pol behind you?" Thomas asked.

She shook her head. "Riese destroyed the ladder to the loft. Pol cannot get out. I am looking for another ladder."

Thomas looked around and then grabbed the arm of one of the rakers and spoke briefly to him before bringing him back to Jackie. "This is the gardener, Miss de Haricot. He shall find you a ladder."

"This way, Miss," the gardener said. "There's several ladders in the shed across the road."

They returned with the tallest, but Jackie knew, even before they tried it, that it wasn't going to be tall enough. Sure enough, it was more than six feet too short, and worse, once Thomas had climbed the ladder—he had insisted on taking her place—he could see that the trapdoor leading into the loft was bolted shut, and he couldn't reach it to open the bolt.

"I will go up the wisteria," said Jackie. "I can take Pol something to break open the trapdoor, and a rope for him to get down."

Oscar had failed in his attempt to burn the place down and Pol with it, though the people who had been mustered to help were still moving the piles of wood, looking for spots that needed to be damped down. The wisteria that grew up one side had suffered scorched leaves within a few feet of the ground but was otherwise intact.

Thomas protested but had to admit he was too heavy for the stems in the upper reaches of the wall. He sent one of the stable men off to find a mallet and a rope. "Preferably a rope ladder," he said.

The man came back with a knotted rope, a hefty wooden mallet, and a feed sack into which he put the other two items, "For the young Miss to loop over her shoulder, my lord, during the climb."

Jackie called up to Pol to let him know she was bringing him what he needed to escape and began the climb. She was halfway to the pigeon entrances when she heard the bark of a gun from the direction of the house, and something buzzed past her ear and hit the wall. *Someone is shooting at me!* Jackie froze.

Another gun barked, this time from the foot of the tower.

"Good shot. You got him," said Lord Thomas.

"*Cochon*," commented a voice that sounded somehow familiar. Jackie did not have time to think about it. Her hands were clenched hard on the trunks of the wisteria and refused to relax. The crisis was over. She had to focus all her energy on moving again. No one was shooting at her. She was safe, and Pol would be, too, if she just kept climbing.

"Jackie," Pol called to her. "Jackie, are you hurt?"

Hearing her beloved's voice was enough to make her fear-caused paralysis disappear. She moved one hand and then the other. "I am perfectly well," she called back. "I am almost there."

She pushed off on one foot and moved the other to a higher foothold, moved a hand, then the other foot, and the other hand, and repeated the movements until suddenly, she was there, and Pol was reaching a hand through the pigeon door for her to clasp.

"What happened?" he asked. "I heard gun shots."

Jackie looked over her shoulder at the house. Oscar lay draped over a window ledge on the second floor. Even as she watched, Thomas and another man pulled him back inside. "Your cousin took a shot at me and missed. The man who fired back did not miss."

"Oscar's dead?"

"I think so," Jackie said, surprised that Oscar's death seemed almost inconsequential to her Oscar had been such a malevolent force in her life and Pol's that his death should be a relief, but dead or arrested and soon to hang, this had been his last wicked act. Oscar was in the past. She and Pol, and their future together—they were what mattered.

"Here." She had managed to maneuver the bag so she could reach inside it. "This is a mallet to break open the trapdoor. And this is a rope for you to climb down."

Fortunately, it was twice as long as needed, for there was nothing in the pigeon loft to tie it to, so Pol fed one end down from the pigeon door and the other through the trap door. With the stable hands to weigh the rope down on the outside, Pol came down, dropping the last four feet to fold Jackie into his arms.

She lifted her mouth to his and for a long moment, they forgot the world. Until someone cleared their throat, and Pol's arms loosened, and his lips lifted from hers. He did not let her go, but he did look over his shoulder when the man in the doorway spoke.

"It is to be hoped, *Monsieur*, you have spoken to the demoiselle's *Maman*." It was the man who had shot Oscar, and he sounded even more familiar than before. Jackie leaned to look around Pol, but all the available light was outside, and his face was in darkness. However, somehow, she knew it was the man who had been watching her.

"The lady is my betrothed, sir," Pol told him, somewhat coldly.

The man stepped back from the doorway as he said. "Betrothed! It does not seem possible, *ma petite*."

As if the words had turned a switch, she knew him. But no, it could not be! Jackie squeezed her eyes shut and then looked again. He was smiling at her. With more light on his face, she knew him, though he was older, thinner, grayer. She stepped around Pol, but continued clutching his hand, his touch anchoring her against the shock. "*Mon Papa?*"

JACKIE CONTINUED TO cling to Pol as she and her father spoke.

"You have been following me," she accused him.

The Comte de Haricot du Charmont nodded. "Yes, *petite*, it is true. I have been trying to decide how to approach you and *ta mere*. And whether I should." He shrugged. "Whether you needed me."

"Need has nothing to do with it, Papa," she told him, her voice sharp. "We want you. Or, at least, we want to know why you abandoned us for ten years."

"Never abandoned, *petite*," he protested. "Not by my choice. Ah! You are so beautiful. So like your *Maman*. How is your Maman? I see you about with this young man, but she does not chaperone you? Is she ill?"

"We are betrothed, Papa," Jackie told him. "Maman is well, but Pol and I do not need a chaperone to see the sights in an open carriage. It is not the eighteenth century, Papa."

If *Monsieur* de Haricot had expected a tearful reunion, he was clearly to be disappointed. Jackie seemed more annoyed than excited. Of course, he had been missing for ten years, but he had popped up in time to save Jackie's life. That alone was enough to incline Pol to forgive him—though Pol's mercy was not what he needed.

Thomas Winderfield interrupted. "Excuse me, Miss de Haricot. I'm sorry to interrupt, but we need to report Oscar Riese's attempt to kill you and his death. Apart from that, Apollo, what do you want to do about the remaining servants? Do you want to keep them on to look after the house until you have a chance to talk to the solicitors?"

Pol hadn't thought that far ahead, but Thomas's idea was a good one. Most of the people who had helped to put out the fire were still standing around. Pol pitched his voice to carry and said, "I am Apollo Riese, the rightful Viscount Riese and owner of this house. How many of you are servants here?"

Several people raised their hands, and one stepped forward and said, "Matt Mitchell, my lord. Footman. You mean Lord Riese wasn't the viscount?"

"That's right," Pol said, making an instant decision not to get into the details. "His parents, my aunt and uncle, lied to steal the viscountcy from me when I was a little boy. Oscar was never the viscount."

"There are eight of us, my lord," Mitchell said. "Me, another footman, two maids, two grooms, a gardener, and the boot boy. We'd like to stay, if it pleases you, my lord. But the thing is, the servants that left took most of the food, and we haven't been paid our last quarter's wages."

Presumably the solicitor would advance Pol enough to pay the remaining servants, or at least to reimburse Pol after he'd given them most of the money he had left. "I'll make sure you are paid and that you have food or money for food. For now, though, I need to write a note, then I need someone to take it to the magistrate. Which magistrate was it, Lord Andrew?"

The last light from the sun had faded from the clouds as they went into the house so Pol could write a note for the magistrate. *Monsieur* de Haricot wasn't keen on waiting for the magistrate to arrive.

"It is not suitable for a lady to be questioned by this magistrate while wearing the garb of the boy," he said. "I shall escort my daughter to her mother."

Jackie squelched that idea. "I shall stay with Pol, Papa."

Thomas pointed out, "The magistrate will wish to speak with the man who fired the shot that saved Miss de Haricot's life, *Monsieur*."

Monsieur de Haricot grimaced but didn't argue.

In the event, however, the magistrate was happy to take the evidence of the witnesses that Oscar had intended murder and had been shot in defense of Miss de Haricot. Bill Whitely had been nowhere to be found, having presumably scarpered as soon as Oscar died. The magistrate would circulate his description, and perhaps the runners might pick him up.

There was nothing more to be done. Within fifteen minutes of the magistrate arriving, the constables were removing the body, and they were free to go. They walked back to Winshire House, Pol, Jackie, Thomas, and le *Comte de Haricot du Charmont*.

"Papa," said Jackie, "you told the magistrate you were a winemaker, here in England to sell your wine."

Pol had heard that, too, but certainly was not about to contradict his future father-in-law.

However, *Monsieur* de Haricot, "Yes, *ma petite*. It is quite true. It is part of the story I must tell you and your Maman."

The explanation was postponed again, though, when they arrived back in front of Winshire House at the same time as a carriage escorted by Drew and his riders. Drew dismounted to open the carriage door and Amanda descended, to cast herself on Pol's breast.

"Pol," she sobbed. "Pol, everything is dreadful."

"There, there," Pol said. Not original, but the best he could manage at a moment's notice.

"You don't understand," Amanda wailed. "Mother is dead, and my Season is ruined!"

JACKIE WAS DOING her best to help Pol comfort Amanda and could spare little attention for the meeting between Maman and Papa. She heard Maman screech Papa's name, "Etienne!" Next came the sound of a slap, and Jackie glanced that way to see Maman's hand leave Papa's cheek as she fell into Papa's arms, repeating, "Etienne!"

"My life is over," Amanda insisted, and Jackie had no more time to think about her parents.

"She really is upset about her mother and her brother," Pol

told Jackie, after they had finally settled Amanda in her own guest room in the care of her maid, whom Drew had brought along when he decided to return Amanda to London.

Jackie thought that Amanda was more upset about what people were going to think about her than about the loss of her nearest but not particularly dearest. "People don't need to know most of the details of what Louella and Oscar did, do they, Pol? For Amanda's sake?"

"They are dead," Pol commented. "Ruining their reputations will benefit no one."

"Indeed, but it will actively damage Amanda."

"Let us talk to their Graces. If anyone knows what Society might think, it is them."

They returned to the family parlor, to find that Maman and Papa had retreated from the company to talk privately. But Drew and Thomas both awaited them, and so did Gran and the duke and duchess.

"How is Miss Riese?" the duchess asked.

"Understandably upset. Her maid knows what to do for her," Pol said.

"We have assured her she will have a home with us," Jackie said.

"Of course," said the duchess. "Fortunately, her immediate family is dead, so there is no reason for their crimes to be made public. I think if she retires to the country and comes back into Society next Season, all should be well."

"Eleanor," the duke said. "She has just lost her mother and brother. I doubt she is thinking about her reputation."

The duchess kissed her husband's cheek. "You are such a nice man, James," she told him. "Amanda, sadly, is not a nice young lady. But she *is* young, so there is hope."

"How did her mother die?" Pol asked Drew.

"Mrs. Riese arrived to find the doors locked against her. We weren't there at the time, but I heard the story from your butler when we arrived fifteen minutes later. Apparently, the local magistrate was at Lady Campion's ball last night, and his first act on returning home was to advise the butler at Burnwood Hall to lock the door against the imposters. He was still there at Burnwood House when she arrived. She told him she had you as a prisoner, Apollo, but the carriage that supposedly held you did not arrive. Her coach driver said they had turned off to head north about half an hour earlier."

"That would have been Pete Whitely. He was charged with keeping me prisoner but released me instead. He said that, since the carriage belonged to me, he'd like my permission to take his brothers home, and I agreed."

Drew gave a nod of acknowledgement. "Mrs. Riese asked to retrieve some of her belongings, told Amanda to wait in the coach, and went upstairs. When I arrived and was told where she was, I went after her. She had taken poison and was dying. We sent for a doctor, but she was gone before he got there. I thought it best to bring Amanda back with me."

"She gave up even without knowing that Oscar was dead," Jackie commented.

"She had not only lost her title, her power, and her wealth," said the duke, "but she also faced going to prison while her murders were investigated, with all the resulting publicity and the noose at the end of it. She must have seen no other way out."

"Whereas Oscar was fighting to the end," Jackie said. "Her Grace is correct. This way is better for Amanda. We can hope that she is not too set in her ways to change."

"She was a sweet child," Gran said, "But Louella and Oscar indulged her, ignored her, and bullied her by turns. Perhaps, now that I am well again, we can find the sweet child once more."

"We shall try," Pol promised.

It was the next day before Jackie heard her father's story. Maman came down to breakfast on Papa's arm, her cheeks flushed and her eyes shining like stars, leaving little doubt that she and Papa had reconciled. "Your Papa did not abandon us of his own will, *cherie*," she assured Jackie. "He was impressed into the navy. Because he was French, he was not allowed ashore for several years, though he assured them he was a royalist, and they would not post his letters, either. Of course, after the first three months, a letter would not have reached us in any case, for we changed our name and moved, *cherie.*"

Because of Papa's debts. And to further confuse those who might be looking for Papa's wife and daughter, Maman had adopted the name Madame La Blanc, and Jackie had pretended to be her employee, and not her daughter.

Jackie narrowed her eyes at Papa, wondering if Papa was exaggerating or making a story up out of whole cloth, but he insisted it was all true. It was not until the war ended in 1814 that he was able to come looking for his lost wife and child. He couldn't find them. Eventually, after the One Hundred Days of Napoleon's return ended in Waterloo, he went to France.

"I expected my estate to be in ruins, or in the hands of parvenus, but—can you believe it? My *grand-mère* had kept it whole for us, and all through the wars, she had been making wine." Papa kissed his fingers and thrust them upward as if releasing the kiss into the air. "And such wine! *Ma petite,* with *Mémé* in charge of the growing and the pressing, and me to market the wine, no great *restaurante* in Paris would be without its *de Haricot du Charmont* wines. Today, the clubs of London. Tomorrow, the world."

"Ah, Etienne," said Maman, fondly. "Always such a dreamer. And Jackie is just like you."

WITH NO OTHER claimants to the viscountcy and eminent witnesses to Pol's identity, the matter was rapidly resolved. The estate's solicitors instructed the bank, and suddenly Pol was a wealthy man.

He bought Jackie a posy ring, set with diamonds and engraved "Only our love hath no decay," which was a line from a poem of John Donne's. He paid all the servants, restaffed the townhouse, and hired a house steward to preside over the establishment. "You and Monsieur may use it as your London home," he said to *Madame de Haricot du Charmont*, who was planning to return to France with her husband after his and Jackie's wedding.

He would have purchased Jackie a whole new wardrobe, except that the ladies insisted that they preferred to make it, "For there is no better modiste in England or France," Jackie told him. Instead, they commanded that he go to a London tailor and buy a wardrobe of his own.

He also suggested hiring maids for Gran and Jackie, but both declared they would rather have a Tissingham girl and would wait until they arrived home. Jackie was a little nervous about how the villagers and tenants would take her elevation to viscountess, and thought bringing home a London maid would just make things worse.

By letter, Pol arranged for the banns to be called in the village church in Tissingham and set the date for the wedding two days after the third calling of the banns. He did not have the bodies of his aunt and cousin returned to Tissingham for interment. Instead, he and Drew attended a joint funeral for the pair at the village near Burnwood House, and they were buried without ceremony sometime in the dark between nine o'clock in the evening and midnight in accordance with the law, in a corner of the churchyard.

For Amanda's sake, for Pol was convinced neither of the pair deserved even that last mercy.

Even the unceremonious interment bothered the vicar, since one was a suicide and the other had died while attempting murder, but Pol gave him a substantial donation to the steeple fund and reminded him that only God knew the human heart, and perhaps they had both repented at the last.

There were no more drugging kisses. *Monsieur de Haricot du Charmont* proved to be a much more diligent chaperone than

Madame, and the best Pol and Jackie could manage was a fleeting touch of the hands or a quick peck on the cheek.

Except in public, for the duchess insisted that they must go into Society, so most of their remaining nights in London saw them at a ball, a musicale, a dinner, or the opera. Balls and the opera were Pol's favorite activities. Balls had the downside that he had to watch Jackie dancing with others, but the upside that she saved all her waltzes for him, and for thirty blissful minutes at a time he could hold her in his arms.

As for the opera, when the gas lights were dimmed, they could hold hands under the cover of Jackie's shawl without being detected. Every night, and especially on nights when they had danced or held hands, Pol went to bed yearning for more. But every night took them one step closer to their wedding.

At last, it was time to travel north to Tissingham, taking their leave of the duke and duchess and all their household, except for Drew and Thomas who were coming to witness the wedding.

Traveling in their own carriages rather than a hired post chaise was a vastly different travel experience. Not only were the carriages more comfortable, but the service at the inns they favored along the way was also exponentially improved— although that might have owed more to name-dropping than to their better class of transport. Pol made certain to mention to each innkeeper that the establishment had been recommended to him by the Duke of Winshire, which was true, but also vastly useful.

They arrived two days before the wedding. Since they had to drive through Tissingham, they stopped at the rectory, for the rector had written in response to Pol's letter, assuring him that all would be organized as he wished, "However, my lord, so that all might be right and proper, I greatly desire that you and Miss de Haricot du Charmont might visit me in person to give me your consent to the marriage."

"I shall go in the other carriage with your mother and father, Jackie dear," said Gran, who had been taking her turn as chaperone. "Don't take too long, my dears, or we shall have Jackie's father running back to the village to check up on you."

As it was, Pol could hear *Monsieur's* voice raised in protest as the other carriage drove away. Jackie chuckled. "Is it unfilial of me to be grateful he was not present during my years as a stable hand and sometime gambler?" she asked Pol.

They were not long at the rectory. The rector exclaimed over the discovery of Pol's true status and the perfidy of his aunt and uncle, confirmed the time they were to be at the church on the day after next, and assured them that the village wished them both well.

That was confirmed when they stepped out of the rectory to find that word had spread and most of the villagers had gathered to welcome and congratulate them.

Pol's mind had been lingering on his plans for the uninter-rupted minutes in the carriage, and how much time he could add to the journey by asking the coachman to drive the ring road around Riese Hall before taking them home. After all, the horses had had a rest while he and Jackie were in the rectory, had they not?

Obviously, his yearning for a kiss and perhaps a little more would have to be put on hold. His beloved was already moving from person to person, greeting the villagers by name, smiling and shaking hands. What a magnificent viscountess she was going to be.

He followed her example and was gratified by how pleased everyone seemed to be with the news that he was the rightful viscount, and that he was marrying Jackie. "You could not have done better, my lord," said the blacksmith. "We always knew Miss Haricot and her mother were quality, but no airs and graces, not like some."

Clearly, Jackie need not have worries about the villagers' attitudes to their seamstress becoming their landlady and the ranking lady of the district.

The innkeeper was there, assuring Pol of his full support. "No more card sharping," Pol told him. "I'll not have people cheated in an establishment where I am the landlord."

"I'll tell my boy, my lord. I never let him cheat any of the locals, my lord."

"No cheating," Pol repeated, before turning to the next person who wanted to congratulate him and assure him that they had always known Louella and Oscar for villains.

The Whitelys were out in force, with Mrs. Whitely but without her husband. Mrs. Whitely had two bruised eyes that must recently have been black and swollen, judging by the broad spread of fading green. She was limping, too, but Pol knew she would deny that Whitely was the cause of her injuries.

"I am sorry to see that you have been hurt, Mrs. Whitely," he said, anyway. "May I be of help."

"An accident with a door," Mrs. Whitely said, predictably. Her eyes shifted to her eldest son.

His eyes hard, Pete Whitely said, "Papa has decided to travel. For his health. We do not expect him to return, my lord. But I trust the tenancy agreement holds good for Ma, me, and the boys?"

"I am pleased to have you as a tenant, Whitely," Pol told him, shaking the man's hand. In the next moment, he was stumbling backward. Pete had shoved him. *No.* First, there had been the crack of gun and the whine of a bullet.

And there went Pete, haring across the village green toward a horseman, who watched from the shadow of a stand of trees. "Bill, you idiot," he was roaring. "Just wait till I get my hands on you!"

Bill didn't take the invitation. He turned the horse, clapped his heels to it, and took off at a gallop.

Pete stopped in the middle of the green, shaking his fist at his departing brother.

Mrs. Whitely grabbed Pol's hand. "You won't throw us out, my lord, will you?"

"Your eldest son just saved my life, Mrs. Whitely. For the

second time. I'll not hold his brother's crimes against him and his family," Pol assured her.

Another voice had Pol's heart sinking. "Jacqueline? Are you safe?" It was *Monsieur de Haricot*. They had lingered too long, and he had walked down to meet them.

Crickets! So much for a little kissing and cuddling in the carriage on the way home!

JACKIE'S GOWN WAS a rose pink figured silk, simply but elegantly cut. It was embellished with a richly embroidered silk ribbon—one row at the cuffs and neckline, and three rows at her hem. Maman had wound the same ribbon through her hair, taking over from Jackie's new maid.

The bridal flowers Jackie had chosen had prompted something of a disagreement between her and her mother. Maman thought the flowers were common. "They are vegetable flowers, Jacqueline," she kept saying. "Why would you want to carry the flower of a vegetable?"

When Maman and Jackie had taken Papa to see the cottage where they had lived, the beans that Maman had thrown out the window had grown, and smothered one side of the house, spreading even up part of the roof. The flowers waved petals of the palest pink on long stems, and a few of the stems already sprouted rows of baby bean pods.

"They are bridal flowers," Jackie had said. "And they go perfectly with my gown." Not only were they lovely but carrying them in her bouquet was a sort of poetic justice. Louella's accusation that she—Jackie—had made up to Oscar to climb from seamstress to the rank of mistress had always been ridiculous, but had smarted a little, nonetheless.

No one she had met since the betrothal was announced had repeated the slur, at least not to Jackie's face. Human nature being what it was, people were surely thinking it.

So, she carried the bean flowers as a symbol of her climb, and to thumb her nose at her detractors, even if they never knew it.

Only a keen gardener would know, she realized, as she looked at herself in the mirror. And even they may question it. She had been right about them complimenting her gown.

"Jacqueline, *ma fifille,* said Maman. *"Tres belle. Tres, tres belle."* Clearly too overcome for words, she hugged Jackie instead, being careful not to crush the gown or the flowers.

Gran was next in line. "Your mother is right, dear one," she murmured. "Very, very beautiful."

Maman was trying to recover her usual brisk self. "Now, *cherie*, the carriage awaits to take us to the church, Clara and me." She brushed a tear from the corner of her eye. "Go down to Papa after we have gone," she instructed, her tone scolding. The arrangements had been in place for days, but if it helped Maman to scold, then Jackie would not challenge her. Not today.

"I will, Maman," she said.

And if she rolled her eyes at Maman's back, no one saw except Bella Whitely, who giggled, but only after Maman shut the door.

"Me own Ma be the same," Bella confided. "More like to growl than to hug but loves us summat fierce. You do look right purty, Miss Haricot."

"Are you coming in the carriage with us to the church, Bella?" Jackie asked. She'd hired the eldest Whitely daughter as a favor to Pete. The girl had the makings of an excellent maid, and the housekeeper had already taken her under her wing, to teach her what was expected of a maid in a peer's household. Jackie hoped she'd not entirely lose her habit of blurting out her thoughts in Jackie's presence.

"Nay, Miss," she said. "It's nobbut a hop, skip and a jump, and it ain't—" she caught herself and tried again. "It is not proper." She even sounded a little like the housekeeper as she repeated what she had obviously been told. Then she, her voice, and her accent relaxed, and she added, "Not today nonewise. Just ye and yer Da, and I'll be waitin' for ye at the church, as will 'bout everyone." She sighed her satisfaction. "And I saw ye first."

They walked downstairs together, and Papa's reaction was as satisfying as Ma's. "*Ma petite* Jacqueline," he kept saying, with a shake of his head as if he could not reconcile the tomboy he had left behind and the bride beside him in the carriage. "*Ma petite jeune fille.*"

What would Pol think? She would find out in a moment, for here they were at the gates of the church. The people standing around in the road and in the church grounds gave a cheer. Papa handed her down, and Bella was there to tidy her slight train before hurrying into the church ahead of them. She must have run through the woods like a hare!

She put her hand on her father's arm, and the men who were waiting by the double doors flung them open. The church was filled to capacity, with the gentry in the pews and every standing place taken by somebody.

Every soul in the neighborhood must be either in the church or outside. But all of them faded from her mind as she looked down the aisle, where Pol waited for her, with his heart in his eyes.

LATER, THE WEDDING would come back to Pol in flashes, each a sketch of a moment in time.

His first sight of Jackie as she entered the church on her father's arm, stepping into a sunbeam from one of the side windows, so beautiful that his breath failed him. Her sideways look at him, almost shy, as they faced the minister. Her eyes on his as she repeated her vows, her voice thrilling through him. Her beaming smile as the minister proclaimed them husband and wife. And then afterward, another broad smile when they came outside to the cheers of those who had not been able to fit into the church.

They had paid the innkeeper and the local baker to put on a feast for the villagers and tenants, and they walked around the green for a while, accepting congratulations and best wishes. It still seemed strange to be greeted as "my lord" or as "Lord Riese," but when people called Jackie "my lady" or "Lady Riese," his heart seemed to swell in his chest. No one mentioned, or even seemed to be aware, that they had known Pol and Jackie as the viscount's bastard cousin and the seamstress.

They returned to the carriage to ride to the Hall to find the carriage had been decorated during the service—every available space adorned with ribbons and flowers. Furthermore, it clanked when it pulled away from outside of the church—several iron posts or the like must have been fastened to the back axle.

Jackie laughed and the horses didn't complain. She was examining her ring. He had had it engraved with another line from Donne's poem. "Let us live nobly." The ring didn't have room for the next bit, but he meant the sentiment—the poem continued, "And live, and add years to our reign." That was his wish for them—that they would live a long and blessed life together and go at last together to the peace thereafter.

Jackie read the sentiment and kissed the ring. "Here on this earth, we are Kings," she quoted, from the same poem, and truly, at this minute, Pol felt as if he had been crowned king of all the world, with her as his co-monarch by his side.

Within minutes they were at the Hall, and the racket was over. Now he just had to endure another hour or so of doing the pretty at the reception the ladies of the house had organized for the local gentry, and he and his wife… *My wife! How good that sounds!* He and his wife would be able to leave in another hour, he reassured himself.

IN THE LATE afternoon, Jackie and her new husband arrived at the cottage in Little Tidbury, which Pol had arranged to hire for a week. "His wife said they would provision it," he told Jackie, as the carriage pulled up outside. "And a maid will come in each afternoon to clean and to prepare dinner."

The innkeeper's wife had outdone herself. The cottage was sparkling clean, and the color and scent of vases of flowers brightened the rooms. In the kitchen, several pots simmered on stands over embers. They proved to contain a pot roast, root vegetables, and a steamed pudding. Jackie found fresh bread and sweeter baked goods under a cover on the kitchen table.

A bottle of wine, too, and two glasses. Pol opened the envelope propped against the bottle and read it out loud to Jackie. "To Lord and Lady Riese, with our very best wishes for a happy future."

"Wine?" he asked Jackie.

Jackie had had several glasses today already. Would more help or hinder?

She was very nervous. Maman had been very vague about what was to happen tonight, saying merely, "Follow Apollo's lead, *cherie*, and if you have any questions, ask him. It is a very pleasant activity. I am certain you will enjoy it. After the first."

The rest of Jackie's experience came from unwanted advances and from watching bulls and stallions at their work. None of that was reassuring.

On the other hand, Pol's kisses and caresses had been splendid, but had left her craving… something. Logically, their coupling was that something.

But what did "after the first" mean? After the first act? After the first month? The first year? Maman's comment was more alarming than helpful.

It was only four of the clock. What time would it be acceptable to go to bed? She wanted the waiting over.

"Would you like a glass of wine, darling?" Pol asked.

She had been fretting instead of answering him. "When can

we go to bed?" The question was out of her mouth before she could catch it back. If he laughed, she was going to hit him.

He put his head on one side and regarded her from solemn brown eyes. "You are nervous," he said, sounding as if he had discovered something surprising.

Of course, she was nervous. "I do not know what to expect," she grumbled.

"Did your mother explain—?"

"Nothing. She explained nothing. 'Follow Apollo's lead. If you have questions, ask him!' Nothing, Pol. I want to know when it is going to happen, for I think I shall go mad without knowing how long I must wait."

Pol had taken her hand while she was complaining, and now he wrapped his arms around her. "In that case, let us not wait," he said, and kissed her.

It was one of the open-mouthed all devouring kisses that melted Jackie's innards and left her weak at the knees, but she still retained her senses enough to ask, when his mouth left hers to cruise down her neck, "Really? Now? I thought it was a nighttime activity."

He stopped what he was doing, the beast, and straightened to smile down at her. "It is an 'anytime we please' activity, dearest Jackie. Now is an excellent time. The best."

Jackie glanced at the foodstuffs on the table. "I can wait if you are hungry," she said, hoping he would not want to wait.

He didn't. "I am hungry for you, my love. Come upstairs, and I shall show you."

He led her, holding her hand, to the largest of the bedrooms, where clean sheets were turned down on the bed, and rose petals were scattered. He closed the curtains and lit the candles, then unbuttoned all the buttons, untied all the ties, and unlaced all the laces on her garments, removing each item with ever more fervent kisses and caresses, and not a few muttered curses when one of the fastenings proved recalcitrant.

The garments that had taken Maman and Bella a full thirty

minutes to put on her were gone in fewer than five, and he was undressing himself at the same time, unraveling his cravat, shrugging out of his coat and his waistcoat, and dropping his breeches.

Next time, she was going to undress him, she decided. But for now, it was all she could do to stay upright.

By the time she was down to her chemise and stockings, and leaning against the bed, for her knees were too weak to hold her upright on their own, he wore only his smallclothes. He went to lift her chemise, but she shook her head.

"You first," she ordered.

He unbuttoned his underbreeches and slipped them off, then lifted his shirt over his head. By the time the hem had reached his waist, her eyes were riveted on what lay beneath. *So, men have hair on their groin, too*. It was a diversionary tactic on the part of her mind. Her true attention was on the shaft that rose out of the brown curls.

So that is what was pressing into me, she thought. And *that is never going to fit inside me*.

Pol dropped to his knees. "I am going to take off your stockings and then your chemise," he said, but he didn't move.

"Yes," she said, and that must have been what he was waiting for. His fingers stroked her inner thigh as he untied her garter and unrolled her stocking, then his hands brushed her sides as he lifted the chemise. He stepped back, after that, stopping two paces away to stare at her body in the way she had gazed at his.

The urge to cover herself was easy to resist when she realized that it was awe she saw on his eyes. Awe, desire, and love.

She took the opportunity to take in the rest of him. Broad shoulders and muscled arms, from assisting in the fields. Slender waist and hips. Powerful thighs. The upright shaft and the color of his flesh, living and breathing, were the only factors that differed from the Greek and Roman statues they had seen in London. He was magnificent.

"You are beautiful," he said, in a breathy whisper. "So beautiful."

Had she been able to muster words, she would have returned the compliment.

"Time to get on the bed, darling," her husband told her.

His sudden indrawn breath when she obeyed had her turning to look over her shoulder. His eyes were wide, his mouth was open, and his gaze was firmly fixed on her bottom. *Oh, so that is the way of it!* Stunned as she was by his naked body, he was even more poleaxed by hers.

The sense of feminine power had her hips swaying more than they needed to as she crawled another couple of times into the center of the bed. Before she reached it, he was beside her, drawing her into another embrace.

After that, Jackie could no longer focus on a single sensation. The touch of his hands, his lips, his teeth and his tongue, the press and slide of his skin against hers, the smell of him—a combination of the soap he used and something indefinably Pol—the sound of his whispered words and his groans as her inexperienced touches grew more confident and more daring—all of those combined to drag her into a maelstrom of feelings and responses.

Taste and sight came into it, too. It was as if her body was a harp, her senses the harp strings, and he the maestro creating a symphony that transcended the flesh on which it was played.

By the time he entered her, she was so far beyond wild for him to redeem the promises his body was making to hers that the slight pinch barely registered and had no effect on the crescendo building within her. Building, building, until she screamed his name, desperate for whatever all this was leading up to. Then, as if her scream had been the final push, she peaked and exploded, in a crash of sensation she could only experience and not explain.

The explosion, or the fall, or whatever it was went on and on, and above her, Pol continued to move. But then he stiffened and cried out in his turn. "Jackie!" She felt a warm gush deep within, and then he gathered her in his arms and rolled to his side, taking her with him, kissing her tenderly now, and without urgency.

"My wife," he said, his voice replete with satisfaction.

"My husband," she responded.

After all the passion of the afternoon, they were at peace together. After all the drama of the last few months, they had found their way home.

THE END

AUTHOR'S NOTE

This book is inspired by Jack and the Beanstalk. The clues lie in Jackie's variant names—Bean, Haricot, Le Gume, but also in the name of the villains and, as it turns out, of Jackie's hero. Riese (the "ie" is pronounced like the name of the letter "e") means "giant" in German.

I also have a golden goose (Oscar calls it a swan, but you and I and Jackie know better), a packet of magic beans (the old woman said they were magic, and who am I to argue), and—if not a harp—at least a harpist. One, furthermore, that my Jackie takes away from the giant's home with her.

Above all, I have the climb, or the climbs, both physical and societal. I—or rather Jackie—explained that in the book you've just read, Jackie did not actually kill the giants, but they certainly died because she dared to climb.

I hope you've enjoyed my take on the old tale.

In Regency England, what was a curate? What is a solicitor?

In the Regency era Anglican church, a curate was an ordained minister of any age who was paid by the vicar to assist him in the parish.

A post as vicar of a parish was called a living, because it guaranteed a fixed amount of property or income (which the vicar would live on). This income came from tithes paid to the holder of the living, either great tithes or small tithes. A great tithe was 10% of all cereal grown or all wool shorn in the parish, and a small tithe was 10% of all other agricultural produce.

A vicar with a big parish, or one who simply didn't want to do the work, could employ a curate to help him out.

In England, to this day, practitioners of law are either solicitors or barristers. A solicitor is a legal practitioner who undertakes a variety of legal work and also prepares cases for a barrister. A barrister is a legal practitioner who pleads cases in court. In New Zealand, where I live, most lawyers are both.

In England prior to the 19th century, the term solicitor was used only for those who prepared cases for Chancery. A legal practitioner who prepared other cases was an attorney at law, or public attorney. This is the term that has prevailed in the United States.

I could have chosen the term lawyer, which simply meant (and means) one whose profession is suits in court or client advice on legal rights. Solicitor is more specific.

Sightseeing in London

Mr. Phillips's guidebook is a real publication that would have been available to tourists in 1820 London. Thanks to Google books, I was able to consult it for the descriptions used when Pol and Jackie went sightseeing.

Pol's rings and their line of poetry

Pol's ring for Jackie took its quote from this poem by John Donne.

The Anniversary
BY JOHN DONNE

All Kings, and all their favorites,
All glory of honors, beauties, wits,
The sun itself, which makes times, as they pass,
Is elder by a year now than it was
When thou and I first one another saw:

All other things to their destruction draw,

Only our love hath no decay;

This no tomorrow hath, nor yesterday,

Running it never runs from us away,

But truly keeps his first, last, everlasting day.

Two graves must hide thine and my corse;

If one might, death were no divorce.

Alas, as well as other Princes, we

(Who Prince enough in one another be)

Must leave at last in death these eyes and ears,

Oft fed with true oaths, and with sweet salt tears;

But souls where nothing dwells but love

(All other thoughts being inmates) then shall prove

This, or a love increasèd there above,

When bodies to their graves, souls from their graves remove.

And then we shall be throughly blessed;

But we no more than all the rest.

Here upon earth we're Kings, and none but we

Can be such Kings, nor of such subjects be;

Who is so safe as we? where none can do

Treason to us, except one of us two.

True and false fears let us refrain,

Let us love nobly, and live, and add again

Years and years unto years, till we attain

To write threescore: this is the second of our reign.

The Duke of Winshire, his entourage, and a couple of definitions

The Duke of Winshire is a character in my joined-up-world, the long-lost love of the Duchess of Haverford. After being exiled from England for daring to love where his father forbade it, he landed himself in hot water in Persia, but he turned it to the good, eventually running off with the Shah's daughter and founding a dynasty in the Kopet Dag mountains north of Iran. *Pari-diaza*, as they called his land, was a kingdom of exiles—the ragtag and the rebels of Europe, Asia, and North Africa. But it worked.

By the time the deaths of his older brothers made him heir to his father, he was a widower. When his father lay dying, he arrived home with six of his ten children, beautiful Turkmen horses (which today we call the *Akhal Teke*) plus a full complement of what I call in the book "foreign retainers"—loyal subjects from his mountain kingdom who agreed to accompany him to England.

The people of Pari-diaza speak a polyglot language, and the two words I use in the book come from slightly different strands of the Turkic languages:

patyşa means king in Turkmen

bey is a Turkic title that roughly equates to the English "lord".

We hope you have enjoyed *Jackie's Climb*, the 9th novel in Jude Knight's series *A Twist Upon a Regency Tale*. Please visit her Amazon page to leave her a review, and to find the rest of the series, her Lyon's Den Connected World books (which are also inspired by fairy tales) and more.

ABOUT THE AUTHOR

Have you ever wanted something so much you were afraid to even try? That was Jude ten years ago.

For as long as she can remember, she's wanted to be a novelist. She even started dozens of stories, over the years.

But life kept getting in the way. A seriously ill child who required years of therapy; a rising mortgage that led to a full-time job; six children, her own chronic illness… the writing took a back seat.

As the years passed, the fear grew. If she didn't put her stories out there in the market, she wouldn't risk making a fool of herself. She could keep the dream alive if she never put it to the test.

Then her mother died. That great lady had waited her whole life to read a novel of Jude's, and now it would never happen.

So Jude faced her fear and changed it—told everyone she knew she was writing a novel. Now she'd make a fool of herself for certain if she didn't finish.

Her first book came out to excellent reviews in December 2014, and the rest is history. Many books, lots of positive reviews, and a few awards later, she feels foolish for not starting earlier.

Jude write historical fiction with a large helping of romance, a splash of Regency, and a twist of suspense. She then tries to figure out how to slot the story into a genre category. She's mad keen on history, enjoys what happens to people in the crucible of a passionate relationship, and loves to use a good mystery and some real danger as mechanisms to torture her characters.

Dip your toe into her world with one of her lunch-time reads collections or a novella, or dive into a novel. And let her know what you think.

Website and blog:
judeknightauthor.com

Subscribe to newsletter:
judeknightauthor.com/newsletter

Bookshop:
judeknight.selz.com

Facebook:
facebook.com/JudeKnightAuthor

Twitter:
twitter.com/JudeKnightBooks

Pinterest:
nz.pinterest.com/jknight1033

Bookbub:
bookbub.com/profile/jude-knight

Books + Main Bites:
bookandmainbites.com/JudeKnightAuthor

Amazon author page:
amazon.com/Jude-Knight/e/B00RG3SG7I

Goodreads:
goodreads.com/author/show/8603586.Jude_Knight

LinkedIn:
linkedin.com/in/jude-knight-465557166

9 781967 169030